FREE FIRE ZONE

Short Stories
by Vietnam Veterans

edited by
Wayne Karlin
Basil T. Paquet
Larry Rottmann

McGraw-Hill Book Company
a 1st Casualty Press Book
New York   St. Louis
San Francisco   Toronto

The editors make grateful acknowledgment for permission to reprint the following material:

"Ben," by George Davis, is reprinted with the permission of Random House, Inc., from *Coming Home*, by George Davis. Copyright © 1971 by George Davis.

"The Interrogation of the Prisoner Bung by Mister Hawkins and Sergeant Tree," by David Huddle, was first published in *Esquire*, January, 1971, and is reprinted by permission of the author. Copyright © 1971 by David Huddle.

"Candidate," by James Shield, first appeared in *Caroline Quarterly*, Spring, 1972.

The quote on page vi by Jean-Paul Sartre is reprinted from his introduction to *The Wretched of the Earth*, by Frantz Fanon, Grove Press, 1968. Copyright © 1963 by *Présence Africaine*.

123456789BABA79876543

Library of Congress Cataloging in Publication Data
Karlin, Wayne.
    Free fire zone.
        1.   Short stories, American.   2.   Vietnamese
Conflict, 1961–   —Fiction.   I.   Paquet, Basil T.,
1944–   II.   Rottmann, Larry, 1942–   III.   Title.
PZ1.K1759Fr [PS648.V5]   813'.01   72–13881
ISBN 0–07–033326–2
ISBN 0–07–033325–4 (pbk)

FREE FIRE ZONE is an American military term used to designate a defined geographical area in which all life is considered enemy. Any humans or animals in this zone are fair game for all of the organic weapons of the U.S. Armed Forces and are destroyed immediately upon detection. Plant and marine life are also considered hostile, and are subject to repeated defoliation by Agent Orange and other chemical toxins.

"In war, truth is the first casualty."—Aeschylus (525-456 B.C.)

ACKNOWLEDGMENTS
The material for FREE FIRE ZONE was collected by 1st Casualty Press. Special thanks are due Francie Rottmann, Sandra Paquet, O. T., Lee Burns, Ned Ryerson, Mr. and Mrs. John Randall, Linda Block, and Lotte Kunstler, whose encouragement and support helped make this book possible.

FOR THE PEOPLE OF INDOCHINA

It is not right, my fellow-countrymen, you who know very well all the crimes committed in our name, it's not at all right that you do not breathe a word about them to anyone, not even to your own soul, for fear of having to stand in judgement of yourself. I am willing to believe that at the beginning you did not realize what was happening; later, you doubted whether such things could be true; but now you know, and still you hold your tongues. Eight years of silence; what degradation! And your silence is all to no avail; today, the blinding sun of torture is at its zenith; it lights up the whole country. Under that merciless glare, there is not a laugh that does not ring false, not a face that is not painted to hide fear or anger, not a single action that does not betray our disgust and our complicity.

Jean-Paul Sartre

Grab them by the balls and their hearts and minds will follow.

The Pentagon Papers

Introduction

Free Fire Zone: Short Stories by Vietnam Veterans is the second volume in a series of veterans' writings coming out of the Indochina experience. *Free Fire Zone,* like *Winning Hearts and Minds* and the third volume, *Postmortem,* is a collection which examines America's policies and attitudes towards Asia through the eyes of the men who implemented them.

The twenty-one writers in *Free Fire Zone* offer a collective insight into the price paid by both peoples when one culture attempts to strip another of its dignity and destroy its gods. The emphasis of each writer varies, but their insight is cumulative. *Free Fire Zone* explores America's attempt to shape an ancient Asian culture into an image that reflects our own physical and psychological needs.

The Euro-American dream of territorial expansion is not simply a predatory instinct for more land and resources. The people of the colonies are always a part of the dream; they have always been a chief resource. *Free Fire Zone* offers the experience of men who as "expeditionary forces" devalued the life of both the people they were sent to subdue and their own lives. This collection of stories explores the psychosexual sickness of cause and result that manifested itself when the Americans came into contact with the "natives." The relationships between GI's and Asian women that are explored in a number of the stories are illustrations of both direct violence and the subtler forms of cultural rape and pillage.

The agent of suffering must believe that the victim and his

world are outside the circle of humanity. This racism is at the core of the soldier's actions and responses to the Indochinese, as it was the operative principle of European colonial activities in Africa, Asia, and the Americas. This collection is about the reality of war for the people who are the victims of the West's twisted ideal of "fulfillment," and about the men who executed their culture's dictates and government's policies. *Free Fire Zone* is about men dehumanizing themselves by imagining the Indochinese as less than human, who victimized their own precious humanity by warring on the "gook."

A few of the "agent-victims" of this war have climbed the tenuous ladder to recognition of what their war has meant. They have broken through the screen image of American Soldier, finding behind the pasteboard mask the demythicized reality—that they were instruments of sick policy, not of humanitarian ideals.

Free Fire Zone's writers treat three levels of experience: the men who operated out of this realization, those who were aware of their loss of freedom but failed to confront it, and the majority who never understood. Sadly and dangerously, most Americans have also refused to understand the sickness and have pushed it back into the nation's psyche, where it grows and engenders new disease. Beyond confronting the implications of America's violation of Vietnam, the writers suggest that the struggle of people in Indochina to maintain and form their own identities has also become their struggle.

Wayne Karlin
Basil T. Paquet
Larry Rottmann

Gliding Baskets

"Eight Six Foxtrot—Eight Six Foxtrot.
This is One One Zulu. Over."

The woman in blue
Carried the weight swiftly, with grace,
Her face was hidden by her
Conical rice straw hat.

"One One Zulu—this is Eight Six Foxtrot. Go."
"Roger Eight Six. I have Fire Mission.
"Dink in the open, Grid: Bravo Sierra,
Five Six Niner, Four Six Five, Range:
Three thousand, Proximity: Eight hundred. Over."

The two heavy baskets
Balanced on tips
Of the springing Chogi stick
Glided close to the hard smooth path.

"Read back, One One Zulu."
"Roger Copy, Eight Six."
"Shot, on the way, wait."
"Shot Out, Eight Six."

A sighing 105mm round slides through its parabola
Then the explosive tearing at the steel which surrounds it,
And the shrapnel catches the gliding baskets,
And they crumple with the woman in blue.

Frank A. Cross, Jr.
near An Trang
August 14, 1969

Contents

The Old Man

By Michael Paul McCusker

He was just an old man. Bent and scabby-legged, sores all over his dark calloused feet; three long chin whiskers curling from his ancient crumbling jaw like nonsensical banners. He was waving one. A flag. Yellow with three red stripes. He was standing beside his hut. Kids were running everywhere yelling at the marines walking through the village. A tiny village alongside a river. Chickens, ugly pigs, scrawny old women with black teeth and frightened smiles because they thought the Americans might kill their men or burn down their homes.

So everybody pretended to be friendly and the old man hid his Viet Cong flag and brought out the Saigon absurdity, waving and smiling to beat hell. But Fat Jack saw him and Fat Jack had never shot down anybody in cold blood. Jack had this thing. He wanted to kill somebody. And there was that ridiculous old man. Who would miss him? Just an old man; he couldn't work in the fields anymore. Just another hungry stomach for a family loaded down with kids. So Jack walked up to him and the old man started bobbing his head up and down faster and smiling wider, but it didn't matter. Jack had the rifle in his face and the trigger pulled before the old man's body knew it was dead. He didn't fall. He just stood there without much of a face. A squashed, dripping berry. The back of his head looked like a busted balloon. Then he fell, old knees buckling on withered legs. His ass hit first, then the rest of him, sitting hunched over for a second, then collapsing on his side. "I don't feel nothin'," Jack shouted. The guys just smiled. The kids stopped running, quiet. The old women scooted back into their huts. A low wailing began to throb through the village, but Jack was walking away, shaking his head, telling his friends he just didn't feel nothin'. The old man, he had a lot of blood for such a small, skinny, used-up old man, he was left to lay there. Nobody touched him, not the kids, not the women, just the flies, coming from all over, from the village, the fields.

Bangalore

by William Pelfrey

"Greeneye four-five, Greeneye four-five, this is Lucy in the Sky, Lucy in the Sky, over."

"Roger, Lucy. Send traffic."

"Roger. Comin on down. We've got a new pinhead, straight from Pleiku, over."

"Roger, where from in the world?"

"New York."

"Fuck me, New York."

"Good copy. We're comin on down. Negative further, out."

Bradley gave Larson the handset, lit a cigarette and began checking the grenade rounds on his chest, making sure he had all HE's on the left and buckshot canisters on the right.

"Lucky you didn't come out for a search and destroy," he said to Gruda.

"What's a greeneye, anyway?"

"Don't worry about it. We got fuckin bangalores laid by the trail, we just set up and hide in the fuckin bush. No humpin at all."

"Except gettin there," said Larson. "You got a girl back in the world, Gruda?"

"I did in college."

"College? Fuck me," said Bradley. "Chamber a round. Let's move out."

Bradley squashed his cigarette and pulled one of the green canister rounds. He tossed it in his hand and rattled the buckshot before sliding it into the breech and clicking the short barrel closed. The hard click echoed. He signaled back up to the machine gun bunker, waving the grenade launcher over his head like Geronimo.

The jungle was triple canopy off LZ Rough Rider, with thick teakwood, vines and bamboo groves. The sun would filter in thin hazed streaks, glimmering on the leaves and rocks from a distance. Gruda heard Bradley's machete swishing above his own panting, which intensified with each step.

Larson turned back to make sure Gruda was keeping up, causing the radio antenna to flap and rattle. He grinned and shook his head, then whispered ahead for Bradley to take a break. Bradley stuck the machete in the ground and stood in place on the slope.

"How much further?" asked Gruda.

The other two stared as Gruda choked his words against the rhythm of his panting.

Bradley laughed. "Shit, this ain't even uphill. You got a ways yet, Cruit. Don't worry. Get the fuckin salt pills, Jim."

Bradley sat down without removing his pack, lit a cigarette and hung his steel pot on the machete handle. When Gruda sat down—almost fell down—one of the grenades on his pistol belt clanked on a bamboo shoot. Bradley instinctively slapped his grenade launcher and whirled; in his stupor Gruda did not react.

"Fuckin ass kicker, ain't it?" grinned Larson as he poured the salt tablets.

"Mother fuck," moaned Gruda.

"Got a picture of yer girl?" asked Bradley.

"No."

"Old Benny had college, didn't he, Jim?"

"Yeah, sorry fucker."

"Who's old Benny?"

"Fuckin dud. You don't even want to let yourself get his attitude."

"He was what you would call your ultimate dickhead," said Bradley. "Never did anything but feel sorry for himself. They finally got him for malingering."

"Did he get court-martialed?"

Bradley took one last drag of his cigarette, stood up and unbuckled the pistol belt to urinate, with the ruck still on his back. "Stuck his ass on permanent KP at base camp. Better start saddlin up, Cruit."

The rolling sweat stained their sleeves and glistened on their bare wrists as they filed down. Gruda's daze intensified, he began shaking his head and let his body fall forward, lunging at the bamboo to jerk himself out of falls. His body would dangle from the trembling hand, then fall to the next tree.

At one point Bradley thought he heard something and halted them. He used the hand signal, like Hollywood cavalry; nodded to Larson and entered the bush alone to check it out. Larson smiled noticing Gruda's face tighten with apprehension.

Nothing was found, but they radioed ahead to Lopez anyway, and walked more quietly from that point on. They formed a football huddle before starting, with Bradley emphasizing to Gruda that he had better quit panting and tripping like a goddammed pussy.

Gruda's spastic panting only increased, but nothing happened.

Lopez had a man on OP to greet them at the base of the hill.

"Ass kick, ain't it, Cruit?" he grinned to Gruda.

Larson pointed his sixteen at the wire for Gruda, so he wouldn't trip over it. The guard lay prone at the edge of the bush, facing the trail on an angle. The hootch was set up in a bamboo grove, fifteen meters back.

"Gentlemen," said Lopez. He lay barefoot on his air mattress, and flashed the peace sign. "Too bad we don't have a batch of hot chocolate to welcome you with."

"You been seeing anything?" asked Bradley.

"I think so, last night. Greyson was on guard. Hey, Greyson."

"I thought I saw flashlights, but it was back in the bush on the other side of the ditch. Nothin on the trail."

Bradley pulled his steel pot off, revealing the tight red stripe cut into his forehead by the sweat band. "I found a trail on the way down, but I didn't follow it. Didn't want to fuck with it."

"Fresh?" asked Lopez.

"Fraid so."

"Fuck me. Guess we'll be lookin good on the way up. We got any mail on the hill?"

"Yeah, letters. No Care packages, though."

"I'm overdue. Is your shit all packed, Greyson? What about White?"

"We're both ready to SP."

"Okay. What you gonna eat there, Larson?"

Larson was punching holes in an empty C-ration can to make a stove.

"Ham and limas."

"What about you, Cruit?"

"What do you suggest?"

"Anything but ham and eggs," said Bradley.

Lopez buckled the faded pistol belt low on his hips, grenades dangling, and glanced inside the hootch one last time before jerking the ruck to his shoulders.

"Okay, young buck sergeant. I guess you're in command. Greyson . . ."

"Hold it, I'll walk with yer and take first guard. Gimme yer rifle and a bandolier there, Cruit."

Bradley took Gruda's magazine out and broke the barrel open, pointing it to the sky and inspecting the riflings like a drill sergeant. He slung the tied bandolier over his shoulder. Lopez and Greyson followed him out.

White whirled as they approached. Bradley grinned and flashed the peace sign to him.

"Okay, Lopez. Bangalores are still in the same place, right?"

"Right, in the ditch."

"Okay, see you on the hill in three days."

Greyson had brought White's pack for him. Lopez called Rough Rider of his approach and dropped in the canister round; clicked the thick barrel closed, gave the hand signal and moved out. He tucked the grenade launcher under his arm, like a hunter with a shotgun. All three stopped and humped their shoulders as they disappeared, trying to get the packs balanced most comfortably on their backs.

Gruda had beans and meatballs for lunch. The food at the bottom of the can was burned and the top not warmed through, but he didn't mention it. He used a cracker to sop the greasy sauce that hadn't penetrated the meatballs. He sat listening to the birds and monkeys, with the sunlight streaking throught just like in a movie.

"What the fuck are we supposed to be doin here?"

"In Vietnam?" Larson was eating cheese and crackers as he spoke.

"No, on a greeneye."

"Oh." He smiled. "We're on an extended OP, really. Spot any movement on the trail and call it in. But take em out if they're not too many."

"How many have you got?"

"With my rifle?"

"Yeah."

"Three. Bradley's got ten, and got an extra R&R for it."

"Jesus Christ."

After the meal Gruda lay back on the air mattress and watched the sun flitter against the leaves. He quickly fell asleep. At three o'clock Larson went out to relieve Bradley. When Bradley came in he kicked Gruda's air mattress.

"What the fuck are you supposed to be doin, dickhead?"

Gruda did not reply, staring and blushing up at him.

"Better act like you're alive, Cruit. Fuckin dink could bring the max on you before you knew it."

"Larson was here."

"He told you to crash?"

"He didn't say not to. He must have left while I was asleep."

Bradley glanced towards the trail, then at the hootch.

"Okay. He should have woke you up before he left."

Gruda kept staring at him. Bradley knelt and began undoing his bedroll.

"So you're from New York, eh, Gruda? I'm from Indiana. Larson's from Michigan."

"Midwest."

"Right. Say Gruda, was college rough? I was gonna go on the GI Bill."

"What do you mean?"

"You have to be a genius? You have to study all night?"

"Not this kid. Christ, anybody can get through if he tries, or has a good fake."

"Well. What about co-eds?"

"What about them?"

"Do they really fuck as much as you hear?"

"Jesus Christ, Sarge. I never had no trouble. I was shacked up my whole senior year."

"You were? Wow."

"Sure wish I was back there now."

"Yeah. I told my dad I was gonna go to college on the GI Bill.

But I ain't goin. No way. Jim says he wants to go, but I bet he don't.''

"It's where the cunt is.''

"And Goddammed rich kids and draft dodgers.''

"Nothing wrong with bein rich, Sarge. Or avoiding the Army.''

"Don't call me Sarge.'' He cleared his throat. "You'd better run a bore brush through that damned rifle of yours.''

Bradley rose before Gruda could reply, and went to urinate. They did not speak again until it was time for Gruda to assume the guard.

Bradley again kicked the air mattress to summon him. He led the way with his M-79 and one canister round. Larson cocked his head hearing the approach.

"Okay, Jim. I'll give him the layout myself.''

"Have you seen anything?'' asked Gruda.

"You gotta be shittin,'' said Bradley. "Dinks don't move during the day. Except ambushes. They don't move till night. At night they own the fucking jungle.''

"They're still around though,'' said Larson.

"Better believe it.''

Larson rolled onto his back and sat up, with the green plastic trigger case in his hand.

"You got claymores?'' asked Gruda.

"Claymores shit,'' said Bradley. "We got fuckin bangalores. There's a ditch five meters back on the other side of the trail.'' He pointed through the leaves. Gruda nodded. "Bangalore torpedoes back there. When the dinks come we open up with sixteens and force them into the ditch. Then you blow it. You know what bangalores are?''

"I think so.''

"They bring the max. If we ever pull it, just make sure your ass is huggin that ground, with your head tucked in.''

"Roger that,'' said Larson. "I'm goin on back, Bradley.''

Gruda laid himself on the cleared pallet by extending his legs one at a time, the way drill instructors did it on the patrol ranges at Fort Polk, Louisiana. He fidgeted to get the grenades on his pistol belt loose at his sides. He held his finger on the rifle's trigger, thumb on the selector switch.

"You wouldn't see anything this shift, Cruit. Dinks don't move in daylight. At night you'll have the radio with you, and call in sit-reps every hour. I'll be bringin it out when I relieve you."

"What if I do see something?"

"You'll have a cord, and it'll be tied to my wrist back at the hootch. Tug like hell, and we'll wake up and get out here. Don't open fire until I get here."

"I mean what if I see em before dark?"

"You won't. Whatever you do, don't ever shoot unless you see em. I mean see live bodies comin at you. Not noises. It's only natural for you to be nervous and jumpy at every noise."

"But if I see em, shoot?"

"Only if you see 'em. And if you do you'd better be damned sure to kill somethin. Higher'll be waist deep in my shit if you give our position away for nothin."

Gruda nodded, and fidgeted again.

"You'll probably get stiff layin there. But you just gotta get used to it. Just say fuck it."

It was a high-speed trail, three feet wide and so well-traveled that no machete was needed to follow it. From his position Gruda could follow it for twenty meters either way.

At first he lay still and held the rifle trigger, with his eyes glued to the trail; but his mind inevitably wandered, even as the eyes pierced ahead. He was copulating with his college girl when Bradley returned, and quivered straining to twist his neck far enough back to see him.

"Think I'd ever get here?"

"Actually it went faster than I thought."

"Then you must have been jackin off or somethin. Don't worry, each time gets slower and worse. No matter how fuckin long you've been here."

"You've got the radio."

"And the string." He pulled it out of his shirt pocket, tied a loop in one end and slipped it over his wrist.

"Here, take this end back and give it to Larson."

"Right."

"Didn't see nothin, did you?"

"No."

"I told you. Dinks don't fuck around in daylight."

Gruda crawled back from the position, and knelt. "How much longer you figure till dark?"

"Not long. Another hour. You better go back, chow down and crash. We pull two on and four off at night. You'll be out here at," glancing at his watch, "ten o'clock. It'll be dark at seven-thirty. Larson starts the regular shift at eight."

"Okay, Sarge. I'll see you when you relieve me again, I guess."

"Don't call me sarge."

Bradley leaned the radio against a rock, lay down and took the handset for his commo check.

"Raider six-niner, Raider six-niner, this is Greeneye four-five, Greeneye four-five. Commo check, over."

"Roger, four-five, Raider six-niner. Hear you lima charlie. How me, over?"

"Roger, same-same. Greeneye four-five, negative sit-rep at this time. Out."

It was dark by 7:15, with a quarter moon, just enough to reflect the width of the trail for five or ten meters out. Bradley had memorized the terrain before dark, and used the silhouette of a tall teakwood thirty meters ahead; concentrating his scanning and listening ten meters left of the tree, where he knew the trail would be.

It had been dark ten minutes when he heard the dinks coming. He wasn't sure of it at first, and leaned forward on his elbows, cocked his head for thirty seconds before hearing the first voice. It was not unusual for dinks to talk and smoke marijuana or opium as they walked at night. They were even known to shine flashlights occasionally. They owned the jungle at night.

Bradley wrapped the cord around his wrist until it was taut, and heaved five times. He took the handset without moving his head from the trail, pressed it against his mouth and spoke in low whispers.

"Break break break, all stations break. This is Greeneye four-five, Greeneye four-five. Have movement to my november, confirmed Victor Charlie. Say again, confirmed Victor Charlie, over."

Gruda lay dreaming on his stomach in the cozy hootch. Larson whirled the poncho liner off, clutched the rifle and kicked him.

"Come on, Cruit. This is it."

"Greeneye four-five, this is Raider six-niner, roger. You gonna take em out?"

"Greeneye four-five, affirmative. Am waiting for them to reach kill zone, over."

"Roger. Estimate size, over."

"This is four-five, negative at this time. They're still too far to tell, over."

"This is six-niner, roger. Okay, just make sure they're in the kill zone before you blow. You will not put your own element in danger. Say again, you will not put your own element in danger, over."

"This is four-five, roger, understand. Stand by."

"Standing by."

Larson dove beside Bradley. Bradley did not speak, grabbed Larson's shirt collar and nodded the direction. Larson heard them talking; returned the nod and low-crawled five meters out on Bradley's flank, along the edge of the trail.

Gruda came low-crawling down from the hootch, like he had been taught to at Fort Polk. Bradley leaned into him until their steel pots touched.

"Okay, Cruit," he whispered, "This is it. We got dinks." He pointed his finger in the direction. Gruda gulped his throat and nodded back. They could distinguish one voice from another now.

"You stay right here with me, Cruit. Don't fire until Larson does. Soon as they return fire I'll blow the bangalores."

"Should I put her on automatic?"

"Who the hell cares?"

There were only five, barefoot, wearing shorts and carrying AK-47's. The leader was the only one with a ruck sack. The other four had tall straw baskets on their backs. Bradley snickered and shook his head thinking how perfect it was. They walked right on each other's heels. He waited until the middle man was directly before him.

"Now!"

He fired his canister round. The hollow thuck echoed over the whiz of the buckshot; the dinks squealing frantic words and Larson and Gruda immediately opening up on automatic. Bradley lay perfectly still with the green trigger case in his hand, waiting for the AK's to open. He heard them yell commands over the M-16 fire, and stared marble, hollow-eyed waiting for the popcorn popping of the AK's. When it came he screamed again, and tucked his head into his arms.

They felt the ground drop, dirt clods, bamboo and bodily remains whizzing around them. The acrid gray cordite hung thick in the air, causing Gruda to choke aloud.

Larson low-crawled back to Bradley's side.

"We brought the max."

"Yeah."

Gruda squinted to distinguish through the cordite and darkness.

"Hey, Jim." Bradley half-smiled as he pointed to Larson's steel pot.

Larson removed it, and saw the patch of cloth from one of the dinks' shorts stuck with blood to his faded camouflage cover.

"Fuckin dinks."

Gruda turned back to the trail and vomited as Bradley called for artillery illumination before moving down to check it.

"College boy," he grinned to Larson.

The Meeting

by Julian Grajewski

There is a blank darkness. Not a void, that sounds like something empty, but a depthless darkness you are confused and get lost in . . .

And then the darkness lightens a little bit and you see a glow on a horizon. And then you go down and you hear somebody being awakened, and you hear their grumbling voices, and somebody mumbling, yeah, yeah, and being awakened and getting up . . . and . . . you know . . . yawning. Like somebody getting up . . . out of a bunk or something . . .

You can't see too much. . . . You can mostly hear things. . . . You can hear this guy getting dressed and putting on his boots. . . . And you can just see him getting up and dragging his boots across the dirt and cracking dry leaves and twigs. . . . You notice that he's got a bright thing in his hand. And his boots . . . his boots are loose . . . not tied on or anything . . .

. . . Walks a few feet. . . . Comes up to this ladder . . . made of logs. The ladder leads up to a tower . . . like a watch tower, made of logs and wood. . . . And it has a thatch roof over it.

. . . This guy climbs up to the watch tower and looks towards the horizon . . . where the sun is coming up. And just as the sun is coming up he puts a bugle to his lips, and blows.

. . . And in the early morning you can see a small base camp. In the jungle . . . you can see this clearing which is not completely cleared. . . . There is a perimeter there, with bunkers and hootches. . . . Guys pulling guard and sleeping. . . . And a couple of ents . . . You know . . . like a command post tent . . . mess tents. . . . And a few trees and some brush. . . . And you come up to one of the tents which is wide open on all sides. . . . There are other guys in the tent, but you only see him . . .

. . . He's got a blanket over him. A poncho or something . . . because it is in the tropics and the morning is humid and chilly. He is sleeping on his back and hears the bugle call and he sort of wakes up. He opens his eyes, and lies there with his eyes open, waking up. Then he pulls the blanket away and you see that he is completely naked. And this guy is in his early twenties. He seems to be in good shape, good body . . . good hands . . . good legs. . . . He's gotten . . . tanned . . . bronzed . . . by the jungle sun. . . . And he looks all right. He . . . he's got a hard-on. . . . It's like . . . it's not—in the morning if you feel all right, you have an erection. It's not lust. . . . It's pleasant . . . a pleasant awareness. . . . That if you feel good you have this.

And he wakes up and he sits up on the edge of the bunk and he pushes away the mosquito net. And he puts on . . . pulls on a pair of shorts without getting up out of the bed without standing up. He just slips them on . . . and buckles up the belt. . . . And then he sort of. . . . He's got his feet on the dirt floor. . . . And he sort of slaps the dirt off his soles and pulls on his boots without putting on socks. He just slops them on without tying them or anything. . . . And he stands up and, he stretches a round a little bit, sort of sleepy. . . . But he's had a good sleep. He feels all right! It's pleasant to get up in the morning . . . he is just slowly waking up . . . letting it drag out.

And then he picks up this piece of soap . . . and a towel. . . . And he's got his weapon hanging from a . . . by a . . . sling from the top of the bunk. You know from the framework for the mosquito net. And the weapon is . . . some kind of an automatic weapon. He's got this and he takes it from the rack, and he puts it on . . . slings it over his shoulder; and he starts walking down this stretch of pretty wide trail . . . a little muddy. . . .

He walks pretty good . . . easy . . . relaxed . . . The weapon dangling from his shoulder . . . under the armpit. His boots are loose . . . he drags his feet a little. . . . He just walks on down to this gully. The gully twists a little bit and goes down to this river . . . not too wide. As he walks down to the river the gully goes up several feet on both sides of him. . . . And he can see these great big roots coming out of the dirt sides. And a wet, heavy, very old smell coming out of it. . . .

... It's a river ... maybe sixty yards across, no more ... a muddy river. And there is a rock there. ... And he puts all his stuff on the rock ... takes his boots off and wades up to his knees. ... And the water is a little bit cold this early in the morning. But it wakes him up. ... And he starts washing his face with soap. ... And washing a little bit on his chest and under his arms ... just washes away the sweat from his skin. And then. ... And then he walks out. He walks out of the water and dries off with the towel. ... Dries his face and dries his underarms. ... Then he sits on the rock and rinses his feet and pulls on his boots. ...

He walks downriver a few feet, opens his fly and starts taking a piss ... takes a full night's load off and it feels good. ... After you keep it in for a full night it stinks. But the stink of his own piss is not too bad. ... And then he notices some movement across the river ...

... And he sees some kind of animal on the edge of the water ... maybe a leopard ... probably came down during the night to drink water. ... And must have overstayed after sunrise. ... This guy is surprised ... He's been in the jungle for a long time but he's never seen that many wild animals. And now he sees a leopard all of a sudden ... it's so startling to see this animal, this wild thing coming down to drink. ... And he looks at it. ... And the leopard looks at him too. ... And they look at each other for a while.

And this guy notices that the leopard has blood on his muzzle and has blood on his paws. . . and a little bit of gore. ... It killed something during the night and then came down to the river to drink water ...

And they keep staring at each other. ... And then the leopard, in its own ... cattish ... way ... turns about the way cats do it, very beautifully ... turns about and climbs the little river bank and disappears into the jungle.

And the guy stares at the spot where the leopard was ... he has a look on his face ... amazed ... surprised. ... He does his fly and walks back to his stuff on the rock. ... Picks up his stuff and ... takes one last look across the river. But there is nothing there anymore. ... He starts walking back. ... He walks back up the gully and this time everybody is awake ... the people cleaning rifles ... getting ready for chow ... and talking and pulling in their booby traps, and flares. ... And a couple of ambush patrols are back. You know, things that soldiers do every morning ...

Medical Evacuation

by Wayne Karlin

Standing by for medevacs, he always had the feeling he was being centered in a movie camera. Flight suits and sun glasses, casually late show and focused in sharply by the magnifying clearness of the Danang air. A loud buzzer sounds with dramatic insistence. A long shot: the crews running self-consciously to the helicopters, loading machine guns competently, talking flight language, sticking their thumbs up. Switch to the interior of the helicopter, the close-up lens zooms in for a really fine shot of his sweaty grease-stained face framed over his machine gun by the open port. Then a full shot of the interior: the black crew chief pumping the A.P.E. then running forward to his gun, the subtle impact of the scene, no racists in foxholes, by God.

The sun sank as the helicopter rose. The gunner looked at its fall and felt powerful and full of height. In its wake, the sun began sucking the colors out of the ground, and the earth seemed insignificant to him.

The crew talked over the intercom, the cords on their helmets linking them together with sound in the darkness. They were flying towards Dong Ha, a flying shovel come to scrape up some of the overflow of bleeding flesh from the Operation. Hastings. Hastily to Hastings, the gunner thought. Where did they get the names? He was trying to slide his sight through the darkness, looking for flashes, for tracers, for anything. For today's trick we will clear the DMZ with Norman cavalrymen. They must be catching shit, he thought reasonably, to be calling for planes on secondary alert. Means the choppers there are very full, and the crews will be cleaning out the insides with hoses, washing away any spare bleeding parts left sticking on the helicopter deck.

The trap door of a gallows suddenly opened, opened right at the moment when he was still counting on more time. A drop and wait for the noose to snap his neck.

The helicopter fell, then began circling downwards more lazily. Leaning out of his port, the gunner could see the flashes of the strobe they were using to mark the landing zone, but the light didn't illuminate the terrain. The aircraft dropped into darkness and the noose never tightened.

They landed hard and the rear ramp dropped heavily. The gunner stayed at his gun while the crew chief ran back to help with the wounded. Looking over the gun, he could just make out part of the circle of infantrymen around the zone. Their green backs looked tense and tired and they were mud-spattered and strangely fragile looking in their hardness. They didn't look as if they had stepped off a tapestry. Backs and sagging asses and legs. Too normal for Normans.

The wounded came through the open rear hatch, touching the sides of the helicopter with gentle, bloody hands. They were already a race apart, consecrated in the eyes of the unwounded, receivers of blows meant for the unhurt. Some whole marines were carrying in those unable to walk and laying them out on the deck. The helicopter was filling up and its blades beat the air insistently as if feeling the danger and straining to go. The interior light dully lit the packed, groaning bodies. The wounded were twisted into one another, holding onto each other, softly bleeding into each other's wounds. The gunner thought suddenly of a pile of clothes crumpled desolately on a cot, cloth arms and legs locked into impossible positions of sad lifelessness. Pudding, bleeding from between its convulsions.

The ramp closed and the helicopter lifted. The corpsman moved among the marines, shooting morphine into them. Many of them hadn't been treated at all yet. We must have landed right in the middle of something, the gunner thought.

A marine, his torn trousers showing shredded meat, was trying to stand up next to the gunner, leaving room for the men on the deck. He put his hand on the gunner's shoulder to steady himself, then looked at him apologetically. The gunner turned his eyes away for a moment, and noticed the black man lying near his feet. The man seemed to have a red gelatinous mass growing from the side of his neck, twisting his head and strangling him. His eyes bulged at the gunner.

All, of course, in a second, a split second, for he was dutifully looking out of his port and didn't miss the flashes below and the green tracers flying up at the helicopter. He fired his guilt down at the flashes and felt it leave him in violent spurts through the machine gun barrel. Just shooting at the noise, he thought, they're nowhere near. His own tracers kept flashing, red. Maybe I hit some NVA, he thought, and he's being dragged off on a hook by his buddy. Who's feeling guilty the hook ain't in his own pudding neck. Fucking fool. The firing stopped.

Then they were dropping towards Dong Ha, and were down, and the ramp dropped again.

The corpsmen came in with some service troops who had volunteered to carry stretchers. See what they'd been missing. The bearers were in respectful awe of the wounded but acted as nonchalant as the corpsmen; I ain't just a cook, seen this stuff every day. The walking wounded began walking and the gunner helped the man who had been leaning next to him walk out, then turned back in.

The corpsmen were going through the men lying on the deck, busily, competently, deciding who was dead. They did that by magic, putting two enchanted fingers on wrists, and bestowing life or death medically. The stretcher bearers began lifting up one man whose pulse was being felt by a corpsman. Save it, the corpsman advised, he's bought it. The dead man was a big blond boy.

"Save it," the economical corpsman said, and gestured impatiently at the volunteers. "Get'm out quick, he can't feel nothin'." One of the bearers grabbed the man's ankles and dragged the body out. The head bounced up and down on the ramp as the body slid, then thudded dully on the ground.

Save what? the gunner thought. The gentleness, I guess. Funny what these two-fingered bankers can save. Sure, he thought, save it.

He walked away from the fuel lines and tried to catch a quick smoke before they took off again.

The Accident

by James R. Dorris

Temple finished pulling a maintenance check on the Major's jeep, and left the motor pool just as the sun was starting to rise. He could see the paved highway clearly as he drove down the company road and parked the jeep in front of the H-shaped building which held the offices of Engineer Group Headquarters.

He left the jeep and crossed the distance to the mess hall, jumping the deeply grooved gullies at the side of the dirt road. He entered the mess hall by the NCO door and told a young Vietnamese girl what he wanted to eat. Some of the other sergeants were sitting at the large center table, talking about the whores they had been with last in Bien Hoa. He sat down at one of the small corner tables and waited for the baby-san to return with his breakfast.

"Didn't see you in town last night, Temple," the supply sergeant said.

"Probably because I wasn't there," Temple said, glancing at the watching sergeants.

"You ever been into town, Temple?"

Temple ignored the question. The baby-san set his breakfast in front of him.

"Thanks baby-san."

"A pretty boy like him must miss those round-eyed broads."

"Yeh, I bet they were hot after his ass in the States."

"Hey, Jack, why don't you take Temple on the mess hall trash run tomorrow morning?"

"How about it Temple? We'll stop at a car wash so you can get your rocks off. It does't cost much," the mess sergeant offered.

"Yeh, and I'll even pay for it," the supply sergeant said.

"Thanks, I'll handle my own sex life," Temple said, finishing his powdered eggs and bacon. The other sergeants went back to their conversation while Temple swallowed the coffee and walked out of the mess hall, leaving baby-san his empty tray to take into the dishroom where it would be cleaned in the greasy dishwater by some of the mama-sans.

He walked down the middle of the road to the shitter at the rear of the company area. There was only a short line waiting for the three seats so he got inside the small louvered building quickly. Dropping his trousers, he plopped down on the hole cut in the wood. While the waste was flowing out of him into the fifty-gallon drum below, Temple thought about how he could have spent his year squatting over open slit trenches in the field. He had been reassigned to the group operations office when he arrived in Vietnam instead of going into the boondocks with a field unit like he was supposed to. Men assigned to subordinate units had to process through the group headquarters and the clerks in personnel were alert for anyone with high test scores.

Temple felt a cool breeze from below his seat as he finished. Buckling his belt, Temple walked out to the rear of the building. An old mama-san gave him a friendly toothless smile as she hooked the can with her iron pole and pulled it out from under the seat. She began dragging it down the dirt road to the rear compound where she poured and ignited oil on the night's runs.

Temple walked to the headquarters building and worked at his desk until the major came into the office. A baby-san had brought over the major's usual coffee and donuts from the mess hall and Temple took them into him. Entering the office, he could sense the major's annoyance. He fidgeted with the papers on his desk as he spoke to Temple.

"Thanks, Sergeant. Did you get the jeep?"

"Yes, sir. It's out front."

"We've got a real problem with the province chief at Phu Cuong. He wants us to pay his villagers for the time they're taking from their fields to build the stinking dam they're helping us put across the stream they have up there. We're supposed to try and reason with him," the major said.

"Do you think he'll listen?"

"He'll have to. They're only giving up one day a week and

they're using our men and equipment to do most of the work. What the hell do they want from us?''

''The province chief gives us intelligence information, doesn't he, sir?''

''Yes. The Colonel wants us to stay on his good side and still try and talk to him about it. We need that intelligence information.''

As Temple left the office, the major started cleaning his pistol. The only time he cleaned it was when he was going out into the field.

Walking to his tent, Temple thought about the major. Adams was a West Point graduate. He had told Temple that Vietnam was the best thing that ever happened to him because he could make lieutenant colonel before he left. He figured that since he was only in his late thirties, he had a good chance to make general if the war continued long enough. He was considered a good operations officer, respected by his superiors and by the men who worked for him. Temple went to his tent just long enough to slip on his flak jacket and sling his well-oiled M-14 on his shoulder. As he hurried back to the jeep, the major came out of the headquarters building. The major liked to drive the jeep whenever they went anywhere. He slid in behind the wheel and started it up as Temple got into the passenger's seat.

They drove through the gate, down the highway and onto the trash-strewn streets of Bien Hoa. They bounced over a rotting railroad bridge and into the boondocks beyond.

The major talked little as he drove. He kept the accelerator pressed to the floor as the jeep bounced and jolted over the dirt roads. Laughing, he had explained his theory on speed to Temple many times before. ''Sergeant Temple,'' he would say, ''the way I figure it, if we ever run over a mine, we'll be at least a hundred yards past it before it has a chance to go off.''

Temple thought about his theory and looked at the sandbags under his feet, wondering how much protection they'd afford if the jeep did hit a mine. The major never seemed to wonder, he always knew for sure. Maybe it was because he had been in the Army so long. He was never at a loss for answers.

The jeep bounced over the cracked and broken pavement which wound through the countryside. Clumps of thick bushes and bamboo trees lined the road, broken by an occasional shack surrounded by rice paddies where Vietnamese families waded under the hot morning sun.

As they approached the small villages scattered along the road, the major had to slow down for the Lambrettas and the carts and wagons drawn by water buffalo which accounted for most of the traffic they saw. The cool breeze which Temple felt driving through the countryside left them as the jeep slowed and the full force of the sun's rays penetrated the canvas into the jeep.

As they passed through the village of Nuoc Lam, Temple thought the name sounded familiar.

"Sir, is this the village where Bohannon and Cameron took the wrong road and hit the mine?"

"Right Temple. They went down the next road on your right."

As they passed the dirt road, Temple looked at the shacks extending for a few hundred feet on either side. There wasn't time to see much before the major sped up again and they were in the countryside once more.

"What do you think Bohannon and Cameron were doing on that side road, major? Knowing the two of them they couldn't have gotten lost."

"I don't know, Temple. They were a couple of strange characters, even for tunnel demolition people."

"Yeh, they seemed pretty crazy."

"It wouldn't surprise me a bit if they were looking for a couple of quickies. Hell, they could have had a harem in this town. It's too bad they got killed. Now the gooks will have to find a new source for their money."

They drove into the Vietnamese Army Compound at Phu Cuong a half hour later. Temple stayed with the jeep while the major went to his meeting. While he was sitting around waiting, a group of scrawny Vietnamese kids gathered around the jeep, looking for handouts. They kept shouting, "GI, GI, you numah one, what you can gimme, GI?" Temple opened a case of C-rations from the back of the jeep and started handing them out.

The major came out of his meeting just as Temple handed the last package to a little girl who had been pushed away by the bigger kids. Swearing, the major told them to get away from the jeep.

The kids ran and the major and Temple started back for the base. Bouncing along, Temple thought of Bohannon and Cameron during Operation Cedar Falls. He and the major had gone out on the operation when tunnels were found so they could see the new acetylene demolition kits in use. Bohannon was a tough little thirty-five-year-old staff sergeant. He had crawled head first into the tunnel with a knife between his teeth and a pistol and flashlight in his hands. Five minutes later he had crawled out again with a rat stuck on the end of the knife. And Cameron—Bohannon called him Pappy—the wiry grizzled old coot who had hooked up the explosive gas pump, filled the tunnel and blown it up. Temple couldn't imagine their bodies scattered around for hundreds of yards outside Nuoc Lam.

Bouncing and jolting and swerving around corners as fast as the jeep would allow, they continued back to the base. As they wheeled around a blind corner, the major saw him too late. Temple felt the bump and the old man hurtled forward into the middle of his small herd of water buffalo.

The major jumped out. "Get out there and drag him into the trees. I'll get the water buffalo off the road. Hurry up, Temple!"

Temple moved slowly and stood looking at the old man. He lay crumpled up, not moving, his blood staining the pavement. Temple felt his wrist for a pulse and found none. He grabbed the old man's feet and pulled him off the road behind a tree, staring at the blood oozing from the man's mouth.

"Hurry up, Temple! Let's get out of here."

Quickly he ran back and climbed into the jeep where the major was impatiently waiting. They took off, leaving the water buffalo chewing contentedly on a patch of elephant grass just down the road from what looked like a forgotten pile of bloody rags behind a tree.

As they continued on the road back to the base, Temple saw the blood on his jungle fatigues and on his hands.

"What are you going to do, sir?"

"Nothing, Temple. There's nothing we can do," the major said without taking his eyes off the road.

"Are you going to report the accident?"

"No, Temple."

The jeep sped along through the countryside as the major continued to press the accelerator to the floor. They passed the families still working in the rice fields, as they continued back toward the base.

"Sir, you've got to report the accident."

"Look, Temple, you'd better keep your mouth shut about this. Nobody will miss him."

"Why won't you report it?"

"I feel bad about the old man, Temple, but nothing can be done for him. It would be useless to report it. Besides, for all we know he might be a Viet Cong. You can't tell which side these people are on."

The major eased off the gas as the jeep bounced over the rotting railroad bridge and wound back through Bien Hoa to the base. The major stopped in front of the headquarters building and got out of the jeep.

"Temple, return this to the motor pool and see that it gets cleaned up."

"Major Adams, I'm going to see the colonel. I'm going to tell him about the accident."

"Okay, Temple. Come to his office when you finish with the jeep."

Temple watched as the major turned and walked into the headquarters building.

The major and the colonel were talking when Temple joined them after taking care of the jeep. He saluted and the colonel asked him to sit down.

"Major Adams told me what happened, Sergeant Temple, and I can understand how you feel, believe me I can. It's unfortunate that people die, but this is a war zone. Sometimes innocent people die too. But that's no reason to ruin the career of a good officer. Look at the overall picture, Sergeant. Major Adams is doing his level best to help the people of Vietnam. One unfortunate mistake can be forgotten. I hope you understand, Sergeant."

Temple walked back to the operations office and sat down behind his desk. He sat thinking for a long time, mulling over everything that happened. He thought about the overall picture. He wondered how that major felt inside about the accident. He wondered whether or not the major felt guilty.

Temple felt someone staring at him and looked up into baby-san's eyes. She was holding a tray of food.

"Major call over for food. You give him?"

"Sure baby-san, set it down on the desk."

The major was in his office and Temple took the tray into him.

"Thanks Temple, I'm starving. It's been a pretty hectic day," the major said as Temple stood watching him gulp down his food.

"You hungry Temple?"

"No. I don't think I could eat anything right now."

"That's too bad. You're taking this whole thing too hard. Take the rest of the day off and get some rest."

Temple walked out of the office and left the headquarters building. He stopped in front of the company bulletin board to see if he was scheduled to pull Sergeant of the Guard. He wasn't on the list for the next three days so he went to the NCO tent. He crossed to his bunk and laid down.

First Light

by Steve Smith

funny how the voice has to start talking to you again maybe dreamt or thought in waking or just limbo between kind of interesting terror dry but must have a wet mouth "Willard Morgan, you know you're not going to make it out of here alive" must probably be fear because only twenty days more and back in the world it seems to crazy to even think about you standing on the street or sitting in soft chairs easy social drinking no what a laugh die now great irony plane maybe crashing on California coast here I am oh motherfucker maybe old Norma Bredon'll be free God she was nice skin so soft smell nice the silk nightie sliding over that round ass Jesus not here in the chopper lean out in the wind maybe it'll go down you're getting so bad you can come thinking nice wind sometimes it can blow everything away especially flying lead like this glad to fly with Sloane again just closer and closer to the ground Mr. Charles pretty good pilot too easy first light today maybe out over the sea just skim on top of the water get away at least from Sergeant Hart and his fucking shaving inspection clean face will win the war it's fine for him sitting all day reading fuck books drinking rye Jesus there's the coconut grove water buffalo were all rigormortis and the black-pajamaed bodies face down big red spots on the backs there's sea

"Hey, Morg," Captain Sloane said, "you want to test fire the guns once we get over the ocean?"

"Roger, sir." *why not nice the way they plunk up water tracers bouncing sometimes up orange skipping over blue evaporating color*

"Four-four, this is four-three, over," Sloane said.

"This is four-four, over."

"Four-four, we're going to test fire when we get about a quarter mile out. You can follow if you want."

"Roger, four-three, will do, out."

"Okay, Morgan and Berry," Sloane said, "don't go tryin' to hit no sampans. Just shoot straight down."

"Gotcha, sir," Morgan said. *still looks fine all the orange tearing down there all six working yes nice ricochet flying orange try the M-16*

The side guns stopped, and Morgan fired the twenty tracer bullets from the automatic rifle. *wonder if they really burn you when they get inside.*

Warrant Officer Charles pulled the helicopter up to the left. Morgan rested the machine gun in his lap again and looked out the door as Captain Dixon's ship began firing.

"Four-four, let's go up the coast a couple more miles, then we'll take it back in."

"Roger, four-three. We're right behind you."

God coast is nice rocks haven't seen before wait there's where Harkness got it

"Sure was too bad about Harkness," he said.

"Yeah," Berry said, not looking at him.

"What the hell happened down there anyway? Were you guys taking fire?"

Berry looked around, then back at him. "Look, Morgan, I ain't startin' no shit, but that wasn't no VC got Harkness."

"What?"

"I heard the medic talking and I seen him too and his chest was all tore up because the bullets went in his back and the medic said it weren't no thirty caliber but M-16."

"What?"

"Could have just been from everybody firing wild when they got out of the ship, but a few people got other ideas."

and nothing more after that but maybe somebody Jesus no it doesn't seem right but I guess the riflemen are different fourteen hours a day in rice paddies leeches Jesus Christ twenty fucking days and they can have it Hart can run it up his funky ass.

Morgan leaned out the door and guffawed into the wind. He came back inside the ship and flipped the intercom button onto private.

"Twenty days, Berry."

"Well, I wish they'd get a replacement for you. You're as happy as a pig in shit this morning. Still drunk from last night?"

"Just feeling good, that's all. Nice sunny day, cool breeze blowing through the ship."

"Maybe you better keep your eyes on the ground," Berry laughed. "It was right about here that Sanders took that fifty caliber through the window."

Okay, man, dig you later." *but that was Sanders sorry sack of shit too bad it didn't hit him damn you feel invincible as hell this morning don't you but Christ if you were going to get it you should have got it by now and maybe it's after all just luck and you've always had that or believed you did anyway and the voice hasn't got you that scared funny never scared the shooting starts maybe because it's finally an end to bullshit talk and lies you've almost greeted it as brother except for others you had to know getting it then maybe the big lie comes across but moment of the shot just clear exhilaration of jeopardy lots must feel you hope couldn't only be you but there should be fear sometimes*

"Well, let's take it back in," Sloane said.

"Might as well," Mr. Charles said.

"Four-four, we're heading back to base.

"This is four-four. Roger, out."

not even out an hour yet but wouldn't mind staying out the extra hour today it's good maybe write Norma a letter when I get in no can't write too good no more maybe show up there a little drunk surprise she'll feel sorry Christ Halsey'll almost have his Ph.D. and you still haven't a degree yet hell maybe go to Berkeley right away not wait till September hell with Princeton too far gone by then hope I get out when I get back but still only two or three months at Benning after leave maybe go down to Mexico or go see Chambers in Minnesota but too much snow now stay home for Christmas anyway it'll be nice having the money for a car maybe a VW or straight eight Packard ask

He flipped the intercom to private again. "You think I could get a straight eight Packard fixed up good enough to go from California to Georgia?"

"Shit."

"No, man. If I got the engine overhauled she'd probably make it, right?"

"Maybe to East L.A."

"Come on."

"It might make it. You'd have to have some good work done on it though. What you want with one of them, anyway?"

"They're kind of neat."

"You can have some fun with those old buggies, but they ain't that good for cross country travel."

Morgan looked up and saw Captain Sloane talking on the radio, and quickly flipped the intercom back.

". . . ger, three, this is four-three."

"Four-three, this is three. How much fuel do you have left?"

"This is four-three. About five hundred pounds, over."

"Roger, four-three. There's a Special Forces Camp about two miles north of that market place on highway one that's taking fire from the adjacent village. Want you to go check it out. You can tune them in on your UH up 1.67 from where you are. It's their discretion on firing."

"Roger, three. Out."

"This is three. Out."

"You hear that four-four?" Captain Sloane asked.

"Roger, four-three."

"Let's go check it out."

old green berets in trouble got to call on us like always sitting up there boozing and farting around with AK weapons on rifle range big tough motherfuckers can stuff their singing staff sergeant up their ass too you can bet he's not staying in any army after making all that bread wonder what the hell's going on here won't be too long not enough fuel probably nothing anyway

Mr. Charles banked the helicopter and turned it to the north when they reached highway one. The road near the market place was flanked by tall palm trees. The market place was full of people in black and white pajamas moving in and out from under the thatched roofs of several small huts. From both directions people moved on the road toward the market place. They were mostly women, who carried baskets on their heads, or poles over their shoulders with bundles hooked on either end. There were also bicycles driven by old men, and an occasional motorbike. At the north end of the market place several children were running around a jeep, pointing and laughing at the MP's who lounged in it. One of the children crawled over the spare tire in the back of the jeep and pinched one of the MP's in the arm. The MP tried to swat the child but he was out of the jeep and laughing by the time the arm came around. *just like an old horse switching at flies damn MP's anyway laid up in town with whores all night but burning you if they catch you after six going to burn some whores when you get back to clear post almost two months now Christ it'll be something me and Martin and Webster and Hancock and Chambers and the others all down there and screw the money I won't need more than a dime when I get to Oakland anyway*

"This is Noble Rider four-three, this is Noble Rider four-three, do you read me? Over."

"Noble Rider four-three, this is Jungle Master six. Read you Lima Charlie. How do you read me? Over."

Jungle Mastermy ass master bater

"Lima Charlie, Jungle Master six. What's the situation? Over."

The Special Forces Camp looked like a cache for sandbags inside barbed wire. There were a few small huts with aluminum roofs, but the compound was mainly bunkers covered with many layers of sandbags. Across a clearing; about a hundred yards north of the camp, was a small hamlet of fifteen mud hootches, some shaded by palm trees, the others blending with the brown ground around them. There was no sign of life.

"This is Jungle Master six. We've been taking fire from one of the hootches in that hamlet. I think they got a BAR and a machine gun. Can't figure out which hootch it is. You want to see if you can draw them out?"

"Roger, six. Four-four, this is four-three. We're going down on the deck and see if we can rouse these birds. You circle around the hamlet and see if you can see anything."

"Roger, four-three. Out."

"I'll take it," Captain Sloane said to Mr. Charles. "You stay ready to take it if we start getting shot at so I can work these guns. Morgan and Berry, you keep your eyes peeled and don't shoot till you're fired at, unless you see VC with guns."

Captain Sloane flew the helicopter back to the highway and banked it high to the right. The ship seemed to hang suspended a moment *like a cormorant before crashing for fish,* then gradually fell back and around, gathering speed, until it was headed directly at the hamlet. *Jesus Sloane can fly this baby bet he misses the roofs by an inch or two they start firing our ass is out*

Morgan braced his left foot against the door jamb and leaned out into the wind. Captain Sloane completed the first pass and repeated the banking movement above a tree line past the west end of the village. *white somebody running from behind that hootch long hair woman must be some people down there.*

"Captain Sloane, I saw a woman down there run from one hootch to another and she wasn't carrying any BAR."

"I saw her, Morgan. She's probably looking for a place to hide."

Morgan looked over at Berry and shrugged. Berry grinned at him foolishly, shook his head and looked back out the door.

"Jungle Master six, this is four-three. We haven't seen anything down there but a woman going from one hootch to another, over."

"Roger, four-three. Probably getting more ammo for the others. Look, four-three, I got a Vietnamese interpreter down here who thinks he might be able to spot the hootch. Why don't you come down and take him up with you."

"Roger, six. Four-four, go down there and pick up that interpreter. We'll keep making passes and keep you covered."

"Roger, four-three."

now what the hell they think they're doing like he'd know sure unless he'd been laying in there at night probably did well only three hundred pounds fuel so not much longer get another team out here quick anyway why the hell don't they just send a couple scouts in there on the ground silly bastards

"He see anything yet, four-four?"

"Negative, four-three. He seems more confused than us."

"Jungle Master six, this is Noble Rider four-three. That interpreter can't see anything. Doesn't look like he knows what hootch it is. Over."

"Roger, four-three. Well, uh, maybe you ought to . . . no, what the hell, why don't you make a couple gun runs over the whole village. Try to get some in each hootch. You ought to smoke them out that way. Over."

This is four-three. You want me to fire at every hootch? There may be . . ."

"Roger, four-three. You read me right. Every hootch. These people been helping Charlie too long anyway. Probably everybody's at market but them with guns and ammo. Why don't you make the runs from southeast to northwest. That'll probably be safest. Out."

"Six, this is four-three. But . . ."

"You heard me, four-three. Southeast to northwest. I can't afford to be losing any men because of a bunch of VC in a village. Out!"

"Roger, six, out!" Sloane flipped the radio switch. "Well, four-four, you heard him. You follow me. Christ, if he wants it, let's give him the whole damn show—guns, rockets, the works."

"Roger, four-three."

so now maybe you'll get to read this one in the paper "friendly village destroyed by accident" just because some fucking lazy lardass screw it okay hang a frag and WP pacification program sure they just love having us around we're so helpful and friendly and guess Sloane doesn't especially want to probably doesn't care that much anyway and what do you do want the experience get it can't call it back so now you know so what buy maybe it should be something like let's quit now it's just been a film you saw but you couldn't accept that either like out of books you've got to taste but I guess like they all say that's done it quits making sense after a while so quitting caring isn't so bad but quitting trying to is so maybe Chambers was right just shutting up but I know he hasn't tried to hit anything in four months he's made his progress and you

"Okay, Morgan and Berry, you heard the man. He's a major and I'm only a captain, but I'm not telling you anything. I don't see any pigs down there, Morgan, do you?"

"No sir." *no pigs like we killed last week just woman like it to be old Special Forces major and Hart let them taste hot licks*

"Okay, four-four, we're going in."

"Roger, four-three."

Charles can't bank it good as Sloane guess he's nervous hasn't seen anything like this yet but'll probably dig it fuck it isn't his fault isn't anybody's god the bank stop is nice holds everything like picture brown green maybe to make it sink in ho here goes like elevators coming to quick stops stomach funny

When he started firing, Morgan realized that he didn't have a target. Captain Sloane was maneuvering the side guns up and down, and from right to left. *God orange flight all over shoot the*

ground okay Jesus hootch rake it right across the top there go
rockets throw WP can't stop feed pull more ammo throw frag

"Anybody see anything?" Captain Sloane asked. Mr. Charles was banking the ship above the tree line on the west side of the hamlet.

"Nothing," Berry said.

"Sure a lot of smoke down there," Morgan said.

"Should be three rockets left on each side," Captain Sloane said.

"Three here," Berry said.

"Same," Morgan said.

Mr. Charles was laughing. "Hey, Morgan," he said, "you see that bird you hit?"

"What?"

"I guess it flew in front of your gun. You didn't see it?"

"No, sir."

"I saw it out of the corner of my eye. You must have hit it right in the chest because it just exploded into a puff of feathers. Looked funny as hell."

Captain Dixon's ship pulled over the tree line. There was so much smoke that Morgan could barely see any of the hootches in the village.

"You see anything, four-four? Over."

"About ten chickens ran out of one hooch, four-three. Didn't look too dangerous."

"Roger, four-four. Well, let's get it one more time, then you can drop that interpreter and we can get the hell out of here."

"Roger, out, four-three."

Morgan was still breathing hard from the first gun run when they began the second. The more he thought about the bird the more absurd it seemed, and he felt his mouth widening into a grin. As he started firing he began to laugh. He had fired about fifty rounds when he saw the three women running from one hootch to another in the northeast corner of the village.

"God, there's people all over down there," Mr. Charles said.

There was something in his voice that made Morgan laugh harder. The knuckles of his right hand were white where they gripped the trigger and trigger-guard of his machine gun. He looked up at Captain Sloane who was bent over the infinity sight which controlled the side guns. Sloane suddenly glanced back at

Morgan, and their eyes met for a fraction of a second. Morgan's mouth was open wide with laughter. *God stop it stop it his eyes are just like glass rock face hand won't open can't guit this funny why it's funny*

The rockets had destroyed a hootch nearly midway across the hamlet. Morgan saw two children peering up at the helicopter from what was left of one wall. *don't ask don't ask for Chirist's sake put your faces down laugh more Jesus stop motherfuck*

He was standing up, firing straight down, when the woman with the baby in her arms ran underneath the ship. She was running for the small hootch at the northwest corner of the hamlet. Morgan watched the tracers from his gun hitting the dirt slightly behind and to the left of her. He watched them move over slightly until they were directly behind her. She wore a white top and black pajama bottoms. The tracers looked better crawling up the black than they did when they got to the white. He laughed at the surprised look on the baby's face, and his laughter became uncontrollable when the woman did three somersaults into the wall of the hootch.

He was still standing up and looking out the door when Mr. Charles banked the ship, and he fell down on his knees and bumped his chin on the machine gun. The laugher stopped when he saw the orange starting out of the tree line. He moved into his seat and reached for the mike button, but Captain Sloane was already on the radio.

"We're taking fire from the tree line. Four-four, they're in the tree line. Keep running straight right over it and try to get some grenades in there."

Morgan climbed outside the helicopter, and stood on the skid firing into the tree line. *the orange starts like pin points racing at you turning into footballs not close enough yet ship turning right now can't see all yours Berry baby there's village Jesus she rolled and the child accused you burned yourself into its face no not laugh again Jesus please stop please what's this back neck feels soft warm moist.*

He put his hand to the back of his neck and turned around and stopped laughing. Berry lay on his back on the floor of the ship. One of the bullets had skinned the bottom of his nose before it split his front teeth and went through his mouth and came out at the base of his brain. Another had shattered his chin. Others had gone through his neck, taking most of it with them, and his head lay on a blanket of blood which kept growing larger and larger. A bright red bubble welled up from where his Adam's apple had been. Morgan popped it with the index finger of his right hand. Then he reached slowly for the mike button.

"Berry's dead," he said deliberately, almost whispering.

Captain Sloane turned around and his eyes met Morgan's. They stared mutely at each other for several seconds. Morgan's voice began low and guttural in the back of his throat, gathering volume and speed. "Can't any of you motherfuckers understand that Berry's dead?"

Captain Sloane turned to the front again and flipped a button on the console. "Noble Rider three, this is Noble Rider four—three, my crew chief's shot up and I'm coming to the medevac pad and you better have it cleared and someone there to get him."

"This is Noble Ri . . ."

Captain Sloane flipped the switch again.

"Jungle Master six, this is Noble Rider four—three, your Victor Charlies are in the tree line not in the hamlet and one of them got my crew chief and I'm leaving. Out." He flipped the switch again. "Four-four, they got Berry, and we're heading for the medevac pad."

"Roger, four-three. They quit firing down there. I think my gunner got a grenade right next to them."

"Tell it to three. Out. Okay, you take it in, Mr. Charles. I'm going in the back." He unfastened his harness and crawled over the console into the back of the helicopter. He pulled Berry's flight helmet out of the socket and plugged in his own. He switched the intercom to private.

The helicopter floor was almost completely red. Morgan was kneeling over Berry, his legs spread so that each knee was a few inches outside Berry's ears. He didn't move when Captain Sloane touched him on the back, and he made no sign of acknowledgment when Sloane said "I'm sorry, Morgan."

Berry's machine gun hung free from the elastic cord, and bounced crazily in the wind as the helicopter moved toward the camp. The belt of three hundred rounds that was left in the box on the floor had been jostled out, and swung loosely from the gun outside the ship. Captain Sloane crawled up on the seat and over to the gun. He pulled it in and secured it against the back of the pilot's seat, and dumped the ammunition back in the box. Berry's calves dangled outside the ship, but there was no way to get them back inside without moving the entire body, so Captain Sloane let them hang. Morgan watched Sloane, and when their eyes met he looked back at the corpse beneath him.

so you'll have to kill Hart and yourself grenade the sorry fucker laid in his tent my god she rolled and rolled while you laughed child accusing forever can't go with that your knees blood-soaked you crawl in mouth of a dead man no just get the grenade Hart's there shaving inspection done now the bastard I'll blow us fucking both to bits he never flew don't need the liquor now at least you've got that far you'll all laugh your bloody asses off the face of the child accusing mother rolling laughing earth face God Sloane don't touch again I've got a fuse my neck turns I explode blow your experience you've got now bags full pockets and eyes forever eyes and branded brain why couldn't the orange pin-point footballs hit you he didn't know or care or couldn't think of this and had fear his neck all wet on yours you couldn't expect but now you wet and hot go flying through that tent mingle with Hart you making bits of you ten thousand Willard Morgan hunks go flying sack them up and send them home to mommy they're bound to tell the appropriate lies "freak accident the grenade dropped and man and his sergeant killed" if only you could see the story printed maybe someone'll drop a paper on the scattered bits no one cleaned up and they can soak it up with flies and ants eating the accusing eyes maybe plucked off your brain by birds pick up the ever rolling woman

The medevac tent was directly behind the area where the aerial gunnery platoon's tents were erected. Captain Sloane leaned out the left door as the helicopter hovered in for its landing. Morgan watched him gesture frantically for the medics to come around to that side of the ship. Morgan took his flight helmet off and picked up a fragmentation grenade. When the helicopter was five feet off the ground he undid his harness, removed his armor-plated vest, leaped out and began running toward the platoon area. He saw Chambers sitting in front of his tent. Chambers started to get up but Morgan ran past him and began screaming when he was ten feet from Hart's tent.

"Okay, Hart, you cocksuckin' motherfucker, you and me are going to see Dennis Berry together!" He burst through the flap, pulled the pin from the grenade, and stopped. He tore the flap viciously and leaped outside, nearly bumping in to Chambers.

"Morgan, I heard. I'm . . ."

"Where's Hart, where's the bastard at?"

"What're you doing with that grenade? Jesus, Morgan."

"I'm going to blow. I'm going to blow there he comes from operations get outa here Chambers I'm going to . . ."

"You ain't," Chambers said, grabbing Morgan's wrist.

"The pin's pulled, baby. I drop this thing, that's it."

Chambers began pushing him slowly away from Hart's tent toward his own. "You don't want to do that, Morgan, you can't."

"I've got to, Chambers. I can't go anymore and I'm not leaving without him."

"You ain't leaving, Morgan—look at me!"

"It's easy for you to say, you got it out of you somewhere sometime but man I just shot a woman and her kid knew and then Berry's neck was all over me and it's just too fucking much. You know Hart doesn't deserve to live."

Chambers had pushed him nearly to the front of his tent. Morgan felt him pulling his arm in closer and moving his hand toward the grenade. "I ain't sayin' it's right what you did or that any of the shit Hart's done is right, or me either, but goddammit."

His arm began to give way, almost involuntarily. He looked at Chambers and blinked twice. He felt Chambers' hand slide over his, holding it and the grenade like a ball.

"Gimme the grenade."

"What's going on over there?" Hart said, standing by his tent flap.

"I got . . ."

"Gimme it."

Morgan's hand began to loosen.

"Everything okay there, Chambers?" Hart yelled.

"Sure, Sarge," Chambers yelled back. "Okay, Will," he whispered, "I got the handle of it, you can let it go now."

Morgan let the grenade slip into Chambers's hand. Chambers tightened his fist on it and Morgan tightened his hand over the fist. He started to say "Thank you." but the words seemed to halt on the dry surface of his throat. He felt his body relaxing. The first sob was nearly to his eyes when he choked it back. His chest heaved violently, and he shook his head as a second sob made his shoulders tremble. Chambers pulled his hand from Morgan's and spread both his arms around him. Morgan pulled his own arms up and folded them on his chest and leaned against Chambers the way he used to lie on the bed when he was a child.

Out with the Lions

by Loyd Little

Through the lotus petals
I drink rice wine
From an artillery shell.

Granny's mains'l popped as a gust of wind from the southwest suddenly filled the canvas. Shielding my eyes from the sun, I squinted at that quilt of a sail and marveled that it held together. A patchwork of mending stitched together by a half-dozen owners and captains over fifty years. Did she care that she now hauled Chinese mercenaries instead of oysters?

Teewee, myself and the Nungs were taking a two-day patrol to Se Toi, north of Giap Phang and the only place in our area still harassed by the Viet Cong. Se Toi was a small outpost, five klicks from the Mekong.

The area was sparsely populated and remote. The few canals there had silted nearly full and the only way in or out was miles of hard trucking through thick grasslands and forests.

I was laying up sorry under the boom, trying to catch some sleep before we arrived at Beo Con, our jumping-off point. The guard duty last night with Hood left me tired. Normally, if one of the team had guard, he didn't have to go on a patrol the next day, but Cranston and Top were giving a rice growing class today with Subchai.

Sandalwood incense drifted back from the Nung's medicine man. The strong perfumes were no longer strange and foreign to us. Like Tiger Balm, they were part of this life. At home my father said grace before meals. And while God and I did not believe in one another, the blessing was, nevertheless, a proper and familiar part of our mealtimes. Now, as I smeared Tiger Balm under my nose to keep evil spirits from entering, it was the same emotional process: a touch of the routine, a mental crossing of my fingers, a token to the god of luck.

"Bac si?" a voice interrupted.

"Yes, An?" I said. It was a Nung gunner who spoke some Vietnamese.

He complained at length about a stomach ache which had troubled him off and on for some time. Evidently, it wasn't anything serious; most likely patrol jitters, so I asked, "Have you had any children before?"

He stared at me a moment and said, "I don't understand."

"Have you ever been pregnant before?"

His eyes crinkled as he caught the joke. He broke into wild laughter, touched my arm and repeated, "Pregnant before?" He raced off to a group of Nungs at the bow. With much elaboration and animation, he told the story to them. The Nungs laughed loudly. Several poked the man in the stomach, while others waved at me.

Shortly, the gentle rocking of the boat stole my consciousness. I dozed off and was awakened two hours later at 10:30 hours when we arrived at Beo Con, a hamlet of no more than a dozen huts. We were five miles south of Phu Duc and Cambodia. From here we would go northeast to Se Toi and spend the night there. Tomorrow we would swing up to the border and return to Phu Duc to meet Granny tomorrow night. If all went well.

We ate a quick lunch in Beo Con and left. A dozen children trailed us for several yards, until their parents called them back. The land was untilled and, judging from the size of the trees and bushes, had lain fallow for ten or fifteen years. That could be explained by the fact that this area lay between the Hoa Hao and Cao Dai territories. Before they formed a loose alliance against the Viet Cong, the two religious sects often were at war with each other.

Two hours out of Beo Con, the tranh grass appeared. The Nungs called it "knife grass" and the Vietnamese called it "elephant grass." I had run into it before. A dull green grass that grew ten to twelve feet tall, the blades were four inches wide at the base, tapering to a thin point. The first time I had grabbed a blade to push it back, I received a quick, deep cut across my palm. The edges were like razors. Now I knew better and used my carbine to push the grass aside. As if that wasn't enough, the stuff also collected, or gave out, a fine dust-like pollen which, on a hot day like today, clogged your throat and lungs and crawled around on your skin like ants. We all had tied handkerchiefs across our noses and mouths.

Because of the thickness of the grass, we moved in a long column, strung out like a picket fence for a quarter mile. I was the tenth man back from the front and Teewee was somewhere in the rear.

The first shot rang out at 13:45 hours and we were flat on the ground before the echo died away. It wasn't close—probably four or five hundred yards away. I crawled back to Wheaty and the Nung commander, Charles. His name was actually Hiung Tse Fau, but he had adopted the name Charles after Charles DeGaulle many years ago. After ten minutes of silence, we decided the shot was a warning or someone hunting supper. Earlier, our point man had reported tiger tracks on the trail.

By the time the fifth shot came at 17:00 hours, we didn't even break stride. They had been fired every forty-five minutes and all came from points several hundred yards northwest of us and slightly to our rear. Obviously, they were signal shots, warnings by sentries giving our location and speed to sentries on ahead. The method was old, cheap and as effective as the quarter-million-dollar helicopters our army used. Even moonshiners back in the hills of North Carolina used the system to warn of approaching revenue agents. It would have been useless for us to chase them. And there was the possibility they were trying to lure us into a trap.

We reached Se Toi shortly before dark. It had been a frustrating day, knowing that we were watched every step of the way and that the Cong knew our exact location at all times, the number of troops we had and how many guns we carried. A proper guerrilla war.

So Toi guarded the intersection of two canals, both overgrown and silted. I wasn't really sure what it guarded the canals against. A hand-dug moat surrounded the outpost and gave it the appearance of being on a tiny island. The camp itself was a smaller version of the other PF outposts around the edge of our area.

The Nungs stayed outside, by choice. They said there would be more room for them and that they would feel more comfortable. I felt more comfortable with them outside, too.

We crossed the plank bridge and were met by the camp commander, a middle-aged, tired lieutenant named Ha Si Phuc. He led us inside, where preparations for supper were underway. Phuc invited us to his house and we sat on the porch. Next to me was an ancient mantis shotgun. I had only seen pictures of them. It was a steel tube, which looked to have been the top cross frame bar from a bicycle, fixed on a bipod. The tube was filled with gunpowder and glass and metal bits. Phuc said the gun had been here since the war with the French and was still used.

Soon, Phuc's wife rolled out a large clay pot of what I suspected was rice wine. Vietnamese rice wine was delicious. The wine was light, with a wet, round taste and a hint of American scuppernong. It was made by placing dried rice kernels in the bottom of a two- or three-foot urn. The fermenting agent, made of powdered roots and rice flour and resembling small, porous white cones, was added next. Then the pot was filled about one-third with water and covered. The wine would sit undisturbed for four or five days. The longer the better. When the wine had fermented, water was added to fill the pot. Although the potency varied from batch to batch, it was always strong enough to fill one's mind with rambling discourse, lecherous thoughts and a sharply modified rational process. It wiped you out.

She poured water from a 120-mm. artillery shell into the urn. Lotus petals floated to the top, along with the rice kernels. The Hoa Hao often added lotus, chrysanthemums and other flowers for flavoring. Sometimes they also added rats.

Phuc pushed a bamboo reed down through the floating kernels and flowers. He spit out the first mouthful as an offering to the spirits and to clear the reed and held it out for Teewee. Wheaty thanked him, took a long pull and, following tradition, offered the reed back to Phuc. He declined, as was the custom. ''Give it to the doctor who walks on water.''

''Cam on, ong,'' I said, taking a drink. ''Ah, tot lam!'' Delicious, I said, and it was.

Phuc asked us about the patrol and Teewee told him of the VC signal shots. Phuc nodded slowly, as if to say, "Ah, yes, it is true and sad. There are VC around here." He told us the Cong had been coming into the few nearby villages at night and forcing the people to listen to propaganda speeches. He thought they came from the direction of the Mekong. They might even be Cao Dai guerrillas, he theorized. That would explain why they hadn't gotten the word yet on the ban on operations.

We chatted about the VC and sipped rice wine for another hour.

A few minutes later, his wife brought a small, live pig to the porch and Phuc placed joss sticks in the cracks on the bamboo floor. The pig, which had its feet tied together, probably weighed twenty-five pounds. We were about to see a sacrifice. In the mountains and in some parts of the delta, animal sacrifices to honor one's ancestors or to please other spirits were still common. Tradition demanded Teewee and I stay.

It wasn't pleasant. After lighting the incense and setting aside wine for ancestors, Phuc and the elders began sticking long, icepick-shaped knives into the pig. Its screams were awful. High-pitched wails filled with terror and death. I looked at the faces of the men. They seemed to be taking no particular delight or joy in it. The stabbings were quick and sure. Their attitude suggested that this rite must be done and must be done correctly. I never did find out exactly what the occasion was. It could have been someone's death or a particular ritual for this village. After a half-hour that seemed like days, the pig shuddered and died. Its eyes were wide and staring. Phuc carefully slid a thin knife into the pig's heart. When the blood rushed out it was captured in a small bowl. Later it would be placed in special areas around the camp as offerings to the spirits. Sacrifices were not sanctioned by the Hoa Hao religion; but rather, were tolerated as part of the animism that permeated all Vietnamese religions.

Only fifteen minutes before, Phuc and I were discussing stock prices.

"God, that's terrible," muttered Teewee.

"Yes," I said.

The pig was taken away to be cooked.

We were exhausted and after a supper of rice, nuts and pig entrails, Teewee and I strung our hammocks between two poles beside Phuc's hut.

I had just made myself comfortable, when Wheaty whispered, "Elliott, you asleep?"

"No."

"Top figures we can leave in two or three weeks."

"Yes."

"What do you think about going back?"

"I don't really want to go. But what I want can't be. I'm not the type to settle down as a civilian," I said.

"That's not what I meant. What do you think the Army'll say?"

"They'll ask if our shot record is up to date. What can they say? The Army abandoned us. They got too wrapped up in their own paperwork and their own systems and their own image to care about what happens to us mere soldiers," I said.

Wheaty said, "Hmmm."

"In a way, it's the same situation that Choi and Hoa Hao are in. They've been abandoned by the South Vietnamese government and the GVN army. For all practical purposes. Carry it one step further and say the people of South Vietnam have been abandoned. The only time anyone cares about them is to move them to a strategic hamlet, to draft soldiers, or, in the case of the VC, to take their rice and bore them to death with political speeches."

Wheaty said, "A year ago, bac si, I would have argued with you. I've forgotten what the arguments were."

"Just as we were left out there with the lions to fend for ourselves, so have the Vietnamese been left stranded." I suddenly wondered why the phrase "out with the lions" was popular. There were no lions in South Vietnam. I went on, "You remember a week or so ago when the radio reported the latest head of the government in Saigon was bragging about the fact that over a million leaflets had been dropped by airplanes to the South Vietnamese in the delta?"

"Yes. Hood had one. It was something about supporting the government and to be patriotic."

I said, "Well, it strikes me as one hell of a note when the government has to communicate with its people by means of leaflets dropped from planes."

"I never thought of it that way."

I slapped at a mosquito that had found its way inside my netting.

A few minutes later, Teewee said, "Still, I wonder what they'll say about us being gone so long. I could really get in trouble."

"We tried to get out. And once the floods started there was no way," I said, yawning.

Teewee fell asleep mumbling something about being a private detective in Norfolk, Virginia. God, of all places to be a private eye.

A few minutes later, sounds of a Nung singing softly and playing a gentle guitar drifted over. I knew one of the young Chinese had been carrying a guitar on his rucksack. The music expressed an awful loneliness and aloneness. It took me back to Methodist church camp as a teenager. Long evenings around a campfire. Soft air and dark woods. We spoke our sins into pine cones and threw them into the fire. Even then there was the twisting hollow in my stomach. That awful aloneness. There are no Buddhas.

We left Se Toi the next morning at 08:00 hours. Phuc wished us good luck and asked me to autograph a picture of me skiing. I did.

We crossed the east-west canal and headed north to the Cambodian border. Today, we might run into real trouble. It would be obvious to the Cong we were heading back to Phu Duc. They had let us go yesterday to see where we were going.

The day was as hot, if not hotter, than yesterday. More elephant grass and dust. The VC sentries didn't pick us up until 11:00 hours. We had reached the border—the only demarcation was a wide canal—and turned west, when the first shot sounded. It was three hundred yards northwest of us in Cambodia. Not only were the shots good military strategy, their psychological effect was devastating. It was subtle torture: we waited for the next one. Hoping that it wouldn't come, or, if it did, it would only be a single shot. All the while knowing that over there a pair of eyes watched our every move.

We stopped at 12:30 hours for lunch. Teewee and I ate C-rations, while the Nungs had cold rice balls. The Chinese were tense. If the VC were going to attack, it would be soon. Before we got within mortar range of Phu Duc.

By 13:15 hours, we were moving again, along an old trail on the bank of the canal. The elephant grass was thinning and the afternoon wore on, hot and dusty and strained. We all expected the attack and perhaps for that reason no one, except Teewee, was hit when it came. He and I had switched positions. He was near the point man and I was sixth man from the rear. My first clue came when handfuls of dirt began exploding in a moving row down the bank. Their guns were low. A fraction of a second later, the noise of the shots reached us and we were already rolling down the bank to our left. It sounded like a full company. Rocks, dirt, and twigs sprayed over my head and I detected at least one, maybe two, machine guns sweeping back and forth along the bank over us.

To our backs was flat, open land. No trees; no bushes; nothing to hide in. The only good thing was the three-foot bank we were lying against. The Nungs were well tucked in, checking their guns and waiting for the first volley to die down.

In a minute it did. Carefully, I poked one eye over the bank. Across the canal was a large empty rice field. The firing came from a large grove of trees beyond the field, one hundred yards away. I couldn't see anyone, only an occasional flash from the shadows.

The Nungs shouted commands to each other and assorted curses at the VC. The Chinese were quite vocal in combat. Frenchy was hollering, ''Death to the Japanese!''

Beside me, a machine gunner was jamming his tripod in the dirt. The man on the other side of him was quickly unwrapping ammo links from his neck, preparing to feed them in. Very professional.

Suddenly, I realized a message was being passed down the line. A Nung a dozen men away shouted, ''The lieutenant wants you, bac si. He's hit.''

I looped my medical pack over my neck, rose to a crouch and ran. Our guns were beginning to return the fire and the noise was deafening. Both sides flailed away at each other. Halfway to the front, something snatched at my back and I almost lost my balance. Probably a branch or a bullet. Finally, I reached Teewee. He lay on his side, one hand behind his back and his face filled with pain. I dropped beside him.

''Where?'' I asked.

''In the ass, of all places,'' he said, turning over on his stomach. His pants were red with blood.

''Unbuckle your pants, sir. What happened?''

''That first volley. One caught my stock.''

The stock of his gun was shattered. A dumdum round had

smashed it and hurled dozens of wood splinters into Wheaty's ass. I hoped the bullet had been deflected or had spent itself.

I slid his shorts down. His right cheek was freckled with punctures. Blood oozed out steadily and I couldn't tell if there was a bullet wound. I didn't think so. As I unzipped my medical bag, I noticed a bullet hole, neat and clean and dead center on the canvas bag. Maybe tomorrow, Cong. I cleaned Wheaty's fanny with cotton and peroxide. There were wood splinters every half inch, but none serious.

I said, "Take these two codeine tablets. That will stop the pain. There's nothing I can do here. You've got a million splinters from your stock in your ass and each one will have to be pulled out. Don't sit down for a while."

"It really hurts," said Teewee, while we both pulled his pants up carefully.

"You may get your medal yet, Lieutenant," I said.

"Captain."

"Captain," I said.

"That's right. Wounded in action. I hadn't thought about that," he said happily.

That would make him feel better. I sprawled out on the bank and sighted my gun on a flash in the woods. The firing was still heavy. Charles, the Nung commander, lay a few feet to my right and was obviously having difficulties. He had tried to send a squad up the canal to see if there was a way we could cross. Their movement caused a hail of fire from the grove. If we tried to back off to the rear, we would be sitting ducks. There was no cover beyond this bank for a good three hundred yards. We were trapped.

"What's happening, Charles?" I shouted over the noise.

"Beaucoup problems," he said. "We may have to wait until dark, unless we can find some way across the canal," he said, never taking his eyes off the trees.

"What if they decide to come over?" I asked more out of curiosity than a fear that they actually would.

"We will fight."

"To the last man?"

He looked around fiercely. "We will fight to the last man because our contract runs until May 11."

That's one way of looking at it, I thought.

A couple of bullets cracked overhead, up and down the line, the Nungs were shouting obscenities to the Cong. Some reviled them in Vietnamese, some in Chinese. Their most favorite was "Do ma," which meant, "You fuck your mother." I guess most people think motherfucking is gauche.

Teewee said in agony behind me, "Goddam, Elliot, how long does it take codeine to work?"

"About twenty minutes. You won't feel a thing."

A message was suddenly being relayed from Nung to Nung. "Stop shooting."

We did and I realized that the gunfire from the Cong had stopped also. A Nung ran up to Charles and spoke with him briefly in Chinese. Charles nodded. Then he stood up, leaving his gun on the ground. Wheaty and I both lunged for him, but he irritably waved his hands at us. The man's crazy, I thought.

He cupped his hands around his mouth and shouted a half-dozen sentences in Chinese. A moment later, one of the Cong answered, also in Chinese. Back and forth, Charles and the man talked. The other Nungs were grinning and whispering to each other. Had the whole world gone mad?

A few minutes later, Charles turned and spoke to the Nungs nearest us. Then he casually picked up his rifle and said, "We go now." And began walking.

"Wait a minute," said Teewee. "What the hell is going on?"

"It's all right, thieu uy, we do not fight any more today."

"What do you mean, 'We don't fight any more today'? What about the Cong?"

Charles said, "That was not Viet Cong. That was Nung. I know them. They know us. They said they were hired by the Viet Cong as soldiers, but since we were Nungs also, there was no need for us to fight. I agreed. We are all Nungs. We are all the same family."

"I'll be damned," I said, helping Wheaty to his feet. "Nungs fighting Nungs."

"We're lucky it wasn't Viet Cong," said Wheaty.

Across the canal in the woods, men were standing and waving at us. There were about seventy-five of them. Several conversations were being carried on across the border. Probably family gossip. How's old Aunt Ling doing? Still alive and mean as ever? Have you seen Cousin Lio lately?

I waved at the enemy and we began walking to Phu Duc. In front of me, Teewee limped along, bloodstains on his ass.

Search and Destroy

by Wayne Karlin

There were fiery needle pricks in his foot, jabs felt through a half dream, and he kicked out. His foot connected with something warm and hairy, and he sat up abruptly, sleep sucked from him like water down a drain. "Shit," Joshua said, and tried to go back to sleep.

He lived in a hut at Marble Mountain Air Facility with ten others. They had a parachute hung under the ceiling and partitions and shelves of scrap wood and straw matting. Home-made, homemaking.

Up to the month before, the hut had been canvas-roofed and almost unbearably hot. The new tin roof made it much cooler inside. "But now we got rats in here," Joshua said to Rodriguez.

"Yes, indeed," said Rodriguez, "and it seems like it's been raining more since you white men invented this tin stuff."

"Rats," Sam said, shaking his head. He was lying on his cot, reading a paperback. "Jesus Christ. Rats."

"Don't let it worry you," Torenelli said.

Eventually it worried all of them.

At least once a night someone would be snapped awake by the feel of a small hot body somewhere in his cot. Usually the rats preferred to attack feet, two naked hunks of meat that tended to become exposed in the night. Sam, for one, could never get back to sleep after feeling a rat. He would begin to drop off, then a mental picture of the animal eating his nose or an eye, jumping across the floor with a chunk of Samface dangling from its mouth, would wake him up. He began to sleep hunched protectively over his genitals, like a man about to fight.

There was a constant squeaking at night. It got on the men's nerves, and they would lay awake listening, feeling the sweat from their backs wetting the sandy canvas of their cots. Often they could see the small dimples the rats' feet made as they ran along the top side of the hanging parachute. The men would throw things at the impressions but the rats were too fast.

It wasn't until Torenelli was killed, actually, that it became an obsession to kill the rats. The night before it happened, he had flipped out at the soft scuffling noises on the silk above his head, and had shot a few holes in the roof with his .45. He would have been court-martialed if he hadn't caught a .50 round that blew most of his chest away, on a medevac the next day.

The rats became a jinx to the men on flight pay after that. They began calling them gooks.

They would lay awake at night, waiting. When someone would feel or hear a rat, he'd yell, gook, and Perez would switch on the light. They would chase the creature frantically, upsetting cots, tripping over seabags. It would have been a funny, Keystone cop scene, except for the hate and fear in the marines' eyes.

At the weekly movie they didn't laugh anymore at the little cartoon mice. They would stare at them with hate-rimmed, sleepless eyes, and look at the people who did laugh as though they were idiots.

Perez almost got one once. He was chasing it with a Montagnard spear he had picked up near Khe Sahn. He cornered the rat and was trying to jab it with the spear, mock-dueling, laughing hysterically. The animal suddenly reared up on its hind legs and drew back its thin rubber lips, exposing sharp, wicked-looking teeth. Its eyes bulged with frantic hate. Perez was taken aback and stopped jabbing for a split second. The rat immediately leaped away and disappeared into some unseen hole.

On the day that the hunt was finally successful they killed eleven rats.

It happened right after Perez and Billings were knocked out of the air while on a resupply to Hill 55. A recoilless rifle round had punched a huge hole in the side of their helicopter, but they were able to autorotate down with no one hurt.

They all sat around that night, telling sea stories about getting shot down. Perez was religiously grateful the round hadn't exploded the gas tank. "Thank fuck it didn't explode," he prayed, "thank fuck." All it had meant was a little time with the grunts for his gunner, Billings, and him. He was shaking his head when they all heard the squeal, punctuating his prayer. "Gook!" Perez yelled, his face hard.

The slick brown body jumped across the room, and they flew after it, yelling. They were surprised to trap the rat almost immediately. It stood on its hind legs in an unescapable corner, squealing shrilly.

Sam was the first to see why the rat was so easily trapped. He heard a soft noise from the opposite corner of the hut and went to look. Billings saw him move and followed. "Damn," he yelled fervently, triumphantly, "it's got *babies!* It was trying to lead us away."

There were ten of them, blind and pink, clutching at each other with small groping hands.

Billings took a long piece of copper wire and, kneeling, stuck its end through each baby's small, pulsing throat. The tinny sound of their squealing gradually died as the wire tore through flesh, until only the squeal of the trapped mother could be heard.

Billings whooped and brandished the chain of dead babies in front of the mother. Then he took them outside and plunged their still-twitching mass into the large water barrel just outside the hut. His face was alight and strained.

Donner, the big silent boy from Kansas, clubbed at the mother. She kept up her high-pitched squealing, her eyes darting towards the water barrel outside. Perez grabbed a canvas sack and dropped it over the stunned rat. The rest of the men stood around him, watching. He picked up the sack and carried it outside to the barrel, then took it by the bottom and shook the mother out into the water. The two ends of the wire on which the babies were dangling had caught on the rim of the barrel, and the bodies just broke the water, next to her face. She was still alive, swimming frantically.

Perez began pushing her face under with a piece of wood. He kept holding her down for longer and longer periods, but each time he let up she would still be alive and struggling. He swore at her.

Donner went into the hut and came back with his can of deodorant. He waited until Perez let the rat's head break the water, then sprayed the deodorant through the flame of his cigarette lighter.

It sent out a sheet of flame; a miniature flame thrower. The hair on her face began to burn off, leaving her with surprisingly pink skin that soon blackened and began peeling off like singed paper. Her eyes changed from alive black berries to small dead ones and then to cinders. They could almost see her blood boil. She kept coming up alive.

Perez and Donner began to look panicky. "Die, goddam you," Perez swore, under his breath. The rest of the men watched silently. Both Perez and Donner were sweating profusely. They held the rat under for impossibly long periods, but she kept surfacing, her burned face coming up next to her dead babies, her mouth opening and closing, grabbing lungfuls of air and fire.

After a long time she died.

Perez and Donner stood there for a while looking at her gently bobbing body. Their mouths were hanging open, and they looked drained and exhausted. Everybody else went quietly back into the hootch.

The Vietnamese Elections

by Wayne Karlin

Once there were dogs in the squadron at Marble Mountain. There had always been a bunch of them wandering around the base, infiltrating in from the highway and from the huts strung like dirty straw beads along the roadside. Vietnamese dogs, skinny and hungry, but with eyes and acts like any dogs, Free World or Communist Conspiracy. They'd look at you reproachfully if you didn't feed them, piss on your tent or the colonel's, all of the things that make dogs so attractive to Americans.

Some became special. Adopted.

The squadron had three dogs. One to Motor T, one to the mechanics and one to Operations. Each dog had one guy who took care of him, but he belonged to all of them. Hanging around the flight line. Watching the crews coming in from missions. Getting in people's way. Getting cursed. Getting their ears scratched and their asses kicked. You know, dogs and Americans.

The dogs were three, thus:

To the mechs: A yellow almost cocker spaniel called Grease.

To ops: Herbert, black and white and three teeth.

To motor T: A large strange half-boxer, half-setter called Ky. He had a habit of farting in formation.

Some permitted pats on the head from outsiders; all would take food from whomever they could get it, and all were completely chauvinistic towards their particular section. It got them a lot of kicks and started a lot of fights.

The order came:

FROM:

TO:

SUBJECT: there are too many dogs here and I'm supposed to do something, after all I'm c.o. of the base and it's unhygenic and what are we here for anyway kill japs kill japs, you'll do your job better if you only have one dog per squadron.

The rest to be shot.

Sincerely yours,

America.

So, they had to shoot two dogs.

The C.O. decided on an election. "First Shirt, we'll have a formation and do it democratically.

"Squadron, atten-HUT!"

Ky farted. So did Torenelli.

The dogs were held in their keeper's arms. They squirmed and tried to jump down onto the flight mat, but were held tightly. They were having a good time.

Democracy started.

The C.O. was in the admin tent signing air medal certifications, so the first sergeant read the order. It was an impressive ceremony.

If you could have seen the entire ceremony from the air, as Lieutenant DeLeon was doing at that very moment, from his helicopter, it would have really looked impressive. The base lying below him like a grid iron knuckle on America's fist, neat rows of efficiency bounding the sloppy sand.

Look. First an ocean (the South China Sea actually), turquoise blue and sparkling, interspiced with patches of deep green. Next to the ocean, and startling in contrast, a large stretch of gleaming white sand held between two mountains (one called Marble, the other Monkey). In the middle of the stretch of sand, a great settlement, rows of tents and tin huts, huge squares of latticed metal, making pads and cryptic runways running to nowhere in the sand. In the middle of it all, something that could have been the center of a military-industrial complex, but was really the messhall.

On the biggest square of perforated metal were rows of helicopters, green and expensive. UH34D's, CH46's, UH1E's. And smack between the parked helicopters and a row of tents, Lieutenant DeLeon could see a geometric formation of standing men, fitting in well with the scene. Neat rows of green men standing at attention, clean, handsome men who had built the order around them. Three of them were holding dogs. One of whom kept farting.

The keepers were each supposed to make a little speech about their dog. So, one by one, they stood with their animal in front of the staring formation, to let them decide.

"Well," they said, embarrassed, "he's a good dog."

"he's a good dog."

"he's a good dog."

The dogs looked at the men and struggled to be free, barking joyously, wanting to run and play around the stiff green legs that seemed like a forest. Then someone said that they should take the dogs away while the voting happened.

O.K.

Ky won. Even if some didn't vote.

They took the other dogs behind the flightline tents and put bullets in their brains. Later they were driven out to the trash dump and burned.

The Interrogation of the Prisoner Bung by Mister Hawkins and Sergeant Tree

by David Huddle

The land in these provinces to the south of the capital city is so flat it would be possible to ride a bicycle from one end of this district to the other and to pedal only occasionally. The narrow highway passes over kilometers and kilometers of rice fields, laid out square and separated by slender green lines of grassy paddy-dikes and by irrigation ditches filled with bad water. The villages are far apart and small. Around them are clustered the little pockets of huts, the hamlets where the rice farmers live. The village that serves as the capital of this district is just large enough to have a proper marketplace. Close to the police compound, a detachment of Americans has set up its tents. These are lumps of new green canvas, and they sit on a concrete, French-built tennis court, long abandoned, not far from a large lily pond where women come in the morning to wash clothes and where policemen of the compound and their children come to swim and bathe in the late afternoon.

The door of a room to the rear of the District Police Headquarters is cracked for light and air. Outside noises—chickens quarreling, children playing, the mellow grunting of the pigs owned by the police chief—these reach the ears of the three men inside the quiet room. The room is not a cell; it is more like a small bedroom.

The American is nervous and fully awake, but he forces himself to yawn and sips at his coffee. In front of him are his papers, the report forms, yellow notepaper, two pencils and a ball-point pen. Across the table from the American is Sergeant Tree, a young man who was noticed by the government of his country and taken from his studies to be sent to interpreter's school. Sergeant Tree has a pleasant and healthy face. He is accustomed to smiling, especially in the presence of Americans, who are, it happens, quite fond of him. Sergeant Tree knows that he has an admirable position working with Mister Hawkins; several of his unlucky classmates from interpreter's school serve nearer the shooting.

The prisoner, Bung, squats in the far corner of the room, his back at the intersection of the cool concrete walls. Bung is a large man for an Asian, but he is squatted down close to the floor. He was given a cigarette by the American when he was first brought into the room, but has finished smoking and holds the white filter inside his fist. Bung is not tied, nor restrained, but he squats perfectly still, his bare feet laid out flat and large on the floor. His hair, cut by his wife, is cropped short and uneven; his skin is dark, leathery, and there is a bruise below one of his shoulder blades. He looks only at the floor, and he wonders what he will do with the tip of the cigarette when the interrogation begins. He suspects that he ought to eat it now so that it will not be discovered later.

From the large barracks room on the other side of the building comes laughter and loud talking, the policemen changing shifts. Sergeant Tree smiles at these sounds. Some of the younger policemen are his friends. Hawkins, the American, does not seem to have heard. He is trying to think about sex, and he cannot concentrate.

"Ask the prisoner what his name is."

"What is your name?"

The prisoner reports that his name is Bung. The language startles Hawkins. He does not understand this language, except the first ten numbers of counting, and the words for yes and no. With Sergeant Tree helping him with the spelling, Hawkins enters the name into the proper blank.

"Ask the prisoner where he lives."

"Where do you live?"

The prisoner wails a string of language. He begins to weep as he speaks, and he goes on like this, swelling up the small room with the sound of his voice until he sees a warning twitch of the interpreter's hand. He stops immediately, as though corked. One of the police chief's pigs is snuffing over the ground just outside the door, rooting for scraps of food.

"What did he say?"

"He says that he is classed as a poor farmer, that he lives in the hamlet near where the soldiers found him, and that he has not seen his wife and his children for four days now and they do not know where he is.

"He says that he is not one of the enemy, although he has seen the enemy many times this year in his hamlet and in the village near his hamlet. He says that he was forced to give rice to the enemy on two different occasions, once at night, and another time during the day, and that he gave rice to the enemy only because they would have shot him if he had not.

"He says that he does not know the names of any of these men. He says that one of the men asked him to join them and to go with them, but that he told this man that he could not join them and go with them because he was poor and because his wife and his children would not be able to live without him to work for them to feed them. He says that the enemy men laughed at him when he said this but that they did not make him go with them when they left his house.

"He says that two days after the night the enemy came and took rice from him, the soldiers came to him in the field where he was working and made him walk with them for many kilometers, and made him climb into the back of a large truck, and put a cloth over his eyes, so that he did not see where the truck carried him and did not know where he was until he was put with some other people in a pen. He says that one of the soldiers hit him in the back with a weapon, because he was afraid at first to climb into the truck.

"He says that he does not have any money, but that he has ten kilos of rice hidden beneath the floor of the kitchen of his house. He says that he would make us the gift of this rice if we would let him go back to his wife and his children."

When he has finished his translation of the prisoner's speech, Sergeant Tree smiles at Mister Hawkins. Hawkins feels that he ought to write something down. He moves the pencil to a corner of the paper and writes down his service number, his Social Security number, the telephone number of his girl friend in Silver Spring, Maryland, and the amount of money he has saved in his allotment account.

"Ask the prisoner in what year he was born."

Hawkins has decided to end the interrogation of this prisoner as quickly as he can. If there is enough time left, he will find an excuse for Sergeant Tree and himself to drive the jeep into the village.

"In what year were you born?"

The prisoner tells the year of his birth.

"Ask the prisoner in what place he was born."

"In what place were you born?"

The prisoner tells the place of his birth.

"Ask the prisoner the name of his wife."

"What is the name of your wife?"

Bung gives the name of his wife.

"Ask the prisoner the names of his parents."

Bung tells the names.

"Ask the prisoner the names of his children."

"What are the names of your children?"

The American takes down these things on the form, painstakingly, with help in the spelling from the interpreter, who has become bored with this. Hawkins fills all the blank spaces on the front of the form. Later, he will add his summary of the interrogation in the space provided on the back.

"Ask the prisoner the name of his hamlet chief."

"What is the name of your hamlet chief?"

The prisoner tells this name, and Hawkins takes it down on the notepaper. Hawkins has been trained to ask these questions. If a prisoner gives one incorrect name, then all names given may be incorrect, all information secured unreliable.

Bung tells the name of his village chief, and the American takes it down. Hawkins tears off this sheet of notepaper and gives it to Sergeant Tree. He asks the interpreter to take this paper to the police chief to check if these are the correct names. Sergeant Tree does not like to deal with the police chief because the police chief treats him as if he were a farmer. But he leaves the room in the manner of someone engaged in important business. Bung continues to stare at the floor, afraid the American will kill him now that they are in this room together, alone.

Hawkins is again trying to think about sex. Again, he is finding it difficult to concentrate. He cannot choose between thinking about sex with his girl friend Suzanne or with a plump girl who works in a souvenir shop in the village. The soft grunting of the pig outside catches his ear, and he finds that he is thinking of having sex with the pig. He takes another sheet of notepaper and begins calculating the number of days he has left to remain in Asia. The number turns out to be one hundred and thirty-three. This distresses him because the last time he calculated the number it was one hundred and thirty-five. He decides to think about food. He thinks of an omelet. He would like to have an omelet. His eyelids begin to close as he considers all the things that he likes to eat: an omelet, chocolate pie, macaroni, cookies, cheeseburgers, black-cherry Jell-O. He has a sudden vivid image of Suzanne's stomach, the path of downy hair to her navel. He stretches the muscles in his legs, and settles into concentration.

The clamor of chickens distracts him. Sergeant Tree has caused this noise by throwing a rock on his way back. The police chief refused to speak with him and required him to conduct his business with the secretary, whereas this secretary gloated over the indignity to Sergeant Tree, made many unnecessary delays and complications before letting the interpreter have a copy of the list of hamlet chiefs and village chiefs in the district.

Sergeant Tree enters the room, goes directly to the prisoner, with the toe of his boot kicks the prisoner on the shinbone. The boot hitting bone makes a wooden sound. Hawkins jerks up in his chair, but before he quite understands the situation, Sergeant Tree has shut the door to the small room and has kicked the prisoner's other shinbone. Bung responds with a grunt and holds his shins with his hands, drawing himself tighter into the corner.

"Wait!" The American stands up to restrain Sergeant Tree, but this is not necessary. Sergeant Tree has passed by the prisoner now and has gone to stand at his own side of the table. From underneath his uniform shirt he takes a rubber club, which he has borrowed from one of his policeman friends. He slaps the club on the table.

"He lies!" Sergeant Tree says this with as much evil as he can force into his voice.

"Hold on now. Let's check this out." Hawkins' sense of justice has been touched. He regards the prisoner as a clumsy, hulking sort, obviously not bright, but clearly honest.

"The police chief says that he lies!" Sergeant Tree announces. He shows Hawkins the paper listing the names of the hamlet chiefs and the village chiefs. With the door shut, the light in the small room is very dim, and it is difficult to locate the names on the list. Hawkins is disturbed by the darkness, is uncomfortable being so intimately together with two men. The breath of the interpreter has something sweetish to it. It occurs to Hawkins that now, since the prisoner has lied to them, there will probably not be enough time after the interrogation to take the jeep and drive into the village. This vexes him. He decides there must something unhealthy in the diet of these people, something that causes this sweet-smelling breath.

Hawkins finds it almost impossible to read the columns of handwriting. He is confused. Sergeant Tree must show him the places on the list where the names of the prisoner's hamlet chief and village chief are written. They agree that the prisoner has given them incorrect names, though Hawkins is not certain of it. He wishes these things were less complicated, and he dreads what he knows must follow. He thinks regretfully of what could have happened if the prisoner had given the correct names: the interrogation would have ended quickly, the prisoner released; he and Sergeant Tree could have driven into the village in the jeep, wearing their sunglasses, with the cool wind whipping past them, dust billowing around the jeep, shoeshine boys shrieking, the girl in the souvenir shop going with him into the back room for a time.

Sergeant Tree goes to the prisoner, kneels on the floor beside him, and takes Bung's face between his hands. Tenderly, he draws the prisoner's head close to his own, and asks, almost absentmindedly, "Are you one of the enemy?"

"No"

All this strikes Hawkins as vaguely comic, someone saying, "I love you," in a high-school play.

Sergeant Tree spits in the face of the prisoner and then jams the prisoner's head back against the wall. Sergeant Tree stands up quickly, jerks the police club from the table, and starts beating the prisoner with random blows. Bung stays squatted down and covers his head with both arms. He makes a shrill noise.

Hawkins has seen this before in other interrogations. He listens closely, trying to hear everything: little shrieks coming from Sergeant Tree's throat, the chunking sound the rubber club makes. The American recognizes a kind of rightness in this, like the final slapping together of the bellies of a man and a woman.

Sergeant Tree stops. He stands, legs apart, facing the prisoner, his back to Hawkins. Bung keeps his squatting position, his arms crossed over his head.

The door scratches and opens just wide enough to let in a policeman friend of Sergeant Tree's, a skinny, rotten-toothed man, and a small boy. Hawkins has seen this boy and the policeman before. The two of them smile at the American and at Sergeant Tree, whom they admire for his education and for having achieved such an excellent position. Hawkins starts to send them back out, but decides to let them stay. He does not like to be discourteous to Asians.

Sergeant Tree acknowledges the presence of his friend and the boy. He sets the club on the table and removes his uniform shirt and the white T-shirt beneath it. His chest is powerful, but hairless. He catches Bung by the ears and jerks upward until the prisoner stands. Sergeant Tree is much shorter than the prisoner, and this he finds an advantage.

Hawkins notices that the muscles in Sergeant Tree's buttocks are clenched tight, and he admires this, finds it attractive. He has in his mind Suzanne. They are sitting in the back seat of the Oldsmobile. She has removed her stockings and garter belt, and now she slides the panties down from her hips, down her legs, off one foot, keeping them dangling on one ankle, ready to be pulled up quickly in case someone comes to the car and catches them. Hawkins has perfect concentration. He sees her panties glow.

Sergeant Tree tears away the prisoner's shirt, first from one side of his chest and then the other. Bung's mouth sags open now, as though he were about to drool.

The boy clutches at the sleeve of the policeman to whisper in his ear. The policeman giggles. They hush when the American glances at them. Hawkins is furious because they have distracted him. He decides that there is no privacy to be had in the entire country.

"Sergeant Tree, send these people out of here, please."

Sergeant Tree gives no sign that he has heard what Hawkins has said. He is poising himself to begin. Letting out a heaving grunt, Sergeant Tree chops with the police club, catching the prisoner directly in the center of the forehead. A flame begins in Bung's brain; he is conscious of a fire, blazing, blinding him. He feels the club touch him twice more, once at his ribs and once at his forearm.

"Are you the enemy?" Sergeant Tree screams.

The policeman and the boy squat beside each other near the

door. They whisper to each other as they watch Sergeant Tree settle into the steady, methodical beating. Occasionally he pauses to ask the question again, but he gets no answer.

From a certain height, Hawkins can see that what is happening is profoundly sensible. He sees how deeply he loves these men in this room and how he respects them for the things they are doing. The knowledge rises in him, pushes to reveal itself. He stands up from his chair, virtually at attention.

A loud, hard smack swings the door wide open, and the room is filled with light. The Police Chief stands in the doorway, dressed in a crisp, white shirt, his rimless glasses sparkling. He is a fat man in the way that a good merchant might be fat—solid, confident, commanding. He stands with his hands on his hips, an authority in all matters. The policeman and the boy nod respectfully. The Police Chief walks to the table and picks up the list of hamlet chiefs and village chiefs. He examines this, and then he takes from his shirt pocket another paper, which is also a list of hamlet chiefs and village chiefs. He carries both lists to Sergeant Tree, who is kneeling in front of the prisoner. He shows Sergeant Tree the mistake he has made in getting a list that is out of date. He places the new list in Sergeant Tree's free hand, and then he takes the rubber club from Sergeant Tree's other hand and slaps it down across the top of Sergeant Tree's head. The Police Chief leaves the room, passing before the American, the policeman, the boy, not speaking or looking other than to the direction of the door.

It is late afternoon and the rain has come. Hawkins stands inside his tent, looking through the open flap. He likes to look out across the old tennis court at the big lily pond. He has been fond of water since he learned to water-ski. If the rain stops before dark, he will go out to join the policemen and the children who swim and bathe in the lily pond.

Walking out on the highway, with one kilometer still to go before he comes to the village, is Sergeant Tree. He is alone, the highway behind him and in front of him as far as he can see and nothing else around him but rain and the fields of wet, green rice. His head hurts and his arms are weary from the load of rice he carries. When he returned the prisoner to his hamlet, the man's wife made such a fuss Sergeant Tree had to shout at her to make her shut up, and then, while he was inside the prisoner's hut conducting the final arrangements for the prisoner's release, the rain came, and his policeman friends in the jeep left him to manage alone.

The ten kilos of rice he carries are heavy for him, and he would put this load down and leave it, except that he plans to sell the rice and add the money to what he has been saving to buy a .45 caliber pistol like the one Mister Hawkins carries at his hip. Sergeant Tree tries to think about how well-received he will be in California because he speaks the American language so well, and how it is likely that he will marry a rich American girl with very large breasts.

The prisoner Bung is delighted by the rain. It brought his children inside the hut, and the sounds of their fighting with each other make him happy. His wife came to him and touched him. The rice is cooking, and in a half hour his cousin will come, bringing with him the leader and two other members of Bung's squad. They will not be happy that half of their rice was taken by the interpreter to pay the American, but it will not be a disaster for them. The squad leader will be proud of Bung for gathering the information that he has—for he has memorized the guard routines at the police headquarters and at the old French area where the Americans are staying. He has watched all the comings and goings at these places, and he has marked out in his mind the best avenues of approach, the best escape routes, and the best places to set up ambush. Also, he has discovered a way that they can lie in wait and kill the Police Chief. It will occur at the place where the Police Chief goes to urinate every morning at a certain time. Bung has much information inside his head, and he believes he will be praised by the members of his squad. It is even possible that he will receive a commendation from someone very high.

His wife brings the rifle that was hidden, and Bung sets to cleaning it, savoring the smell of the rice his wife places before him and of the American oil he uses on the weapon. He particularly enjoys taking the weapon apart and putting it together again. He is very fast at this.

And Even Beautiful Hands Cry

by John M. Kimpel

The bar is a cave no it's a tunnel and I'm on a goddammed slow train going nowhere closer and closer. I see a light dim way down far away through the fog the fog is everywhere and cars splash rain from the puddles on the cracked concrete speeding by this slow train and I get off at the end of the tunnel by the light and walk up the stairs dark and lonely the boards creak and dust falls on my face below so many steps and then down another tunnel shorter but slower with many doors. There are so many doors. I walk through one door and then there is another door I keep walking on this moving sidewalk planting my cleats in the turf to keep my balance door after door and then silently I begin to hear noises voices music faint and still through all the doors I have to walk my legs are so fucking heavy through all the spiral doors I still have to open and close like a giant sphincter until almost there the noise is quite loud now behind the next she gave me the key so I open it and walk in and like a million shattering icicles the light explodes into waves of color and music and green everything is green. I smell the lusty green and feel it next to me like a flood of water rushing from a broken dam and all the people are there and I know them all the people and all the people know me we are one and wrapped together in lush earth our hearts in our hands rocking back and forth when like a blackjack a baby cries and even beautiful hands cry.

It's raining. Of course. There will always be rain.

But inside the bar, he didn't care. He'd been coming to the Starlite Bar on Hai Ba Trung almost every night for months now.

He was a Saigon Warrior, with MACV out at Tan Son Nhut, and after eleven hours of work each day, he was a free man and the war went away.

He had written his mother that he was safer in Saigon than he had been in Chicago. For so many GI's, the war was the main theme, they couldn't escape it, but for Frank the war was only a setting. His job was assignments, sending MACV advisors to the field. Across the hall from his office in the MACV Annex, his friend Mike, who worked in Casualty Reports signing General Abram's name on condolence letters, informed him of how many didn't come back. Frank had a good head for names, so he always remembered which ones had been his, and sometimes he remembered the faces too. Like the aging captain he'd assigned to a Mobile Advisory Team who had almost begged him not to be sent to the Delta again—he'd been there three years ago and watched his best friend die. So Frank had sent him to II Corps near Kontum, far from the bad memories of the mud and rain and rice paddies to the south. So he got to die in the Highlands instead of the Delta.

But it was not the kind of thing Frank liked to think about, so he didn't.

The cool breeze from the air conditioner felt good on his shaggy brown hair as the old woman lit another stick of incense in the corner next to him. The Starlite, like all the bars, was poorly lit, small, narrow and dirty. Tu Do Street was too much of a hassle and too expensive, and Plantation Road too sleazy and too close to the base, so he had settled in on Hai Ba Trung. He was familiar with all the bars on the block, but he always came to the Starlite now. He knew the people there. They were his friends.

The old woman smiled at Frank, her lips discolored from the numbing red herb ball in her toothless mouth. How come you live here so long, old woman? Maybe Quasimodo thought his hump was beautiful.

He'd worked his ass off yesterday, even though he'd had the afternoon off, the first one in almost a month. And he'd still put in six hours. Sometimes, most of the time, it was like working the night shift at Rockwell or a Saturday afternoon shopping with your old lady at Lazarus' Department Store in Columbus, Ohio.

He was waiting for Luong.

He'd gone down to Luong's apartment on Truong Minh Giang after work yesterday. It was past the railroad tracks and the city boundary coming in from Tan Son Nhut, but before the market and the bridge. She had put a black light in her one room apartment. All of the rooms are built around balconies. The building was three stories high, which gave them a view from the roof. Louvered doors and windows let in a little sun and a lot of mosquitoes, and the fan in the middle of the high ceiling moved the air around.

"Look in the freezer," she said, her hair black and falling almost to her waist, dark and deep. She'd remembered. Christ, when was it? It must have been a month ago that he'd mentioned to her what kind of wines he liked.

In the refrigerator he saw a nice tossed salad—tomatoes, lettuce, hard-boiled eggs sliced thin. The tomatoes were even red. There was a loaf of French bread on the table, warm from the bakery across the alley.

Luong went downstairs to the common kitchen, on the first floor of the building, and brought up the curried chicken. Her mother's mother was from India, as her father's father was from China.

"This is good." He'd never eaten curried chicken before. It was hot, spicy hot, but not so hot that all you tasted was the hot. The curry sauce was everywhere. He wanted to eat his fingers. The sensuous aroma of the curry entered his nostrils and glazed his brain with honey.

My whole body smells like, tastes like, curried chicken.

He ate two legs and two breasts. When he had finished those, Luong handed him the pieces from her plate.

"Aren't you hungry?" With a paper towel, he wiped at his green fatigue pants leg where the sauce had dripped.

"No." Luong cut the meat from the bones and soaked it in the sauce left on his plate. "I stay up last night playing cards at Mimi's. Not go to sleep until maybe five o'clock this morning. And all day I cook for you. I too tired to eat."

She filled his glass with more wine and fed him salad and broke off pieces of bread for him, while all the time Frank ate the curried chicken with a hunger that he hadn't realized was there.

"It is your last meal," she smiled. "After you eat all this, you die for sure. I poison you for sure."

He was never sure when she was kidding. She was so jealous. More than once she had said, "I will kill you first. I not let you go home to her." And more than once, in his dreams, he believed her. But now he laughed, and said, "No sweat. At least I'll die happy."

Curried mustache, curry stains on his shirt. Curried breath and curried sound. Then they made curried love.

And her eye makeup gets all over her face my face our bodies and silver sparkles like stars in the black light.

Afterwards, they just lay there. Her head on his stomach, her long black hair covering his chest. So nice, he thought, my mind is lost in long black hair. "You know, Luong, I don't think I've ever been happier in my life." Listening to Rod Stewart sing "Mandolin Wind" on the portable cassette player, they smoked a joint from Mom's, and then Frank fell into dreams.

Mosquitoes. Always mosquitoes. Especially here. Luong woke when he rolled over to slap at his neck.

"You don't love me, Frank. I think you hate me, make fun of me." She had been dreaming. He was walking down Tu Do Street with his wife when she saw him, she said. She called to him, but he ignored her. She just stood there on the street while he and his wife walked from shop to shop. He bought his wife many things. Coming out of a shop near her, she called to him again, and this time he saw her. He whispered something to his wife, and then pointed to her. Then he and his wife started laughing, louder and louder, it ricocheted down the busy street, slapping her full in the face.

It doesn't matter what I say, he thought, she wouldn't believe me. Believe what she wants to believe. And we'll sing in the sunshine, we'll laugh every day, and I'll stay with you one year, or something like that. When you're not with the one you love, love the one you're with. But who do you love? "Who's making love to your old lady while I make love to you," she asked. Until it's time for you to go. Roberta Flack sings it the nicest, and his wife Mary saw her last week in Washington with Donny Hathaway and Cannonball and Les McCann and Eddie Harris. For two dollars.

My mind is shattering into fragments, like the small patterns of this tiled floor. I think now only in phrases from books or lines from songs. Like cracked ice, I wish I would melt and be whole again.

"And what'll you do if you go home to United States and your wife she be pregnant?"

"Du ma, Luong, why do you want to talk like that? I don't know what I'd do. Maybe I'd be happy, I don't know. And you know how I feel for you."

A flat stomach. I love a flat stomach. And her legs are so nice, firm and slender and dark. She really is the most beautiful girl in Saigon.

"I have to go down to Starlite, Frank. Poppasan he owe me 50,000 pi. I no collect from him because I not need it." He brushed her hair back and kissed her neck, noticing the thick scar behind her ear. But he never asked her about that. "Don't do that baby, you make me horny." He laughed.

Never trust anybody. She didn't trust him. Anybody. "Can't trust people that always laugh," she laughed as she stepped out of the bed.

The helicopter buzzes overhead snapping pictures as she suns herself naked on the roof and doesn't grab a towel. I love your beautiful body. "Don't look at me like that, I am ugly."

"Goddam it, Luong, let me in." He had gone out on the balcony to the shower after she'd finished. "I knew you'd lock me out," he shouted through the louvered door.

"Come back after I sleep."

Tammy, the girl upstairs, walked by, but she was fucked up on speed and didn't see him standing there with the pink towel wrapped around his suntanned waist. "Please let me in, Luong," he tried.

"How much you love me?"

"I'll show you when you let me in." She let him in.

And the hospital was incredible. Like Luong's apartment build-ing, it was three stories high. It reeked of urine and chloroform, reminding him immediately of the time he had hitched a ride to the Annex in an Army hearse. People were on the floors and on benches in the hall, it was so crowded. Dying. He climbed the narrow stairs to the third floor. The babies were all in one small room. Dying. All of their mothers, and other relatives, were in the room too, watching and waiting.

What am I doing here, Frank wondered. He and Luong had taken a taxi to the Starlite and the girl there had said it was her cousin's baby girl. The girl was a friend of Luong's, so he had listened. She had said the baby was dying and the Vietnamese hospital would do no more. "Would you take her to the American hospital?" Frank had said he didn't think he could get her into the Third Field Hospital. "But you can try." Now he wished he'd stayed at the Starlite with Luong, but he'd said he would try.

"If you take her to your hospital, will they give baby back to mother when it die?" the nurse asked. He hadn't been able to find a goddammed doctor in the place, and this nurse was the only one he could find who spoke English.

"I don't know. I guess so. I can't promise, but what would they want to keep the baby for?"

"Sometimes before," the nurse chose her words carefully, "baby die in your hospital, but you no give it back to family. That be very bad. Number ten for sure."

He didn't understand. Maybe the Third Field hadn't known whose baby it was. "Look, I think they'll give the baby back if it dies. But she's not dead yet." Frank looked at the baby girl. "What's wrong with her?"

She was in a tiny crib, lying on a dirty sheet. The baby was two years old, but so damned small. Thin clear tubes brought fluid from two bottles on the bed frame into her frail body at two infected incisions in her thighs and through her nostrils. Her lips were a dry purplish white and her eyes were closed. But she was breathing. "She be very sick," the nurse answered. "She have a cold, very bad cold. Temperature 106 today. And she lose much fluid, too much fluid. Also she vomit. She will die very soon."

"Well, will it do any good to take her to the American hospital?"

"I don't know. You have beaucoup medicine, beaucoup doctor. But she be so very sick. I don't know."

"Will she live through a taxi ride to the American Army Hospital?" Frank asked. The sweat was thick on his forehead. He had never wanted to kill anybody. But he didn't want anybody to die. Goddam, I wish I'd gone to Canada, he thought.

"I don't know."

"I want to do what is right," he pleaded.

"Will they give baby back when it die?"

"Damn it, I think so. But will baby live through the taxi ride?"

And it's sort of like a quiz game and I'm standing in front of two doors, and there's a prize maybe behind each one of the doors, and I have thirty seconds to beat the clock and open one of the doors (and then close it behind me). BUT I CAN'T DECIDE and I stare at those doors, one to the other as THE CLOCK TICKS and the crowd yells THE FIRST DOOR! ! ! or THE SECOND DOOR! ! ! confusing me even more than I was before and then BUZZ! ! ! goes the bell and the announcer (he's from the Firesign Theatre) says, "Oh, I'm sorry, Mr. Jarrell, you didn't beat The Reaper." And the doctor says, "After my careful progthesis, I have determined that you have the plague." And I say fuck the goddammed Army, they give me plague shots every six months and I still get the plague.

There it is.

"I don't know. I just don't know," the nurse finally shrugged.

Frank motioned to the girl from the Starlite, and she went downstairs to get a taxi. The nurse carefully removed the tubes from the discolored body, and the baby's mother quickly wrapped her in an old Army blanket. The nurse took Frank's hand and said, "If she stay here, she die for sure, very soon." All of the other women in the small room had crowded around, and their deep brown eyes made Frank wish he hadn't been born in America.

The baby's heart and breathing stopped somewhere on the way to the Third Field. She was so damned small and the blanket so big, he hadn't noticed. "Was she still breathing when you took her out of the Vietnamese hospital?" the American Major asked.

Frank, breathing heavily from carrying the baby at a sprint from the gate, where the girl from the Starlite had to stop and leave her ID card, to the emergency room, answered, "Yes." It was only a five-minute ride from the Vietnamese hospital to the Third Field. So they tried.

Artificial respiration. Closed heart massage. A tracheotomy. Respirator. Finally, the renal dialysis unit. He was surprised that they had one.

"It looks like an irreversible kidney malfunction," said the young doctor, an American Captain, in the Vietnamese ward. Frank had sat outside the emergency room for four hours with the girl from the Starlite, he never did ask her name, but the doctors had done all they could do. And now they had moved the little girl to Ward 1. The Vietnamese ward. It was very large, but half the beds were empty. The baby, in a high crib, with the dialysis unit by its side, plasma bottles overhead, and all of the tubes connected to her body, looked like a miniature astronaut. "It doesn't look good," the doctor continued. "I don't think she'll live, but then, she's still alive now, so maybe."

The girl from the Starlite and an American nurse had gone outside the hospital to bring in the baby's mother, who had been waiting outside the gate the entire time because she did not have her ID card with her, as the MP had explained. Now the three of them were inside the ward talking to a Vietnamese nurse. When Frank left, the baby's mother was asking if they would give her baby back when it died.

But that was all yesterday, Frank thought, and tonight, still, I wait for Luong. He put ten dong in the jukebox and The Rolling Stones sang "Love in Vain" for him. He ordered another vodka after he sat down. His friend Lok, who owned the Starlite, came over and sat next to him. He shook Frank's hand. "We say man can buy ten pagodas, it mean nothing. But save one life, that be number one. You good boy."

Bullshit, Frank thought, I know you're a goddammed Catholic. But he smiled as Lok stood up and walked over to Kim, one of his girls, to get his 2,000 pi from her before she left with the tall GI standing next to her.

Still he waited. How long would this go on, how did I trap myself like this, he wondered. He smiled remembering the drunk GI here last week who'd asked him where he was from and he'd said, "Saigon."

"No man, I mean in the world."

"Saigon," Frank had repeated. "I was born here. My old man worked at the embassy."

And this dumbshit GI had put his drink down, saying, "Goddam. Let me shake your hand man. I never met anybody before who'd admit he was born in this fucking place."

And Luong had laughed. Luong. She had taken him to the zoo, an island of lush green amidst this grey city, and to the Cholon Market and the nice shops along Pasteur. In the small market on Truong Minh Giang they had bought crabs and shrimp and she had cooked them on the small charcoal stove in the kitchen of her apartment building; it tasted so good. And sometimes they'd gone to Chinese movies at the Eden and eaten ice cream, or sat in the Continental Palace, sipping beer, pretending that there was no war.

But there was a war out there somewhere, he thought, and he remembered one night on the roof of Luong's apartment, three stories high, smoking some dope and drinking a beer, watching the flares, a light show over Saigon, listening to the far off low constant whump! of the outgoing artillery somewhere past Tan Son Nhut, and she'd said to him, "You better lover than you are soldier." And he thought of his M-16 in his locker, unused except for zeroing it at the range and an occasional meaningless guard duty at the Annex. And he remembered the night, shortly before the elections, there had been automatic weapons fire in the streets nearby. There had been a lot of firebombings and they'd blown up the Tu Do Nightclub, and of course there were rumors, there were always rumors of an "imminent attack on Saigon," and in bed next to him Luong had said, "I hope goddam VC do come to Saigon," listening to the quick bursts outside. "Outside they go bang bang, inside we go boom boom."

Luong, you beautiful woman, he thought, where are you tonight? Mike had warned him and he laughed and told him not to be corny. This country, these people, have gotten into me, but it's no good. Like the hospital last night, always the pain. Like Luong, when her brother was killed in Vinh Long. Beautiful eyes cry. And he had held her hand, so soft to touch, the nails neatly manicured and polished, but there was nothing he could do, and why do beautiful hands cry, he wondered.

And Mike, you son-of-a-bitch, you were right, buddy, but I think it's too late.

"You didn't know that?" Luong looked up from her drink. She had finally come. "The baby die at three in the morning." Frank slowly sipped his vodka. "What time you leave? She not dead then? It was too late. I sit with friend from Third Field this afternoon, he tell me. He say it was too late. Nobody tell you? Don't look sad, baby, it is nothing. Everybody be dead someday. Buy me another drink?"

"No."

"Why do I sit with you? You spend no money. Lok mad as hell, he say, 'Luong, why you sit with him, he buy you nothing.' "

"Oh bullshit, you know damn well I bring all of my friends here and we all buy a lot of drinks."

"I know. I tell him that. But he say he never see me like this before. Why I sit with you? If you think for your money, you are stupid. If you think that, you be very stupid."

"I know, Luong."

"I don't know why I like you so much, Frank. Forget what I say tonight. I go to Mimi's house in Tu Duc today, and I drink too much. I am ding-a-ling for sure. I want you to sit with other girl. Something I want I can't get. This never happen before. Before, Luong want something, she get."

"You know I don't want any other girl. I only like you. You're the only girl I want to see. I mean, Jesus, there's no one else like you in Saigon."

"I don't want your money. But people talk. Everybody talk about Frank and Luong. But I do what I want to do. If you need money, I give to you. I help you. Understand? I don't give a damn about money. My heart like table, hard like rock, cold like ice. I have no feelings. I don't give a damn about anything. Understand?"

I understand, Frank thought. Hard as granite, soft as wax. Always changing. So many nights they fell into this. Trying to kid each other. But maybe tonight it's different. Quickly, rapidly, almost whispering I love you. No, forget that, forget everything I say tonight. I am a ding-a-ling. What to do, what to do. And fuck you, Mike, you were right, and fuck my brother, he was right, and fuck me, because I don't know what the fuck to do. Melting wax inside the granite.

Standing in front of her mirror naked looking at herself playing with her tits. A little girl in her mother's dress she looks at me on the bed looking at her and she knows that I will go away in three months.

Lederer's Legacy

by James Aitken

Don't bother me
with stories
of your evenings spent
at the bedside of an
alcoholic priest in Cleveland.
There is very little I can do about it,
and you lie outside my sphere
of interest. (Lederer)

Lederer is leaving in seventeen days. That means he's been here
for 357. They give you one day off on your way back, or it has
something to do with the dateline. But it's too many days all the
same, and I have to admit I envy him a lot. Lousy year in Nam any
way you get it.

He hasn't put much time in the office since he got pissed about
a month ago and left the hootch. Got pissed at Howard who put
ice on top of his mosquito net and it melted down during the
night. When Lederer woke up, around four in the morning, both
he and his mattress were soaked. I thought it was a pretty good
trick, but I was just new meat and nothing bothered me. Lederer
went stomping around, banging on the lockers and waking up the
juice freaks while he moved his stuff out.

I wasn't sure of where he was sleeping then. He was slipping
into the office there for a while, mostly at night, and filling in a day
or so on his short-timer's calendar. It's a crazy magic marker
dream with seventeen blank spaces left on it running down into
the bowl of a little pipe stuck in the mouth of a guy stretched out

in bed—made up by a Red Cross girl with a good head or a sense of humor.

He pretty much quit last month. That hurts, because there is a lot of work to do, and even though nobody does very *much* work you get more work done when you have three guys not doing very much than you do when you just have two guys not doing very much. He did leave us Lederer's Legacy, though, a little book he put together, and that makes it easier. I have a copy of it, open and taped down under a sheet of plastic on the top of my desk. Fifty or so stock phrases for use in any situation when writing an award.

Not that he left it for me personally. He left it for me, Chassen, and for Howard and Loving and whoever it was that was coming in after he went home. Along with the right to buy his interest in the two-foot-square Sanyo refrigerator we use to keep the Cokes in. And a little bitty fan that blows hot air on you when it gets up over one hundred, which has been every day so far this summer. And the last four months of an attractive calendar from an electronics firm in Japan that sent it to him free with his tape deck and speakers. And a collection of fantasy paperbacks and a couple of H. P. Lovecraft weirdies. And a guide to Taipei. And the four hundred awards in our In boxes and the five cardboard cartons of more awards that are getting moldy in the storage room, and thirty to one hundred new ones showing up each day for action.

This awards business is all pretty standardized, which seemed funny to me at first, because you would have thought that was the kind of thing which really required individual action in every case. In a way, it does, but when you have so many, it has to get a little routine or you would never get anything at all done.

You get an Army Commendation Medal if you get shot at and don't get killed. You get a Bronze Star if you get shot at and somebody else gets killed. Or if you step on a mine and they don't know what to say. Or if you kill two or less dinks.

You get a Silver Star if you get shot at, kill two dinks, and save a man's life. Distinguished Service Cross if you're a lieutenant colonel or above.

You get a Medal of Honor if you're really crazy, and it doesn't matter whether you get hit or not, although the only two we've processed were for dead guys who did spectacular things and must have been really all right. I mean, *really* all right.

We take the proposed texts for the citations that come in from the field and turn them into Army English. Then other guys type them up and you have orders and we have one less in the stack to do.

Lederer is really good at it. He doesn't even seem to read the things anymore, just checks the guy's name and fakes it. With the help of the Legacy.

tenacious devotion to duty
his intrepid actions
with a total lack of regard for his personal safety
ever intensifying barrage of hostile fire
in an effort to deny the enemy access

Oh yes.

You would like Lederer, though, in spite of the fact that he was a little stingy and given to throwing fits whenever discovering that one of his sodas had been stolen and scarfed down, ordinarily by Howard. He's got a Midwestern, buck-toothed, split in the middle, open appearance, sandy hair, and a pair of aviator's sunglasses—the kind that look like a mirror from the front—that he wears all the time.

He comes from a little dusty town in Texas and plans on going back there. I once asked him what he did when he was back in the world, and he said, "Not much." I thought that this was probably true because he struck me, you know, even when I first met him, as the kind of guy who was willing to let things happen in his head while events and stuff slid by on the outside.

Pressed further, he owned up to the fact that he worked for his father as an expediter in a shipping company. Light Freight. Odd lot work. He said it seemed like a reasonable thing to do after he got out of college. I said, yes, but not when you got a degree in Chemical Engineering. "Goddam, man," he said, "Fat lot you know about it." Which didn't clear up very much, but it kept me from asking many more questions.

It was hard to get Lederer to just sit around and talk, which made him different from the rest of the guys, who couldn't stop talking about how great they used to be before they came into the service. I thought it was a shame that Lederer wouldn't open up a little more, because there were a lot of things I wanted to ask him about. He was, for one more thing, a conscientious objector. Refused to carry a weapon.

Now, we *are* in a rear area. So far removed from the shooting and all that few of us would be able to recognize an enemy soldier unless he walked into the office and started lobbing hand grenades under the desks. Why a man lets himself get shipped to Vietnam and then decide that he's a conscientious objector is beyond me. Something of a real question there. So I asked him: "Why are you a conscientious objector?"

"If you're a conscientious objector," he said, "they can't put you on guard and you don't have to sit up all night."

Which ended that line of inquiry.

ATTENTION TO ORDERS:

GENERAL ORDER 3647

BY DIRECTION OF THE PRESIDENT, UNDER THE PROVISIONS OF EXECUTIVE ORDER 11046, 24 AUGUST 1971, THE BRONZE STAR MEDAL WITH "V" DEVICE IS AWARDED TO:
Specialist Four Blake Christianson for heroism in connection with ground operations against a hostile force in the Republic of Vietnam. Specialist Christianson distinguished himself by extraordinary heroism on 7 February, 1969, while serving as a rifleman with Company B, 4th Battalion, 21st Infantry. On that date, the company was conducting a search and clear operation near Ap Hai when it came under a heavy volume of enemy fire. Although most of the company was pinned down by the insurgents, Specialist Christianson ran to a bomb crater twenty meters in front of the enemy emplacement. With complete disregard for the danger involved, he attacked the hostile position with hand grenades and placed intensive suppressive fire on the enemy force. He then exposed himself to the hostile fire, assaulted the position, and destroyed it completely. Through his timely and courageous actions, he contributed significantly to the defeat of the enemy force. Specialist Four Christianson's personal heroism, professional competence, and devotion to duty are in keeping with the highest traditions of the military service, and reflect great credit upon himself, the Americal Division, and the United States Army.

Hundreds and hundreds of them in the cartons in the storage room.

The first time we got together was over at the 523d Signal Club across the road from Division Headquarters. I like it there. It has all the warmth and atmosphere of any sleazy dive in East St. Louis. And only one of the bar girls is hopelessly pockmarked.

I walked in and heard a guy call my name and say, "Buy a Bloody Mary." I was pretty sure it was Lederer, even though I'd only seen him once or twice before, and then only as he passed through the office on his way to wherever it was he went to screw off all day. Still, we'd been sort of watching each other out of the corners of our eyes.

I brought him his drink.

"You sorry bastard," he said when I sat down at his table.

"Why me?"

"Everybody asks himself that question at least a thousand times while he's here, but it doesn't do any good."

"That's not what I meant. I know why I'm here. I'm here because I didn't want to go to jail or Canada. Why am I a sorry bastard?"

"Oh, that. Because of the way it's going to get to you after a while. Wait until you see the dead guys coming across. Posthumous awards. Guys you went through training with, or sat between on the plane coming over. The skinny crazy eighteen year old grunt you met at the replacement center. His name sticks in your mind because he drank too much and passed out one night and had to be carried back to the hootch. He's dead now, and you have to write him up. A guy you knew. Damn."

Silence for a minute, and I try to get the sense of what he's working toward.

"It hits you in three stages. First you think: this is really rotten. Here I sit in this office, completely removed from whatever it is they're doing out there where they're shooting and killing each other. Phew. And I'm supposed to make up some kind of coherent award about a man who knew so much more about what was going on than I do, or did, or will. Like the man I had to write up for the Medal of Honor. You might see one come through. It takes about a year to get it processed.

"He's twenty years old, a medic. They're always the screwiest. They get inspired or something. The healers. Anyway, it happens.

"This whole company is getting zapped from four sides of a rice paddy. They make it back to this little island, but five men are shot down and lying out in the open. Medic makes five trips out to get them. The temperature is maybe 110 degrees and he is constantly under fire. On his last trip in, he gets killed. You wonder what the hell he could have been thinking about. Not so much the first and second trip. That's sort of reflex. But what does he think about after three times? Or four times?''

"He has the power, now. He knows he can do what has to be done, now. He's been doing everything that he's been trained for, that they want him to do, that a man can *possibly* do. Think of the sense of elation he must have felt. He has passed beyond fear. He is off somewhere else in his mind now, feeling the strength of himself flash out of his pores and crackle in the humid air. It's louder than the bullets and the grenades; the sound of his own power. He is really making it, he is on top.

"He gets killed on the fifth go round, but that is not where the interest is. What are you going to say about a man like that? That would make any sort of sense? In 250 words?

"Maybe the problem is being too close to the words for too long. For a year you sit and write about courage and valorous actions, about gallantry and heroism, and when something which screams of it comes along and you only have the same words left to try to make it come alive.

"And you start thinking about what a bitch it is to have come all this way to sit it out, to never really know what is going on around you. If you felt that your time in the States didn't make much sense, wait until you've been sitting around here for a couple of months.''

"There was a line in *The New York Review of Books,* in a poem. It had to do with artificial respiration and went something to the effect of, 'I get tired of kissing the dead.' Maybe that isn't relevant here. I don't know.''

He stopped talking for a minute and I ordered another round of drinks from My Lee. Her little son was in the club, a two- or three-year-old trailing around after her or sitting on the bartop staring at the television set.

"The second stage is when you start to laugh at it. You laugh at the deadies. Look at *this* stupid son of a bitch. Tripped a booby trap and got himself greased. A Bronze Star for screwing up. Must have been some kind of a dud.

"I guess that's the easiest part, and it lasts for the shortest period of time.

"After a while, the horror of it starts to sink in. These are guys, man, just off the block. And now they're nothing anymore. It comes on you suddenly, just how dead they are. They simply are *not* anymore. Everything they might have been has just been erased. Wiped off. Whatever they might have been just isn't going to happen.

"And for what? In stage two you would answer, 'So that I can write awards about them.' In stage three you don't have an answer. The varieties of death that we invent for each other are almost endless. The reasons why are almost always vague, false, or nonexistent. You work that over in your mind for a while and you start to feel pretty rotten."

There was nothing I could say to him.

Lederer did not so much take part in a conversation as launch into an occasional tirade on one subject or another. He ended these outbursts when he felt he had said enough.

I don't know why he had been in the club that night in the first place. He didn't like to drink, unless it was to keep himself occupied during a movie. There was supposed to be a film that night, but he walked out before it started. I guess that talking himself out a little made it unnecessary to get lost in a flick for a couple of hours.

I am pretty sure that was the only time I ever saw him over at the club. He was a grass fancier. Every time his name came up in the office, Sergeant Reeves would stick his arm out and pretend to be an airplane.

"Cruising at 45,000 feet, ground speed approximately three-quarters of a mile an hour, and going up."

It was supposed to be funny, and I guess it was, the first five or six times. They all kidded about it, Lederer's smoking dope. They made out like he was high all the time. He wasn't, though.

continued to resist by all means available
denied himself medical attention until
inspired leadership
unremitting dedication
by displaying the utmost of personal bravery/courage/intrepidity

Howard is barking like a dog. He does this exceptionally well. When I first got here, he would do it when I wasn't looking and I would always make a remark about it, how I wished the dogs would go away. Everybody got a kick out of that, but managed to hide their smiles, so it was about three days before I finally caught on.

Howard can also cackle exactly like a chicken. He places the backs of his wrists against his kidneys, waves his elbows, thrusts his chest out, cranes his neck, bobs his head, takes one tentative, jerky step after another, and puk pawwk! Puk pup puk!

He never could stand Lederer.

"That silly-ass freak! What do you want to know about him for? Damn guy's always flying. Grooveeno, you know. Shambling around with his head a million miles away from here. And he's a stingy bastard, too. I stole a Coke of his one afternoon and I didn't hear the end of it for a week. That measly can of Coke, you'd have thought it was gold or something."

Howard goes out of his way to inform you that he is from South by God Carolina, stand when you say it, and seriously believes that people don't go far enough out of their way to do things for him. It is his contention that anything left unattended in the communal refrigerator is fair game, and is genuinely surprised at the number of people who do not share his views. He doesn't share Lederer's hangups about the job, and is probably no worse off for it.

"Screw him! I was going to give him the damn dime, but not after he put up such a stink about it. I mean, it was a can of *soda!* And *then* he tried to sell me his lousy radio for eighteen dollars and got mad when I would only give him fifteen. I swear to God, he didn't even want to *give* me the thing after I paid him for it. I mean, three lousy dollars. You'd think it would break the guy.

"What the hell did he want? It wasn't the only radio around. It wasn't even the best radio around. He could have sold it to me for ten dollars and still come out better than he was before.

"Or the time we put ice on top of his mosquito net. I never saw a guy get so mad over nothing. I mean, we were drunk, kidding around. What did he expect? We should go out and buy him a new bed because his old one got wet? I sure ain't going to miss his ass when he drags it out of here."

Well, yes, Howard, I had to say, I'm sure all of that is true, and I hoped he'd quit rapping, but like as not he'd go on for another half an hour about the crimes Lederer had committed against him. He'd go on until he noticed that no one was listening anymore. Then he would look at the ceiling and yell, "Hey, ceiling, can you hear me?" If the ceiling ever heard, it didn't let on.

intrepid actions at the cost of his life
gallant display of heroic action
courageous and decisive action at great personal risk
resolute personal determination
reflect the utmost personal credit

"And you think you lucked out, but you're wrong," Lederer said. He walked into my plywood walled area in our hootch and lay down on my bunk. I was sitting at a rough desk I had built, writing a letter to a buddy of mine from Basic who'd pulled a MAG assignment in Iran. I wasn't too sure whether he'd lucked out either.

"And you think I don't know anything about you, but you're wrong about that, too. You sit there and act dumb, stupid half smile on your face, detached, and all that good stuff, but the first thing you do when you get here is build a bookshelf and put books in it. Your priorities give you away. Those are not the actions of a fool."

He had a soft West Texas way of speaking, like Henry Fonda in *The Rounders.* A little half lisp, and he talked with his teeth clenched and his lips hardly moving at all. You would wonder where the sound was coming from unless you stared closely at his mouth. Anything suits you—howdy—just tickles me plumb to death. He was western, all right, and had that certain independent big-goddam-deal way of speaking and moving and half smiling that said he just *knew* more than you did, and it came from growing up on the dry dusty plains where there is no shade from anything, and he just might tell you what he knew, if you were listening right.

"I often wondered," he said, "who it would be that would come in and take over my job after me. I cared about it, you know, even though I can't say exactly why. Shouldn't have bothered wondering, though, because the next guy in was Howard. Couldn't say anything to him at all. Crazy mother drunk. Can't see living a life like that. There's enjoyment, and there's disease. He's got the disease.

"So, whatever I worked up went out the window on his arrival. Be that as it may, I will tell you an apocryphal story, meaning that parts, or all of it, don't have to be true. Maybe some parts aren't."

I turned my chair around to face him. His uniform was filthy. He could have put it on a week ago, or fresh this morning. Nothing here stays clean longer than an hour.

"It occurs in the EM Club, one night last February. I had gone over to watch a movie, despite the fact that I detested that rat-infested hole. It was a terrible old Lee Marvin movie that I had seen before on television in the world. And hadn't liked. But it wasn't raining for the first time in a week, and we could sit outside and watch a film. The smell of the cesspools immediately to the west hangs heavy in the air."

He half laughed at his attempt to draw the story out, like a grandfather trying to soothe shadows that danced on his grandchild's wall with his soft, old man's voice.

"There were a lot of other men in the club that night. Because of the rain. It was such a relief to be able to do something, even if it was only to watch an old, bad movie. I think all our nerves were a little shot. It was just after Tet, and there was a lot of shelling going on. Two days before, they had blown away the finance building. I think that may have been the only time our company area had ever been hit by anything. There was that, and the boredom, and the rain.

"These guys came by. In a truck, or a jeep. Grunts. In out of the field, with long hair and beads and Montagnard bracelets. Maybe been out in the woods one hundred straight days and scared to hell. You couldn't hear them coming. You don't hear just one more truck going down the road when you're watching a movie and there are trucks going by all the time.

"They hate us because we're back here at division and have very few opportunities to die. I guess it makes them feel better, and I don't hold it against them. You see a lot of fights when they come in for stand-down and decide to raise a little hell.

"So these guys, for fun, you know . . . they threw a smoke grenade into the club. Everybody panicked. I can't tell you how frightened I was, mostly because it was so confused. The grenade landed where we were sitting, right in the middle of the open courtyard in front of the movie screen. It was impossible to get out through the exits. They were packed. I could hear the men yelling and what I thought was bones being broken though I realize now that it was only chairs toppling over and beer cans being crushed underfoot.

"Somebody broke down part of the plywood wall that closes in the courtyard, and maybe sixty people got out through there. I was caught in the middle. I was at the end of a line trying to get out through an exit, and then I turned and was at the end of the line trying to get out through the hole in the wall. This is all taking place in seconds. Not ten seconds have gone by now, maybe not even five. I am still expecting that another round of whatever it was might be coming in, and I would be trapped in the courtyard. I hadn't even realized that it was only smoke, yet.

"Then I saw these fellows going by. They had picked up Lee, one of the bar girls. Hose-momma. Oh boy, she'd been tromped on by the guys running all over the place. They didn't know where to take her. We were caught, all of us.

"I stayed with these men, and we stood in the middle of the area waiting for everybody else to clear out.

"By now we know that it was just smoke, but I am even more frightened. What keeps going through my head is 'Good Christ, what if we've killed somebody?'

"I had to stay there with them, because I was part of it. I couldn't get over the feeling that I might have been the cause of it. There was a chance that if I hadn't been afraid and gotten up and tried to run, no one would have been afraid. There was always that chance.

"It seemed like we stood there for a long time. I know, though, that it couldn't have been over twenty seconds before we made it through the hole in the wall.

"We didn't know what to do with the girl. She was not conscious. We brought her to the far side of the building, in the shadows. Some of the men were moving back into the club now, realizing what had actually happened, and we didn't want them to see her. I didn't, anyway. She was mine now. I had made her my responsibility, and it was strange, but I started to get selfish. I didn't want to share that responsibility with the other two guys.

"They placed her down on the ground and asked me if I thought that she was dead. I said no, but that we should call the

MP's right away. They didn't want to stick around for that, and I was actually glad to see them slip away. It would be easier to feel that you had nothing to do with it, and I think they wanted to get away because they actually knew better. The reason I had to stay with her was because, I don't know, if you're going to be a real person, then you do the things which people should do. It was up to me to save her in some way. Save her from what, I don't know. She wasn't dead, which was fortunate. I can't keep people alive. It's not part of my MOS.

"She wasn't dead, but when I picked up her arm I could tell that it was broken because her wrist was twisted at a funny angle, and I didn't know what else might have happened to her. And I started to worry about whether she might be broken up on the inside and we had hurt her worse by moving her out of the club. But there was nothing else that could have been done. Nobody knew what was happening at the time, and it was right to move her.

"They are a very small people, the Vietnamese. Not only short. That never surprised me, because I expected them to be short before I came over, but they are so slender. There is really nothing to them at all, and not just the girls. When you see the men you don't think of them as being well, fully grown up or something. Until you are used to seeing them around all the time, it is hard to think of them as regular people. But after a while, I don't know, you get protective. You think that might be why we are fighting? Because these are charming little people in need of a brotherly arm around their shoulders? Weird theory, that, but I suppose it makes as much sense as anything else.

"Then I heard the MP's. Everybody else was moving back into the club, or already there. The girl was still unconscious, but nobody was around her or anything, so I left her for a minute and went and got one of the MP's.

"I told this one guy that there was a girl hurt, and took him to her, and he decided we should take her to the hospital. I don't know why I didn't think of that before. I guess I had it in mind that someone would say something or do something right there and she would be O.K. again.

"They put the girl in the back seat of their jeep. I decided I would go along with them to the hospital. I think I felt that if I went along with them that it would make a difference, and that she would get better quicker, or be any better for my presence. I didn't know the girl particularly. I'd only been at the club once or twice. I may have talked to her, but in no special way. It was a crazy feeling, like I could make her all right by wanting her to be all right, because if you wanted something bad enough, then it just had to be so. Your force could make it happen.

"When I got to the hospital, they asked me if I had seen anything, and I said no, you know, and explained what I could about the grenade and how we carried her outside. They told me to go back to the company. I didn't want to leave. I just knew somehow that if I didn't get to see her again she was going to die. It was the closest thing I've ever had to some kind psychic experience."

He stopped talking and stretched out on my bunk and stared at the ceiling. I waited.

"You see," he said after a few minutes, "you're predictable. I knew even before I started that you would not ask me whether the girl died or not. You're too tactful. Willing to sit there and wait to see whether I'm going to tell you or not, and figuring it's my business whether I do or don't."

I didn't say anything.

"She did die," he said, "about two days later. She was all messed up inside, and I don't know whether we helped her along or not. I know that it had to be in some way my fault, and it is something that has become part of me. And, of course, the nice thing about the story is that now that you've heard it, what happened is part of you, too."

Lederer got up and left as abruptly as he had entered earlier. I tried to figure out why it was that he had chosen me to talk to. It was probably something as simple as the fact that I was new, and wouldn't have any preconceptions about him, and that I was not close to him. I hadn't lived his life. There was nothing I could say back.

outstanding professional competence
a definite asset and contributed immeasurably
reacting to the extreme danger
imminent pending death
inspired by his courageous actions

Howard came in screaming drunk that evening. "Piss on it!" he yelled. "Do you hear me? Piss on all of it!"

He walked up and down the length of the hootch, banging on all the wall lockers and plywood partitions with his fists and waking everybody up.

"Go to bed, Howard," somebody called.

"Do you think that makes any difference? To me?" He continued to shout as loudly as he could. "Do you think that makes any difference at all?"

"Go to bed, Howard," said the same voice, with the same effect.

Howard stomped through the hootch, bringing his feet down as hard as he could on the echoing floor. "Do you think that makes any difference? Do you think you make any difference at all? Puk Pawwk! Puk puk puk puk. Piss on all your stinking ass holes."

Howard crashed out of the hootch. I don't know where he went.

exceptional courage and daring
demonstrated exceptional resourcefulness
long arduous hours
disregarding the danger involved
during the initial exchange of fire

I didn't see Lederer again until the night before he was leaving, about four days after his last visit.

"Let's go out and sit on the bunker," he said when he came into my area. "I can't stand the smell of these freaks."

It was about nine o'clock and I had been lying around in my underwear trying to get involved in a long adventure novel from the PX. I put on my Ho Chi Minh sandals and followed him outside. There was a lot of noise in the hootch. About three different guys were running with their tape recorders. He raised himself up on top of the green nylon sandbags which cover our bunker and I did the same. It was hot out, hot being away from the fan, but quieter.

"I have left you a document," he said, "which purports to be Lederer's Legacy, a compendium of deathless phrases to be applied with discretion both to mortals and to those who have transcended their earthly remains. Specifically, those guys who either make it back to Mom and Dad, or get greased. Do not be misled. It is neither Lederer's true Legacy, nor does it work, in most instances."

"I don't know," I said, "I think it comes in pretty handy."

"Did you know I was married?" he asked.

"No," I said, a little startled. Lederer just always seemed like he was only himself, not part of something else. I didn't know whether he was telling the truth or not.

"Aptly put. Forthright, direct, and to the point. You might also gather that I am half lit. No matter. It is my last night, and I intend, if not to really enjoy it, at least not to hate it. I am making my fond farewells to this delightful place. No matter. But I wanted to gass with you for a while before I crashed. You got time?"

"Yeah, sure," I said to him. Most of a year left.

"Yes, my friend," he said, launching into a bad imitation of W. C. Fields, "I will be going to a little corn-silk, touseled-topped, blue-eyed darling mine. Little girl from Wrens, Georgia, by way of the University of Tennessee and a disastrous summer at Corpus Christi where she worked as a waitress and had the good fortune to meet and marry mine own self. Beautiful little girl. Salt of the Earth. Salt of the Sea. Salt of the Shaker. Shit. I love her anyway.

"Makes me nervous, it does, this thought of returning to the world. Can't get properly prepared for my hero's welcome. Do you think they will do that, you know, have the high school band out, and we'll half a dozen of us or so march down the main street of the tree-lined town, and everything will turn to technicolor, and all have been worthwhile? Are there any towns left underneath the trees?

"Still, it will be better than the shakes over here, even if everything is still dun brown and dusty.

"Sometimes I wonder what she is thinking, because you never can tell. I just never have been able to get inside a woman's imagination. Trying to play like you are part of their mind and know what she is up to, it just doesn't work out.

"Lays back there in old El Pas-ay-o in the little air-conditioned apartment she picked up while trying to finish her schooling, and dreams about me consorting with flesh peddlars, pimps, whores, and willing boys. A very bad place, the Army is, for clean young men. But that is neither here nor there. Particularly not here.

"I, of course, dream of her constantly. Abstinence makes the heart grow fonder."

He lay back and looked up at the stars.

"Did you ever wonder where the Southern Cross was in all

those stars? That's the four stars on our patch, in case you didn't get the orientation on the history of the unit. I'll be damned if I could ever find it up there in all that space."

I was starting to understand a little of how tired Lederer was, of how disgusted. I could see it happening to me, maybe, just the time starting to wear you down, eat at the edges of your mind.

"I was on the verge of cracking up," he said. "There was nothing particularly dramatic about it. Chalk it up to my being a slightly weird guy. At any rate, nothing came of it. When I first got here, I wanted to be a door gunner. Listen to this, now, it's almost like a poem: I wanted to fly in the mad helicopter skies and piss death with my machine gun, streaming death from between my legs. Wear a red Day-Glow helmet and kill people on the ground . . .

"But that was before I had the realization, before I knew that no matter what I did, unless I killed myself, I would not die here. I realized that I was somehow protected, that *nothing* could happen to me, that I would have to live through it, live with it, and that was all there was. So I decided that I would not kill here. It was only fair.

"And after a while, they decided that I was crazy. Not too crazy to do my job, but certainly crazy enough to keep away from a weapon. No sweat. We all have to make it on our own terms.

"But it didn't help much.

"I think of my wife at home with a Lesbian lover. That is the substance of my erotic dreams. My subconscious is a bitch. Make of that what you will. I dream of my wife and her Lesbian lover who looks exactly like herself, and they roll about in the slowest of motion on the couch and split and fuse, split of fuse. What is the source of these midnight creep shows? They hold each other so tightly that they are just one person, then come apart and make intense, explicit, pornographic love. I can see it, and feel it, and it hurts me very much."

We smoked a cigarette. I had to light his for him because he only had those green Army matches and couldn't keep one lit long enough. He started talking again after a few minutes, but it was different. Whatever he had been working up to was over, and I don't know whether he had said what he wanted to or not.

"So, you spend a long year here. At first, it doesn't seem that way, when you are fresh, and angry, and can think of ways to pass the time. But it grows longer and longer and you close up inside yourself and have visions of the little woman. And you don't want much to be an Indian. No hunting, no trespassing.

"I sleep outside, now. I shipped everything I want to keep back home, because I didn't want to be attached to this place anymore. I sleep outside, down by the beach, with the rats and the lizards and the night noises that I refuse to be afraid of.

"There was another story that I was going to tell you, and it made sense earlier on, but maybe it's not important. It wasn't a very unusual story, and maybe a little maudlin. I need to go home, now, and get my head straight. But it's no sweat, GI. I'll see you in the morning."

Lederer climbed down off the bunker and walked away.

I saw him again in the morning when he came in to pick up his service medal, and Loving drove him down to the airport in the office jeep for his flight to Camn Ranh and home. He didn't say anything.

Now, sometimes, when Howard is beating on his desk with both fists and the Marines are running up their jets down at the airport and everything is so loud that you want to scream, I think about his remarks, and hell, maybe I almost understand him, and I almost understand the little poem which I found neatly typed on a three-by-five card. Lederer had signed it and paperclipped it to an award for a medic who had saved this guy's life by fishing out and tying off the arteries in the stumps of his blown-off legs.

Once in a while I get a notion to write him a letter, even though I don't have his address, and tell him about this crazy scene I've been envisioning. It's Howard, stripped naked, in a room where the light is intensely bright and the walls and floors and ceiling are covered with mirrors, and he's screaming, "Can't you hear me? Can't you hear me? I'm Howard, Goddam it, from South Goddam Carolina! Can't you hear me?" Lederer would probably understand.

while he kept the enemy occupied
continuing his advance
neutralizing the hostile fire
closing with the insurgents
overrunning the enemy positions
his courageous actions at the cost of

The Courier

by Igor Bobrowsky

He knew the world was empty. After the liftoff, after the crushed grass had sprung up to gently sway tall again, and the billowing dust had settled down, scattered along the hilltop, he sat and stared blindly out through the open door at the vague greeness that was streaking by below.

It had been a month or so down in the valley—a month called Essex, after a month called Swift, but before the days which would be called Christmas when they came, if they came, in a month yet unnamed. Days and nights had gone by in whole week groups that fused together and overlapped and blurred into an uncertain twilight. Within this twilight, the individual days had remained nameless, except for those few that came right after one another or were placed in an arbitrary sequence that began with Sunday. Sunday was a good and easy name to remember because it was the first, and one could always add to it.

Now as he looked down, the earth seemed suddenly to spin up crazily towards his face. As it came with reach, he lurched out from inside the helicopter and stumbled away, like a drunk on rubbery legs. The ground heaved up at him in violent, heat-washed waves, that swirled around him, and crashed over him. His brain in the dizzy haze behind his sweat-burned eyes.

"Rock . . . dust . . . ground . . . hot . . . oh . . ." and again, "oh . . .," he mumbled, as blurry shapes melted into forms around him, imprinting themselves on the blank walls of his mind. He found his mouth with his sleeve and half-wiped the caked grime from his lips with the quick, thoughtless gesture of a spastic.

"Wire," he thought fleetingly, as he saw the officer's form waving at him from in front of the barbed coils that lay strung around the helipad in a maze of intricately confused patterns. As he suddenly perceived himself moving quickly toward the gesturing man, he thought "run," and shuffled into a heavy trot.

"Run . . . run . . . run . . . run . . ." he panted out rhythmically, each time he exhaled into the resisting air. The heavy helmet with its tufts of bobbing grass and leaves jostled his brain and pulled at his scalp at each step, and the equipment, draped and strapped all over him, kicked and beat him on the sides, and up and down his back, as he ran. "Running," he mumbled, conscious of his forward movement, and of pushing the pebbled, dusty earth back behind him with his heavy feet. As he ran, he stared fixedly before him at the fluid shape ahead—desperately trying not to lose sight of the man in front of him. "Running in the dust," he thought— "Running."

He remembered that one of the very early days, not long after the news camera had filmed him, with wet socks tied around his helmet, drying, and holding the perforated canteen with the star on it—he had punched one of his team leaders. He had run up and punched crying Elliott in the face because Elliott had filled his gas mask pouch with cigarettes and extra rations, and had run down the hill screaming and vomiting when they had all been gassed and had to stay. Sometime around then too, either before or after Aaron had blown out his own eardrums firing the .45 inside the tunnel, he remembered watching the old people walking slowly out into the fields where the gunships were firing. They were all wailing. One old man could not straighten out his arms which were very thin and deeply scarred up to the elbows. He kept bowing and begging until a gunner came up and kicked him from behind to get him moving. Out in the fields, the old man still turned from time to time to look back at them all, putting his hands together and nodding his head.

He stopped, hunched over, sweating and heavy, in front of the officer who stood shimmering in the heat. "Shotgun," the officer said, thumbing at the vehicle behind him. The officer gestured with his arms for him to climb in. "Jeep," he said to himself softly, then repeated, "jeep," as the green man with the dispatches climbed in beside the driver in front. "J-E-E-P . . . J-E-E-P," he spelled out in his mind as he felt the hardness of the seat beneath him, and watched the two heads and necks and backs in front talk to the officer whose mouth was moving and who was sweating and squinting in the sun. "Hot," he thought.

Where was the AK he had captured from the men by the well— the captain had sent it in on the Medevac . . . where was it? Willard had shot two men carrying rice up the trail and laughed at the reporter who was furious. That was one day, a different day. Those two didn't have any weapons, only rice that day. But where was his AK? He got it in the valley—but where was it now?

His feet had been dry up in the hills, and when they came down into the valley, where Golf and Hotel were waiting for them, he wanted them to stay dry. So in the valley he walked on the dikes, even though it was the wrong thing to do, and stepped on the back of the man who was face-down, dead, in the irrigation ditch. The man sank down under his steps. His feet got wet anyway and it disgusted him.

At Golf Company he saw what the mortars had done the nights before when he had been in the hills watching the flashes in the dark. He didn't look closely at the dead faces because he didn't want to know. At Golf, after the airstrike, he threw a stiff grey kid out of the hole he was taking for the night, and then had to walk out and prod him down the slope because he wouldn't roll. Jenkins had malaria by then, Darden had the rot, Nicholson needed a hospital for what his bowels were doing to him, but Michaels, the corpsman, said his feet were in really great shape. He also had to go down to the river to fill the canteens because someone had thrown somebody down the green well—somebody who stank when he looked in. The bunker where he got the brass belt buckle with the star was near there. It had been dirty when he got it, but he had cleaned it against his shirt until it was shiny.

The jeep lunged forward and bumped its way out of the perimeter on past the wire and onto the narrow dirt road that lay beyond and stretched across the paddies. Pieces of a truck, scattered alongside the road in tangled heaps, fell past his gaze. The wind pushed against his face, and his eyes narrowed into slits against the sun's glare and his own salty sweat that streaked his face and seeped into the corners of his mouth. His eyes darted from place to place along the distant tree line, and his body tensed in vague anticipation. "Riding," he thought, as possibilities of ambushes and snipers and mines rubbed in dark contention.

*After sneaking up on the village through the tall wet grass—
when Skootch had been the first one in, darting at a crouch from
hedge to hedge—they had eaten all the peanuts in the house by
the red brick wall, and then thrown all the shells at the wrinkled
woman who sat squatting under the fence staring. While the rest
ate, the gunners had braced their guns on the wall, and shot all
the bellowing water buffalo out in the paddy, where they later lay
stiff and massive, half-submerged in putrid water. James ran
down and killed a chicken in the yard while the other men were
shooting at pigs in the shed. They had leapt and squealed, trying
to break out, and splashed blood over everything. One pig was cut
in half and stuck on a pole behind the staring old woman.*

*The gunners were crazy anyway. They had killed men from
second platoon on the rainy night when he had slept in the water-
filled hole with Scott and hadn't heard a thing above the splashing
gentle patter of the rain. It was hard to be a gunner though . . . to
have to hump all that ammo around all the time. Some of the dead
buffalo had rings through their noses and bells strung on ropes
around their necks. Some of the dead men were almost naked, or
at least they had looked like they were. The dead dragged out of
the bunkers had looked naked . . . naked and filthy.*

The jeep slowed down gradually, rocking and bumping from rut to
rut as it neared the river. On the far side, across the wooden
bridge, guarded by its rag-tag band of barefoot irregulars, stood
the village. It lay, half-hidden in the lush green foliage that grew
thick along the top of the embankment which rose in an easy
slope from the flat sand of the water's edge. From between the
thick thorny hedges that ran parallel to the meandering river, the
white walls of the village hootches peeked out intermittently. Here
and there the dull red of tile or bright silver grey of tin roofing
showed itself briefly through the leaves of palm, mango and ba-
nana trees.

The village spread, dreamy and drowsy, in the heat of afternoon, with only the buzz of flies, dragonflies and gnats' wings
beating at the air, and the sound of the river tumbling pebbles
along the shore or lapping around the pillars of the bridge, to
break the lulling silence. The tall grasses rustled as they nudged
against each other, prodded gently by a breeze, and the palm
fronds scraped together softly. The smells of rice, fish and ma-

nure rose into the air above the village, there to blend and hang together in the still, wet, heavy atmosphere. Only the occasional shrill laugh or the splashing slap-slap that came up from beneath the bridge could be identified as human sounds. But even these sounds served only to heighten the pervasive silence.

On the bridge itself, its half-dressed guards, dwarfed by their foreign rifles, walked listlessly back and forth along the sand-bagged catwalk. From time to time they stopped to chat, to light a cigarette together, or sighing, to rest their elbows on the railings and gaze absent-minded smiles down at the women washing their children and their clothes below. Their comrades, not on duty, meanwhile slept in crumbling, shallow holes, dug in a rough, casual semicircle around both ends of the bridge . . . or lay sprawled out beneath the shade of hastily staked-down ponchos scattered here and there.

The guards on the bridge turned unhurriedly at the noise of the approaching jeep, and then, perceiving its occupants, began to grin and wave, and point down at the women, busy along the riverbank. A few of the sleepers, disturbed from their slumber, momentarily glowered, out of their half-sleep, at the jeep, and then, as if overwhelmed by their efforts, dropped back into their dreams.

As the jeep edged on to the bridge, he found himself gazing with a strange feeling of apprehension, at the village. It appeared to him as an unfathomable and disturbing mystery. "People," he thought helplessly and uncomprehendingly. As the jeep went by, one of the guards on the bridge gave him a thumb's up and a broad grin. "Mouth," he noted fleetingly, as his gaze passed over the smiling face . . . "Teeth."

Beneath him along the river bank, he saw the small, black-haired women squatting in the shallow water. A constant, high-pitched chatter rose up from them and blended into a harmony of sing-song cadences of laughter and children's squealing. His ears filled with a confusion of sound. A question half-formed briefly in his mind, but fell apart before it could assume a form, exhausted in its genesis. It fell apart like all his thoughts and dissolved in the whirlpool of incongruities, inconsistencies and unresolved ideas that floated suspended in his mind.

The splash of wet clothes on the rocks below grew increasingly troublesome, assailing his ears, and threatening to swamp his overburdened senses. "Wash . . . wash . . . WWWAAAASSSHH," he repeated, seeking to connect the sound with a word, the word with a feeling, and the feeling with a meaning—hoping to wring sense out of repetition. Every thought led him nowhere endlessly—"they bathe . . . I ride . . ." Each concept which he tried to build into a structure was immediately shattered by its own pointlessness. "I ride . . . they walk . . . they bathe."

Yet the questions now assaulted him in ever-increasing numbers, with ever-increasing persistence. As he tried to form them into patterns and to manage the torrents of their numbers, he found that they smashed aside all his efforts at control, and swarmed in, with increased fury, to clog up the narrow passageways of his mind with their flood of debris. He felt a need to open his mouth, to ease his breathing. He felt a need to scream to keep from suffocating with the mass of his own brain. He found that he could not control the muscles of his own face or jaw which remained fixed and rigid. His mouth grew dry and he fought to gulp down the air.

He had shouted and screamed along with the others until he was choking and coughing as they fired madly from the hillside down at the five dark green men desperately seeking cover behind the dikes in the open paddy below. The corpsman, who was always checking everyone's feet, later cut the wounded man's throat and then rolled him over to stab him between the shoulder blades when he still wouldn't die. After that, the corpsman was very angry and no one said anything when he finally pushed the bayonet into the inside of the dying man's ear. The corpsmen were good and compassionate and it was a miracle that they lasted as long as they did because they lived so much sorrow and embraced so much grief. Their world was always dying around them.

As they rode into the village with its winding, shady paths, and its clustered houses, images rushed out at him from around its corners, from behind its trees and bushes, from within its thorny hedges. They rose up from the ground and raced down the narrow paths to pounce raging at his eyes. They leapt up at him in violent fragments, crashing into his vision pushing him down. The green driver's back seemed to recede, too far away for him to reach or to touch. House, well, waved hand, dirt yard, face, face, tree, tree

. . . tree, flashed before his eyes and passed him. Nothing stayed. He wanted to ask what was happening around him but the driver didn't stop, and the green sweaty courier was waving his hand at the road, and the rushing trees and faces. Fence, house, and man scurrying aside flitted by—and he recoiled from them. Pieces. Everywhere, and here, and there . . . Pieces, pieces, here and there—pieces, pieces, everywhere, he chanted rhythmically and mindlessly under his breath. Clenching his teeth tightly, he sat jerking and swaying with the motion of the moving jeep, and tried to give each thing he saw a name and a place within his mind.

They had been going down the hill most of the day when the word came up from behind that the men in front had found water. He had fought desperately not to be crushed in the rush of men around him . . . and the officers screamed and punched and hit at them with their rifles. He had clung to backs, necks and arms to keep from going under, and pushed his elbows and fists at the mouths and faces around him.

They should have gone down to drink by squads, but the thought of water had made them half-mad, and they fought and cursed one another, falling and stumbling down the steep, slippery path. They fell over each other into the shallow stream, and drank its water greedily. The water felt good soaking their clothes and washing over their ears and eyes, faces and hands.

Later, they were passive and dazed when the officers dragged them out of the stream and shoved them down the path again to where they had seen the green tracers streaking through the darkness. In the valley they drank the greenish, stinking water in the paddies . . . and some got sick.

The jeep rolled to a stop in a large dusty courtyard, some dozen yards off to the side of the main road and in front of a large grey building surrounded by sandbagged bunkers and strands of rusty wire. Torn sandbags lined the outside of the building's veranda and the dull red paint of the windows and doors was cracking and peeling. A number of dogs lay dozing, tongues out, in the shade of some steel culverts, stacked up beneath the porch. Groups of soldiers in tight tiger-striped uniforms sat talking and playing cards around their fighting holes. On the far side of the grey building, clumps of women crowded behind open stalls selling cigarettes, ice drinks, fish, rice, tea, peanuts and bananas, jabbering among themselves and shooing away the persistent swarms of hovering flies. Children scurried here and there all over the courtyard chasing balls and yelling, arguing and laughing. A few of the older boys stood or squatted around the tiger-striped soldiers, intently watching the older men's card play.

The driver and the courier climbed out of the vehicle, stretched, and walked up the white chipped stone steps to the porch. An officer met them at the door and the three of them spoke among themselves for a moment before disappearing inside the grey building. The tiger-striped soldiers, who had looked up briefly from their cards at the men on the porch, resumed their game.

In the back seat of the jeep he sat feeling increasingly afraid and terribly alone. When he noticed the children approaching, a feeling of desperate panic churned up inside him and twisted up his stomach. He felt himself grow rigid and the numbing fear spread through him.

The children, great and small, big-eyed and curious, closed in around him from all sides. Hesitant at first, and very careful, once they perceived that there was no hostility directed toward them they moved forward more boldly. Swiftly then, they formed an almost solid throng around the jeep—kicking its tires, crawling over its hood, and honking its horn. They laughed and screamed at each other as they elbowed their way nearer the jeep and its silent occupant. Intrigued, a few of them even ventured to reach out to touch the filthy, bearded, form in the back seat. But catching a glimpse of the glazed eyes within the shade beneath the helmet, they hesitated and withdrew. The dark sweaty face beneath the helmet did not move, and the weary eyes passed over all of them and through them all, unseeing.

He sat in the back of the jeep and stared at them, uncomprehending and unfeeling aware of their presence only through their noise and conscious of their existence only through the movements of their bodies. Beyond this there was nothing. He tried to think—"children"—to form them into a reality in his mind, but found the resulting concept meaningless and lifeless. Looking at them, he saw only a confused mass of parts that crowded one another and merged and fell apart in endless disunity. Faces, hands, ears, eyes, noses and mouths swam and surged and plunged on the air before him, filled with a constricting terror.

The man with the grenade lodged in his jaw was propped up against the corner of the hootch. He was moaning, and from time to time, his head lolled from side to side in a series of jerking motions. He had run out of the hedge with a grenade and thrown it at Dubois. Whittaker had spun and fired the M-79 at his running face and knocked him clear off his feet and into the bushes with the unexploded grenade in his face. They had propped him up and fired at him from inside the irrigation ditch until the grenade went off. It had taken awhile, because they were jerking their shots and constantly ducking—for fear the grenade would go off prematurely. After the explosion they came up to look and found a gold ring on the left hand. One of them took it.

The man with all the children, who lived by the river, had looked strong and unbending as he watched them pass by. Wright came up to him and screamed in his face and broke raw eggs on his head, while his children and his wife stood off to one side watching and shaking.

It suddenly seemed to him that everything was closing in on him—the children, the cackling women behind their stalls, the tiger-striped men, the flies, the sky, the heat, the light, the air. He felt the panic inside himself. With increasing desperation, he searched his mind for something that would sustain him above the turmoil around him and show those nearby that he still needed time before he could learn how to speak.

The old woman sitting by the well was blind. She couldn't see who or what they were or what they were doing. She was also deaf and couldn't hear them when they yelled their curses into her ears. She didn't know that Purdue had wrecked her house looking for peanuts or that the hamlet had been burned. By the afternoon, when they were pulling out of the hamlet, she was dead. Someone had stuffed her into a wickerwork basket and the bottom of the basket was deep red and wet. The rice that had been in the basket was scattered all over the floor.

He tried to conceive of a way to let them know that that very morning he had still been in the valley. He wanted to tell them that it took days merely to wash away the grime, days more to sweat out the pollution from within, and still more days to learn to find lost pieces and to fit together patterns out of parts. He wanted to say that he needed time . . . he needed water . . . he needed . . .

When he heard the round smash into his helmet he sat down back on his heels, thinking he was dead and waiting for the pain. But it was only White who had come up from behind and hit him on the helmet with a .50 caliber round to get his attention through the racket and confusion. He vomited when he realized that he was alive—and White stayed with him and kept holding his arms.

"I need . . . I need . . . I need . . ." he repeated over and over, as he stood up in the back of the jeep and saw the bewildered children stepping warily away and the tiger-striped soldiers looking up at him with sudden surprise. "I need," he said again—but found that the words would not take shape and that his mouth would not form the sounds. And then it was all he could do to stand rocking gently before them, to stand staring at nothing . . . to stand silent and straining and numb . . . and to try not to crumble.

It was hot and humid and the sun was high when they went to gather up the bodies from morning. He had held the legs up in the air and looped the coarse rope around the stiffening ankles. The explosion had shorn off the upper part of the body in a ragged diagonal that extended from under the right armpit across the chest and over to the left shoulder. The chest cavity was exposed and the gaping hole was caked with moist dirt.

They were on the sandflats that day and he had dragged the body through the loose sand and thorn bushes to the collection point. Along the way, the body had caught on the thorns and he had had to jerk it loose. The weight on the rope had numbed his fingers. The thorns had cut the body and torn off its clothes.

He had sat on the dunes eating and watching it as it was buried along with the others. The holes had been dug deep and the dead were buried upside down with their legs sticking up into the air. And his hands ached and were sore from the rope.

After a long, awkward moment, he slumped heavily down into the seat and sat limp and heaving and crushed by his efforts. Slowly he took off his helmet. He could faintly hear the children approaching again and gathering once more around him. He could hear the officer on the porch yell down to him, "Hey. You all right, Marine?" And then, "Hey you! You down there! You o.k.?"

He could not answer. He hid his face as deep as it would go inside his helmet, and mumbled, "oh" and again, "oh" into its sweat-damp darkness. The world was empty . . .

Candidate

by James Shields

Delay: it is raining. The rain falls over a low graded bank that divides an open field. On top of the bank there are railroad tracks. At the foot of the bank on either side there is a marshy area. There is one man standing at the top of the bank, between the rails. His right hand is on a .45 on a web belt on his right hip. Beyond the bank, in the field, the point man stands watching. To the near side of the bank, in the field, the rest of the squad stands watching. A single man is climbing the near side of the bank, stepping heavily in the gravel. Everybody in the field is watching the top of the bank. It is raining. The rain falls . . .

interview

Pellegrini, you fucked it again . . .

It wasn't me, sir, it was them niggers . . .

. . . We were very careful, the Colonel and me, we told you exactly where to put it, and you fucked it . . .

. . . it was them niggers, good workers them niggers, but you can't let them work alone, they laugh, they sing, they forget things . . .

. . . the Colonel drives around the bunker line in his jeep, see, and he points with his swagger stick and says, I want a bunker here, and I want a bunker there, and o let's see now, how about a bunker way the hell over there . . .

. . . a nigger needs someone to tell him how to do things, he needs someone to watch . . .

. . . and then in two or three days the Colonel drives around the bunker line in his jeep again, see, and wadda ya know, there's a bunker here, and a bunker there and even a bunker way the hell over there, magic, see, and then the Colonel goes back to Brigade TOC in his jeep and he's happy, see, and when he sees me in the Club he smiles just like this, see . . .

. . . I showed them right where I wanted it, where you wanted it, sir, where the Colonel wanted it, and I went to supervise another detail and them niggers put it in the wrong place, them niggers . . .

. . . now when the Colonel drives around the bunker line in his jeep and sees Bunker One fifty meters to the west of the old tree, instead of fifty meters to the east of the old tree, do you think he will smile when he sees me in the Club . . .

. . . you got to stand there and watch a nigger, sir, I see that now, good workers though, real good workers, but you got to stand there and say, Okay, you niggers, put it right here . . .

. . . as long as I command this company the Colonel's magic will work, and he will stay happy, is that clear Pellegrini . . .

. . . it is just a matter of watching them niggers from here on out . . .

. . . now then, you know where the Colonel and I want that bunker, you may, of course, relax your Light Discipline . . .

. . . then we will get on it all night, sir, me and my niggers, we got lots of Coleman lanterns, we will get on it all night . . .

. . . you assure me that tomorrow Bunker One will be where the Colonel wants it, where I want it, where . . .

. . . all night, sir, workinest damn buncha niggers you ever seen, sir, just need somebody to stand there and say, Okay you niggers, put it right . . .

. . . that is all.

Delay: It is raining. The rain falls over a low graded bank that divides an open field. On top of the bank there are railroad tracks. At the foot of the bank on either side there is a marshy area. There are two men standing on the wooden ties at the top of the bank. One, the one on the left, is holding a .45, tightly, with both hands. The other, the one on the right, is leaning backward; his hands are drawn to his chest; his steel pot is rolling down the bank, toward the marshy area. Everybody in the field is watching the top of the bank. It is raining. The rain falls . . .

interview

Where Tweety?
He comin
I said four o'clock
He busy, got to hump some bags, at the CP, for Tow White.
I said four o'clock
He comin
He late
Here Murray
I would die for you
I would die for you
I would die for you
Sit there brother
Where Adonijah?
He back in the corner
Say Home, I'm back in the motherfucking corner
Smile, so we know
Sheeet
Somebody stop that water drippin
It's the roof
Them niggers fucked the roof—built this house so *fast*
You got to watch them niggers
Sheeet
Where Tweety?
Comin
Say Home, what on?
Business, got to take care of business
Business?
Been some smoke, you all know, now come the heat
Here Tweety
I would die for you
I would die for you
I would die for you
I would die for you
Where you been?
Baggin, for Tow White, at the CP
Jive
Truth, you know that
Gather round me
Talk to us Home
I hear you moved a bunker last night

Yes
Wet?
Yes
Heads bad?
Yes
You a bunch of niggers?
Yes
Yes
Yes
I want him off
Yes, but who will . . .?
Yes, but who?
Who?
Got to be somebody get the heat in close, work fast, not afraid of nothin
Who?
Who?
Who?
Tweety
Why yes, Tweety
Of course, Tweety
I don't want to shoot no-fucking-body
Tweety
Tweety
Tweety
Delay: It is raining. The rain falls over a low graded bank that divides an open field. On top of the bank there are railroad tracks. At the foot of the bank on either side there is a marshy area. There are two men on the bank. One is standing: he is holding a .45 with both hands. The other is face down on the rails. At the foot of the bank, to the far side, in the marshy area, there is a steel pot. It contains bone and hair and yellow brain. Everybody in the field is watching the top of the bank. It is raining. The rain falls . . .

candidate

We are crossing an open field. It's raining. No matter. It's always raining. Up ahead; beyond the point man, there is a bank. It comes out of a forest to the left, runs across the field, and goes into a forest to the right. Harris is closest to the bank. He is walking point because Sergeant Pellegrini does not like him. On top of the bank there will be railroad tracks. This is truth: you find tracks everywhere, even in the boonies. You never see a train though. It's hard to understand. Tracks and tracks and more tracks, but no trains. Once in Tourane I asked an old man if he had ever seen a train. Tracks run right through the middle of Tourane, and so I figured here was the place to find things out. At first he just smiled and gave me tea, so I asked him again. He tried to sell me his daughter. He smiled and made the boom-boom sign but I said, No thank you. Then I asked him if when he was a little boy in Tourane did his mother ever take him on the train to visit relatives in the mountains or something. He smiled again and called his daughter who came into the dark room in her panties and felt my cock. I told him about when my mother and I would wait in Penn Station for the train to Atlantic City with our shopping bags full of canned beans and rice and clothes straight from the laundry. He smiled and so did the daughter, but I wonder if they understood. I told them I often thought about the tracks, where they came from, and what happened to the trains. I told them that I had never seen tracks without trains before. I asked them if maybe the tracks had been built first and then the track builders ran out of money and went home, without making even one train. Then I said, No, the trains are here, someplace. The old man smiled and gave me tea. The daughter felt my cock. There were stains on her panties. Harris is close to the bank now. Pellegrini starts yelling from behind me in the column. He tells us to spread out and stay low going over the bank because we will be vulnerable. Crossing hills and banks is dangerous, day or night. A man framed against the sky makes a nice dark target that is easy to zero on. Once I saw a man sniping with a fifty caliber from a little woodline. The man set his gun up to fire single shot and clamped a spotter scope to the square part of the housing. About a mile away a gook officer was giving a briefing to some other officers on a little hill near some bushes. The man with the fifty caliber shot that gook officer's head off. I watched through binoculars. Later the man told me those officers had not even heard the shot. I wonder what they thought. One minute a man is talking and you are bored and daydreaming and thinking about home, and the next minute the man's head falls off and lands at your feet. High places are dangerous in daylight, at night too, unless you have position. But we have no position here, we are just walking across this open field. Until Harris crosses over the bank we can't know what's waiting for us on the other side. Pellegrini is smart about some things, real smart, and he is smart here. If we bunch up or stand going over the railroad tracks we will be taking a risk. Railroad tracks follow Highway One for most of its length. Tall Oakes told me that. I'm not so sure, but I hope it's truth. Tracks are important. But so are trains and I haven't seen any. I've never been all the way up and down Highway One, but I know many miles of it. Especially the part that runs through these sandy plains. I know that wherever you stand in Highway One, there are the tracks. Sometimes they lie right up against the road, and you can walk them on rest halts. Sometimes they lie two or three hundred meters away, but if you look hard you can see them because they are always there. I always look for the tracks. I know that if there really are trains somewhere, then following the tracks is the way to find them. Sometimes in places where there are a lot of troops around, crummy little villes grow up right on the highway. The people need wood to build their houses and so they tear up the tracks and use the ties. This makes me sad. I don't really know why. Maybe I do. It's just that, you see, if they take the tracks up then the trains can never run again, that is, if there are any trains. This is hard to explain, but I know that if those trains start running again, start carrying people from the city to the seashore, and from the plains to the mountains, then everything will be right again. Okay. I have been here long enough to know that this is truth. But what is there to be made right again? I'm not sure. You get feelings about things. Just like the feeling Pellegrini had before he told us to spread out and keep low going over the bank. Or the feelings those guys had when that gook's head fell off and landed at their feet. I get these feelings about the railroad tracks. Once, in one of those crummy little villes that lay across Highway One, I told a woman about my feelings. I said, Find those lost trains and things will be alright. I know, believe me. I said, Leave the ties where they are, I will steal you wood to build, and I will help you build. Later when I lay over her big soft stomach with my cock still inside I told her again how important it was that those tracks not be torn up. I said, If the tracks remain good, useable, then when we find the trains everything will fit together, trains on tracks. And with tracks on the ground we will see them lying there and we will remember and hope and keep looking for the trains. Without the tracks, we might forget, and stop looking. I guess she was sleeping. She had come hard under me and she was tired. The next day I saw her in the road carrying ties. She couldn't have heard, she couldn't have understood. I helped her carry the ties though. Once they were off the ground and rails kicked into a gully, what matter? Besides, she was old and couldn't be carrying ties around her shoulder like that. And I didn't want to lose her. She was old and none of the other guys would touch her so I had her all to my self, and I didn't want to lose her. Once I went in on a young snapper that Harris told me was good. She just laid there like a bear. I felt somebody else's come on her crummy bed. It was still warm. So I helped carry ties. This has bothered me. I needed that good steady woman but a man needs other things besides. Things to believe in, maybe. I believe in the trains. This has bothered me. But how much track could one forty-year-old woman tear up? Still there is the idea of the thing. She was tearing up track and I was helping her. When the brigade moved north and I knew that I would never see her again, it began to bother me even more. She was a warm and steady fuck and she let me stay inside her all night if I wanted, but I couldn't take that part of her with me. All I had was the track we had ripped up together. I can see Harris at the top of the bank. Why does he stand like that? Get down, Home! Now he goes into a crouch, like an Indian. What can he see in the rain? I wonder if the gooks have scopes that can see through the rain the way the Starlite can see through the dark. Maybe Harris's head will fall off. It would make a splat in the marshy place below the bank. Now Pellegrini yells at us again to spread out and keep low going over the tracks. In a lot of ways Pellegrini is the best NCO around. He's as good in the field as Harris, almost. Harris is the best. But Pellegrini is good. He's made some mistakes though. He's said things he never should have said. One thing about Harris, he only talks when there's business to take care of. When we pull the ambush, when we are in the site and set up, and it's dark, some of the guys talk it up, jive mostly, but they are scared and I understand. But Harris can sit like a stone all night. He doesn't even fart. Adonijah Jones farted once when we were set up on that little hill that overlooks the place where all the narrow buffalo trails come together into one big trail. It was such a loud fart that I thought Oake's .45 went off by itself again. Pellegrini kept running around in the dark saying, Who farted? That Adonijah. Harris puts his foot on a rail. He doesn't appreciate railroad tracks the way I do. I told him about my idea once, about how all we do is find those lost trains and things will be alright again. He grinned and handed me the jar of Jim Beam but I don't think he liked my ideas much. You never know about Harris. Once the whole platoon rode shotgun for a big convoy going over the mountains south to Tourane. Harris and I sat like a couple of big shots in beach chairs on a long flat bed. As we went along Harris drank from his jar and I watched the tracks. Coming south, just before the mountains, there was this Shell gas station. The tracks ran right behind it. I was wondering who bought gas way out here when I noticed that the gas station guy had built a little shed out of railroad ties. I was pissed, about as pissed as I've ever been. I wanted to walk right in there and explain to that guy about how much wrong he had done. Harris said to kill him. Then I remembered all the track I had torn up. I didn't go in. I was glad when we got away from that gas station and started up into the mountains. As we climbed, the tracks followed us, or maybe we followed the tracks, all the way. They were always there, even in the mountains. When we got high up, the road became nothing but a buffalo path zig-zagging up a stone slab. But the tracks kept climbing. Harris drank from his jar and said that maybe there would be trains up here, hiding in the mountains. I said that we had better wait and see. In places where there was no flat land at all, the tracks hung from long spans that stretched out over deep green valleys. I never saw such good bridges. Stillman used to talk about when a king or somebody wants something big built, he gathers together all the men in the place. Stillman said that there was nothing in the world you couldn't do, nothing you couldn't build, if you had enough men. Gooks are small. It must have taken the sweat of a lot of gooks to build those spans out across the valleys. Maybe every single gook helped out. Each gook carrying one bucket of cement, or hammering one nail. Those bridges were beautiful. In places where a mountain stood too tall and thick to go over or around, the tracks dug right in. They disappeared in dark holes that ran through the rocks and the dirt. I wondered if maybe the trains could be somewhere in those tunnels, just waiting in the dark for somebody who cared about things to go in there and drive them out. All the trains sitting quiet in the middle of the thickest mountain. I wanted to look inside but Pellegrini wouldn't let me. I asked that old man, the one in Tourane, about the tunnels. I told him that there could be anything in those holes, but somebody had to go in there and look. He gave me tea. I don't like tea much. Then I asked him if when he was a kid did he ever ride the train to the seashore with his mother. I told him about how my mother had to stand up all the way to Atlantic City because the people who got on in New York City took all the seats. We got on in Newark and we stood all the way. We didn't care though, because we were going to the seashore. Then the old man's daughter bent low and took my cock right down to the root. I could smell her hair. I don't think the old man even understood what I meant by Train and Tunnel. He never answered my questions, he just smiled and poured tea. Later I drew him a picture of a mountain with a tunnel going in. He smiled. In the mountains above Tourane we took a rest halt over an old tunnel guarded by concrete bunkers. We made a small fire and heated rations and boiled water for coffee. I walked the tracks a little. Sergeant Pellegrini said, Tweety, stay the fuck out of that tunnel. They were good tracks. The ties were firm and the rails were shiny. No rot, no rust. I began to think that maybe the trains were around after all, maybe they just ran at crazy hours. Else how could the rails be so bright? Maybe in the dark, say between midnight and three in the morning, a train loaded with people going south to visit their friends in the big cities or at the seashore passed right across the long spans and through the dark tunnels, whistle blowing. But if the whistle blew, then somebody would hear. The old man in Tourane would have told me if he heard any whistles blowing early in the morning or late at night, if he understood. And what about behind the Shell station where fifty feet of good track went into a stupid shed, or farther south, where I helped hammer good ties into a crummy hootch for an old whore that nobody else wanted. How could the trains pass through those places? I walked back to where Harris sat by the fire. I ate turkey loaf and crackers and drank coffee. If Harris hadn't been there, I would have cried. The bank is steep going up. There is gravel scattered over the sides. Gravel? Maybe there were real railroad people here laying tracks, not just gooks. Did they go home and take the trains with them? I should have asked the old man in Tourane. But he wouldn't have answered. He would have smiled and given me more tea. And after his daughter began to choke on my wad I wouldn't have heard him anyway, if he had answered. She seemed surprised, the daughter, as if she had been sucking for years without ever getting a wad. She drank a lot of tea. There were stains on her panties and she smelled bad. Good suck off though. I tried to ask more questions about Tourane in the old days, but the old man wanted to talk money. Not trains. These tracks are shiny too. Not as good as the ones I saw in the mountains, but these are good tracks. These tracks can handle a train. If a train should come out of the woods right now, full of people going to the seashore with their kids, these tracks would be ready: I get a good feeling just knowing that the tracks are ready, that all we have to do is find the trains. Pellegrini and I are side by side on the ties now. I wonder if Pellegrini would have understood, about the importance of the trains that is. He's been around a long time and he knows a lot. I should have asked him while there was still time. Now it is too late. And it's raining. No matter.

Thi Bong Dzu

by Larry Rottmann

It was the day before his birthday, and Thi Bong Dzu was a little bit excited. However, he knew it was important that he keep such feelings to himself, for if he failed to control his emotions, he could compromise the entire unit's mission that night.

Dzu rose early, for he had a lot of other work to do before the pre-arranged meeting time. Since the death of his father nearly six months before, Dzu had been the man-of-the-house to his mother, three younger sisters, and grandmother. As he crossed the packed earth of the yard on his way to the well, he could see faint luminescent trails of parachute flares low in the northeast sky. And a moment later, from somewhere in the south near Saigon, came the groundshuddering rumble of a B-52 bomb raid.

Drawing a full bucket, and holding his breath, Dzu doused himself with the cool water. He soaped his lean body vigorously, rinsed off with a couple more buckets, and shaking dry, trotted back to the hut shivering a little in the chill morning air.

He dressed quickly, pulling on a pair of faded trousers, a much-mended shirt, and his sandals, which he'd made himself from some rope and an old jeep tire. Moving quietly, so as not to wake his family, Dzu started a small fire in the cooking pit just outside the door. Into a battered tin pot he placed a few handfuls of rice, a few tiny dried minnows, and a bit of salt. He placed the pot on the low fire, and stirred it slowly until little bubbles started to appear. Dumping a small amount into a chipped bowl, he began eating it, pinching the rice between his thumb and forefinger.

As he ate, he watched the huge, blood-red ball of sun rise slowly. The air remained cool, and a thick mist hovered low over the flooded paddies surrounding the house. The sky was clear though, and Dzu knew that within the hour it would be steaming hot. Worse yet, the sky would probably still be clear that night. He frowned slightly at this prospect, for it would make their operation all the more difficult.

Swallowing the last few bites of breakfast, Dzu gently began to wake his family (all except grandmother, who'd been known to bite anyone who interrupted her sleep). As his mother and sisters began to move about, he took the rice sickle from the tool shelf, and squatting on the stoop, began to sharpen its well-worn cutting edge with a small sandstone. Back and forth, back and forth he moved the stone along the gentle curve of the blade, recalling how he had always been fascinated by the way his father had done it. Back and forth, back and forth, Dzu felt himself slipping into an almost hypnotic rhythm. Suddenly he was snapped from his near trance by a loud squawk from grandmother, who'd been playfully awakened by Dzu's sisters. Testing the sickle's edge, he was surprised to see a fine red line appear on his thumb where he'd drawn it across the steel. Satisfied, he replaced the sharpening stone and made ready to leave for the fields.

His mother had put some of the cooked rice in a small bucket, along with a piece of bread, for lunch. As Dzu took it from her, she noticed the blood on his thumb, and made him sit down while she washed out the cut and tied a too-large bandage around it. Dzu realized that she was making a lot of fuss over nothing, but he knew she was trying to let him know how much she loved him. Because he was now the head of the family, it wouldn't do for her to kiss him or fawn over him, so she expressed her concern in subtle, less obvious ways, like all this bother over a small cut.

But it was getting late, and already Dzu could see the other men of the hamlet heading for the fields. During rice harvest, no time could be wasted, and he was anxious to get started, especially since he'd have to stop a little early that day in order to get ready for the mission. He kissed each of his sisters, made a face at grandmother who was still grouching around, and took off down the path.

Dzu felt good, and for the second time allowed himself to think about his upcoming birthday. He knew that no matter how early he arose the next day, his mother would already be up, fixing a special breakfast. Even though they didn't have much, she would always manage to come up with a small bit of eel, some extra spices, or even fresh melons on birthdays. The girls would have some small, but hand-made and priceless, gift—like the red scarf from his last birthday that he wore on patrols. And even grandmother, despite her pretended gruffness, would have something for him too. But Dzu cared less for the presents than the special feeling of closeness that came on birthdays. Their home always seemed to have extra warmth and happiness then.

Dzu's thoughts were suddenly jarred by the roar of tanks. The path to the paddies paralled Route 13, and a long U.S. convoy was approaching. Dzu paused as the vehicles rumbled by, and remembered the first armored task force that had passed his village, and how, as a small boy, he had stood clutching his father, frozen by fear at the sight of the seemingly endless parade of huge war machines. He recalled how the calloused hands of his father had trembled with fright, and yet how his jaw had clinched in anger and hatred. And he would never forget the words his usually quiet father had spat out at the disappearing Americans: "Bastards! Murderers! Animals!"

At that time, Dzu didn't know what it was that had caused his father to react so vehemently to the hairy strangers, but now he knew. As he watched the column roll by, and carefully counted the number of tanks, APC's, and supply trucks, he remembered the first air strike on his hamlet. The black, screaming planes had suddenly knifed through an overcast sky one afternoon, and for almost an hour had raked Ben Cat with rockets, cannon fire, bombs, and napalm. In the attack, Dzu lost his older brother, his grandfather, two cousins, and a half-dozen playmates. The village's market place, temple, school—as well as over half its homes—were destroyed. Almost half the villagers were killed or wounded, and many still carried the scars caused by the sticking fire. That night most of the hamlet's able-bodied men joined the 271st Viet Cong Regiment. Dzu's father was among the volunteers, and he participated in many operations against the enemy. He was a brave fighter, and at the time of his death during the attack of an artillery fire support base, was still recovering from a wound suffered in an earlier action.

When his father was killed, Dzu took his place not only as head of the household, but also as a scout for the 271st recon platoon. In less than six months he had participated in nineteen separate engagements, had been decorated for bravery twice, and had risen from private to corporal. The platoon had lost nearly a third of its original men during that period, but had also recorded several surprising victories, each time against overwhelming odds and firepower. Dzu was the only man in the unit who hadn't been wounded, and had come to be regarded by them as something of a good luck charm. "Keep bullet holes out of Thi's shirt and we'll all be safe" was a frequently heard remark within the platoon.

Dzu's pulse was pounding as the end of the column approached. He thought of the night's mission and a bitter smile formed on his lips. As the last tank, laden with GI's, passed, Dzu raised his hand in a mock salute. One of the soldiers on the vehicle shouted "Hey, gook, you want smoke-smoke?" and laughing, threw a pack of C-Ration cigarettes at him. Grabbing them out of the air, Dzu stripped off the cellophane, removed the cigarettes, and turned the pack inside out. Taking a pencil stub from his pocket, he scribbled down the unit designations and makeup of the convoy. He folded the small paper, tucked it away, and puffing on one of the stale Camels, strode off down the path, his lunch pot and sickle flapping against his thin legs.

Arriving at the fields a few minutes later, Dzu stripped down to his shorts and went right to work. Again and again the sickle flashed in its smooth arc, severing the heavily laden stalks of rice from their submerged roots. With each easy swing, another sheave would slide neatly into Dzu's crooked left arm. When the shock felt exactly the right size and weight, he tied it about the middle with a piece of twine and laid it on the dike, away from the water. He worked tirelessly, his spare frame bent almost double and his legs immersed in water to mid-calf. He loved the squishy feel of the mud around his toes, and the rough tickle of the stubby, already cut-off rice shoots.

Dzu worked without a break until a little past mid-day. When he finally paused, he looked at the pile of shocks and realized he had already finished the day's quota. Taking his lunch, he walked to the bank of the nearby Hoc Mon River and sat down to eat. On the opposite bank, a young man about his age was fishing with a long, limber bamboo pole. It looked like the fish were biting well, but they were apparently too quick for the fisherman. Each time the float bobbed, he'd jerk the pole, but all he ever came up with was an empty hook which he'd rebait and throw back in. "Xin loi" laughed Dzu, "Too bad." For a moment he felt sorry for himself, wishing that he too could try his luck at catching the elusive cam roa. Perhaps on his birthday . . . ? But that thought lasted only a moment. Dzu remembered his responsibility to his family and to the liberation, and chided himself for such selfish reverie.

He finished his bread and rice and stretched out under a low pineapple scrub for a two-hour nap, just as he had done every day of his life. He knew the strength of the afternoon sun, and wondered to himself why only monkeys and U.S. soldiers dared defy it. He noted many similarities between the two, and was in the process of enumerating them when he fell asleep.

Dzu woke with a start to find his uncle standing over him, pointing a stick at his head and shouting, "Bang, bang, you're dead, you dirty Vee Cee!" "Don't make bad jokes, Uncle." Dzu replied as he jumped to his feet. Angry because he had allowed himself to be sneaked up on, Dzu grabbed the stick "gun," threw it into the stream, and without a backward glance, ran over to the road where his uncle's ox-cart was sitting and led the big water buffalo off toward the paddy.

When Dzu arrived at his pile of shocks, he immediately began tossing them one by one into the cart. By the time uncle had walked over from the river, they were all loaded but one. Dzu paused for a long moment, scanning the horizon and listening intently for the "whack-whack" of patrolling helicopters. Taking the remaining shock, he walked out to the middle of the paddy. He felt around a moment with his feet, then with a swift motion snatched an oblong object wrapped in plastic from beneath the water and concealed it within the rice bundle. Dzu placed this shock deep in the middle of the loaded cart, slipped into his shirt, and calling to uncle, "Make sure you deliver that load on time," he headed down the path for home.

As he made his way back to the village, Dzu noted that it was beginning to cloud up a little to the east. "A good sign," he thought to himself, and quickened his pace. His sisters saw him coming from a long way off, and ran to meet him. He was pleased, for he loved them dearly, but he also knew that part of their jubilance was due to their sharing of his birthday "secret." He embraced them all as they descended upon him in a maelstrom of laughter, and with one girl holding each hand and one riding piggy-back, he trotted the last hundred meters or so to the house.

Shouting and giggling, they burst into the yard, almost tumbling over grandmother. "Not a very grownup way for the head of the house to behave," she groused, but she knew of Dzu's mission that night, and so she said no more.

A few minutes later mother returned from the market place where she'd been shopping for a breakfast treat. Out of sight of the girls, she handed Dzu a tai tom. He opened the hollow pineapple, removed the two dozen .45 caliber shells that had been hidden inside, and with an oily rag, carefully cleaned each one. Moving the sleeping platform to one side, he uncovered the entrance to a small tunnel. Wrapping the bullets in the rag, he put them in the families' tiny bomb shelter, then replaced the bed and went outside for supper.

Everyone else was in a gay mood during the meal, but Dzu couldn't keep his mind on the swirling conversation. He kept running over the plans for the night and casting anxious glances at the clearing sky. As they finished their supper, uncle arrived with the load of rice. Dzu removed his special bundle and took it inside while the rest of the family helped unload the cart. He again moved the bed and dropped into the tunnel beneath it. By the light of a small candle he unwrapped his package. With the skill that comes only from long practice, he broke the submachinegun down into its various parts and cleaned and recleaned each one. When he was satisfied that the weapon was spotless, he lightly oiled each piece, then quickly reassembled it. He also loaded his two magazines with the recently acquired cartridges.

Emerging from the tunnel, he could see that it was nearly dark outside, and time for him to leave. Dzu put on his black cotton shirt and pants, and a pair of black rubber-soled shoes. He tied the red scarf around his neck and fastened two hand grenades to his belt. He locked one loaded magazine into the gun and stuck the other in his waistband for easy access. Choosing a moment when the girls were busy at play, he slipped outside, and after pausing only long enough to make sure mother had replaced the bed, Dzu disappeared into the darkness.

Alert and careful, Dzu padded silently along the path toward the rendezvous point. The sky was again overcast, and a thick fog was forming along the ground. Dzu's spirits rose, and he anticipated another successful operation. He felt sure he would be home in plenty of time to get some sleep before his birthday breakfast. Dzu started thinking about grumpy grandmother and didn't see the first soldier's slight movement. He was imagining the antics of his sisters and didn't hear the faint click of the safety on the second GI's rifle. He was seeing the shy smile of his proud mother and didn't feel the tug of the flare trip-wire until too late.

Dzu stood paralyzed by the sudden explosive blaze of light, and in the instant before his body was riddled by the bullets of two machine guns and a dozen M-16's; in that half-moment before thousands of razor-sharp fragments from Claymores and grenades tore at his flesh, Dzu realized that he wasn't ever going to have another birthday. He realized that he was never going to be twelve.

Temporary Duty

by Oran R. Pitts

The night before, Smith, Foster and myself had drunk a bottle of cheap Scotch that Foster had procured on the laundry run that day; the next morning in formation, I threw up. At noon, my section sergeant told me I was wanted in the orderly room.

"Specialist Michaels," our first sergeant said, "you seem to be drinkin' a little more than is good for you these days."

"Yes, First Sergeant," I said.

"Is anything in particular botherin' you?"

"No, First Sergeant," I said.

"Nothin's bothering you, huh?"

"I didn't say that. I said nothing in particular is bothering me."

"Meanin'?"

"Everything about this dump bothers me."

He sighed.

"How long have you been here, Michaels?"

"You know that. A year and four months. You know that."

"You came back for six months voluntarily, right?"

"Yeah."

"Why? You hate it so bad."

'When my year was up, I still had a year and six months left in the Army. I didn't want to go back stateside and play stupid games for a year and six months. Then, too, I make more money here."

"You been in this company the whole time?"

"Yeah."

"Ever been to the field?"

"We used to handle the aid station on brigade operations— until C company took over."

"What do you think of the company's function now?"

"What function? Washin' ambulances? Standing tall when the colonel strolls through? Piddlin' sick call: This is no medical company."

"Games, huh, Michaels?"

"Damn right, First Sergeant. We got nothin' to do with nothin'."

"How's your medical work, Michaels?"

"It's been so long I've forgotten."

"Well, you're gonna get a chance to do some, Michaels. And I'm happy to tell you that you're goin' somewhere that has somethin' to do with somethin'. We've made a deal with the Evacuation Hospital. We're sending them fifteen medics for thirty days temporary duty. They're short-handed up there, so we're doin' them a favor—and they're doin' us one. I'm sending as many new men as I can; the experience will help us in the long run, particularly if we go to the field, although I'll admit that don't seem likely now. I'm sendin' you along as rankin' man."

"Top, I've heard about this thing already. I thought it was strictly voluntary."

"It is, except for you. I have to send an E-5, and you're it."

"What about Axel?"

"He's trainin' NCO."

"Casselman?"

"I need him here."

"And?"

"Draw your own conclusions. You'll get TDY pay for thirty days. It's a little cleaner up there than it is here, the chow is a little better, and maybe you'll feel a little more involved. I won't change my mind so there's no need to talk about it any more. You won't be lonesome. Smith and Foster have volunteered to go. That's all."

"Yes, First Sergeant."

"Take the rest of the day off to get ready. Take all your clothing and your footlockers. We'll have a deuce and a half to take you up after breakfast tomorrow mornin'. Michaels?"

"Yes, First Sergeant."

"They expect you to be *clean* up there. You look like a piece of shit."

I found Smith and Foster and we talked about the trip.

At first I was reluctant to leave our little slough of despond. I had reached, through strict adherence to our daily routine, a sort of mindless state, the comfort of which I had grown to like. Most of our time was consumed by stupid details and hiding from our NCO's during duty hours; they didn't really try very hard to find us, either. Others had voluntarily transferred to line units in order to escape the ennui, but as much as I hated the place, I couldn't bring myself to do *that*. I had resigned myself to doing the rest of my time on the furthest periphery of the Vietnam Conflict.

Smith and Foster forced me to concede that a change of scenery might not, after all, be a bad idea.

"I don't know, though," I said. "A new situation. It will force me to think again."

"You can't think," Foster said, "or you would never have come back here in the first place."

"You'll get used to it," Smith said.

"Well, maybe. Did you get one or two bottles of that poison yesterday?"

I.

Nights in Vietnam are cool, but the damp residue they leave fades fast; the sun was already bearing down pretty hard by the time we turned off the dirt road from division base camp onto the highway. A staff sergeant from the company was riding shotgun in the cab of the truck and he made us wear our helmets; that made things worse. I sat between SP-4's Smith and Foster and we talked. I lit a cigarette but the wind whittled it to nothing by the time I had taken two drags. We passed an overturned Lambretta on the highway; farm produce was strewn across the road. The body of a Vietnamese man lay, doll-like on the pavement, one side of his face in a pool of blood. Two MP's stood by the Lambretta, waving traffic around the wreck. There were seventeen medics on the truck, but the MP's said to keep movin' and we did. They had no way of knowing we were medics.

The truck wallowed on, immersing us in the odors of the countryside. Unused to the smells because of our confinements to base camp, we felt queasy at first. The smells hung over us, heavy and damp, almost solid.

"Why don't base camps smell, man?" Foster said.

"They do, they just smell different."

Women wearing round conical hats squatted on their haunches in the rice paddies and in front of their hootches. Water buffaloes rolled in mud-holes. Naked and half-naked kids stood along the road jeering. When the Hondas and bicycles on the road caused us to slow down, the kids surrounded the truck.

"You give me chop-chop, GI," they shrilled. "You give me one cigarette." They banged one hand across the fist of the other and screamed, "Boom, Boom!" "Goddam Sonofabitch muthafuck," one yelled, a lone spokesman, perhaps for the true sentiments of the countryside.

"Be nice," Smith said absently.

A pedicab rolled by, a fat sow lying on its back strapped to the seat.

"Why'd you volunteer for this?" I asked Smith. He had been to the line and collected his two purple hearts before he had come to our company.

"For the change. I get tired of lickin' battalion's ass and salutin' all the time. Stupid goddam company."

"It'll kill thirty days," I said. "I guess."

"They got women there too," Foster said.

"Yeah," Smith said, "Officers. I used to have a friend worked where we're goin'. He started nosin' around one of those nurses and she was goin' for it, but the hospital exec. officer, some major, liked her, too. So he transferred my friend to another hospital. Nice hospital, too—up north. 'Course it gets mortared every two or three days."

We stopped at a bridge that only one truck at a time could cross. As we waited our turn, some little kids selling slivers of pineapple on toothpicks climbed the side of the truck. One little girl, gold earring gleaming against her brown cheek, stood by me rubbing the hairs on my forearm back and forth with her hand. She smiled, displaying already decaying teeth.

"Cute little girl," Foster said.

The truck began to move. "Di Di," I said. "Go away." The kids jumped off the truck, screaming and laughing. Because of a traffic jam, we were forced to stop again on the other side of the bridge. One old man led another, leaning on a crooked stick, to the cab of the truck. He extended a tiny can through the window.

"You gib, you gib," he wailed as we drove off. His eyes were gone.

"This is no war, it's a whorehouse," I said.

"You make that up?" Smith asked.

"No, it's in a book I read."

"You sure read a lot."

"Yeah, for all the good it does me."

I had forgotten what the countryside was like.

"Shit," I said later, "I got a hangover."

"Top get on your ass about that little exhibition in formation yesterday?" Smith asked.

"Not really. Said I was drinking too much. I get by with a lot because I've been here a lot longer than him. To him, that means something. This trip is my punishment, I guess."

"That was pretty funny. Puke squirtin' through your fingers."

"Oh, shut up."

We arrived at the hospital shortly. The unit's first sergeant met us in front of his orderly room.

"You men get settled," he said, "and come to the orderly room after noon chow. You will be assigned to the wards on which you're gonna work at that time."

Smith was assigned to neurosurgery.

Foster got the emergency room.

I got orthopedics.

II

The hospital itself was rectangle-shaped; there were seven wards on each side, the emergency room, pre-op and recovery, and surgery at one end; the mess hall was at the other. There were sidewalks all the way around, shaded by tin roofing. White four-by-fours supported the roofing and gleaming No. 10 cans painted red hung from them; butt cans. It was a cool, quiet place and after looking around we expected to enjoy our stay there. The mess hall was spacious and clean, all the KP's were Vietnamese civilians, and we were exempted from perimeter guard. There wasn't the omnipresent cloud of red dust we'd had at base camp; all the area roads were blacktopped. We lived in aluminum buildings with concrete floors. Every barracks had two mama-sans to make our beds, shine our boots, and do our laundry. There was a small E.M. club behind our barracks; we drank beer there when we were off duty. The wards were air-conditioned. There was a movie every night in the quadrangle. There were nurses, the first English-speaking women we had seen in a long time. Patients wearing blue PJ's, swathed in plaster and bandages, with tubes running in and out of them sat in wheel chairs or leaned on crutches, waiting to go to Japan and then home. It seemed further removed from the war, at first, than our base camp had, and, I thought then, made infinitely more sense.

III

After our first day of work, Smith, Foster, and myself gathered in the EM club.

"How did it go?" Smith asked me.

"I don't know what I'm doing yet," I said, "I feel pretty ignorant. And there's a kid on my ward. Christ."

"What's the matter?"

"He's missing one leg and one arm. Three fingers missing on the hand he has left. And a temp. of 105°. They think he has malaria."

"Umm."

"He's got a picture of his wife next to his bed, you know? And his tool is all chewed up from shrapnel. He just lays there looking at it. Says he can explain the arm and the leg, but how is he gonna explain *that* to his wife?"

Foster laughed.

"Foster fainted today in the morgue," Smith said.

"Didja really?"

Foster hung his head over his beer can. "Yeah," he said, "The doctor had to sign a death certificate and he asked me to go with him when he looked at the corpse. He was laying on a litter with a poncho over his head. 'Pull it back,' the doc says, and I do. Lord, one whole side of the guy's face and body was burned black, and his arm had been ripped off. There was a big hole under his ribs and tripe comin' out of it all over the litter. He had like a snarl on his lips like a growlin' dog, his mouth was open like he was tryin' to scream and bugs were crawlin' around on his teeth. Clunk, over I went."

Smith said, "You know, all the guys in neurosurgery are pretty helpless. They don't even know what's goin' on. Lay there and play with themselves. You can put a sheet over them and they throw it off and start flongin' their dongs again. They're all cathe-terized because they can't piss by themselves. So we tape rubbers to the ends of the catheters and just slip them on instead of catheterizin' them. They had me pokin' holes in the rubbers to-day. I told one of the nurses, 'Ma'am, this goes against my natural instincts.' 'What does, Smith,' she says. 'Why pokin' holes in prophylactics,' I said."

"Shit," I said.

"I did, too. I said it," Smith said, giggling.

IV

We had been at the hospital for about two weeks when the MP got shot in the latrine.

Smith and I were sitting in the EM club that evening after work, drinking beer.

Whack! Whack! Whack! Three smacking noises broke the air.

Smith dove under the table. I followed him.

"That was an M-16," Smith said, shook.

"Where'd it come from?"

"I don't know. I'm gonna look, though."

There was a stockade and a POW camp across the road and an MP unit that manned them both. I waited and Smith came back.

"You know that blue MP shithouse across the road?" he asked.

"Yeah?"

"Somebody just shot a guy in there who was taking a shit right off his seat."

"Who was he?"

"I don't know. Some MP. He looked in pretty sad shape. Three bullet holes in his groin."

"Anybody know who did it?"

"No. Shit, it could have been anybody. MP's have a lot of enemies. Whoever did it was runnin' down the road by the time anybody got there."

"Wha'd they do with him?"

"Took his ass to the emergency room. Foster can tell us about it when he gets off. He's workin' tonight."

When Foster came in, he told us that the guy was dead on arrival.

"His femoral artery was severed. Bled to death. Hell of a thing.

Comin' all this way to get gunned off a shitter because they made you an MP and somebody's got the ass at you."

V

The day before we were to go back to our company, there was a big inspection conducted by a two star general, the medical brigade commander. That night we all sat around the barracks talking about it.

"We were supposed to look busy when he came through, so we made all the beds on the ward," Smith said. " 'Course, we'd already made 'em all once, but that didn't matter. It's no fun changin' beds in there either. Those guys are like logs."

"He didn't bother us much," Foster said. "We got two chopper loads of DOA's right before he came through, so he didn't dally."

"He pinned a purple heart on that double amputee I told you about," I said. "On the bandage around the hand he's still got. The kid just looked at him."

"You should have seen what happened on *my* ward," a kid named Waters said.

"Where do you work, man? Maxillo facial?"

"Yeah?"

"What happened, man?"

"You know about the guy with no face?"

"Yeah," Foster said, "When he was in the emergency room, I had to pull blood out of that hole in his face with a 100cc syringe so he wouldn't drown in it."

"That's the guy," Waters said, "They took off all the bandages the other day and all the corpsmen and nurses were gathered around to watch and all the patients rolled over so they wouldn't have to watch. Remember the other day when that big TV star, the cowboy, was here?"

"Yeah."

"Well, he started cryin' when he saw this kid. Then he got sick—turned green—and they had to call off the rest of his tour of the hospital. Well, anyway, the kid's face is gone. He writes notes to the corpsmen all the time. He wrote me a note once, 'Have I got a tongue?' he writes."

"Christ."

"Yeah, and he makes the nurses hold his hand all the time. Well the general came stompin' through with all his brass behind him, noddin' and smilin' to all the patients. When he comes to this guy with no face, he stops and sort of nods his head and starts to move on, but the kid grabs his note pad and starts writin'. 'Please kiss my hand,' he writes and hands it to the general. And the general did it. He looked pretty silly, but he did it. He bends right over and kisses the kid's hand.''

''Oh, hell.''

''Then he says, 'In my twenty eight years in the medics, I've never had to do *that*.' ''

''Profound remark,'' I said.

Smitty and I lay awake talking for a long time after the lights had gone out.

''Smitty,'' I said, ''what was the line like?''

''You know something,'' he said, ''I'd rather do a year out there than do another month here.'' Then he went to sleep.

I lay in bed looking at the ceiling. I had gotten into the medics because of some half-formed idea that it would make my life more meaningful. The draft had been on my ass anyway, so I enlisted. I had learned *something* on this trip, but I was damned if I knew what it was.

''Well,'' I said to the ceiling, ''It'll come to me someday.''

But it was a long time before I went to sleep.

VI

The sun was falling into the jungle when we got back to our base camp the next evening. The first sergeant met us, was standing at the tail-gate when I jumped off the truck.

''How was it Michaels? Everything go all right?''

''Well,'' I said, ''in the long run, I don't think this assignment will have much effect on my drinking problem, if that's what you mean.''

Then I looked for Smith; I wanted to catch him before he started on the bottle of scotch he had bought at the Class Six store before we left the hospital.

R&R

by Wayne Karlin

The marines landed at Tan Son Nhut and filed out of the rear ramp of the plane. Joshua was with them, like them. Faded into the faded men in jungle utilities and sardonic eyes. One of the filers, as it were, in the same drawer.

The men descended self-consciously into the sunlight, blinking. Joshua looked at the red hair and freckled neck of the man in front of him. He wondered idly how many backs of necks he had come to know since being in the Corps. "Lookit this," the voice attached to the neck said, and he looked, struck also by the concrete solidity of the airbase, an absence of tents strange to the northerners.

They were herded between rows of offices and abutted planes. Inside the offices they could see clerks at work. Some of them were wearing Australian bush hats, the brims pinned up on one side and inscribed, Air Commando. The office doors were inscribed Air-Conditioned, Keep Shut. "Oh shit, oh dear," the red head snickered, and the other marines laughed softly, suddenly and smugly aware of who they were.

They were: hard, lean combatants coming down strong on soft, southern Saigon. They all felt like that. Even if they weren't all grunts, even if some loaded bombs for long hours on baking runways, or even stroked typewriters themselves. Least they stroked them under sweaty canvas, shit in a hole in the mud and stood perimeter guard. Least they'd been shot at and mortared. Shot at and missed, shot at and hit. Least they were from the north, from I Corps, the boonies, my man. The grunts and aircrews were doubly disdainful. It was one of their few pleasures, rubbing the hard sight of themselves against the soft white skins of rear area clerks. Let them bleed a little.

They boarded buses and began the ride into the city. Joshua found himself sitting next to the red-haired boy and put it to fate or alphabetical order. He glanced around the bus, automatically. There was a staff sergeant in pressed and ribboned tropicals standing near the driver. As if feeling Joshua's gaze, the staff raised the bull-horn he was holding and began talking about venereal disease. Joshua turned his face away and leaned his forehead against the window. He watched a mad procession of cars and pedicabs lashing around them, and dully felt the vibration of the bus tap the sticky glass of the window into his forehead.

"Same old shit, huh?" the red head was saying to him, and he turned to look. Red was wearing metal corporal chevrons on his collar. Revealed under a rolled up sleeve was a tatoo; the Marine Corps emblem done as a vulture squatting obscenely on an 8-ball with a screw through it. "Sure," he replied, listening to the lecture. The staff was talking about a disease with no cure. Hell, he'd guessed at that a long time back. He and Red grinned at each other, the mutual bullshit recognition society.

"They oughta get a new script," Red said, "I didn't come here plannin' to look at no pagodas."

"Yeah? What did you plan?"

"Plan on getting outta this green amphibious motherfucker."

"No shit?"

"No shit."

He listened vaguely to the ritual, wondering at himself for letting another military acquaintance start. What the hell. Neil, Neil Hanson, the red-head was saying, mortars, First Marines. Well, no alphabetical order in Hanson, so it couldn't be a military plot anyway. His name? Martin, Josh Martin, and the wings over his pocket were because he flew gunner. No, his MOS was utilities, engineers, but he had a secondary machine-gun. Spent most of his time on flight pay, that's how it worked out.

"Good duty?"

"Better'n ground poundin'. Swing with the Wing, you know."

"What kinda choppers you got? Thirty-fours?"

"Naw, forty-sixes; seaknights."

"Yeah. You guys were on Hastings a little while back, huh?"

Everybody was on Hastings, Joshua thought, looking back out the window.

The bus pulled in front of the Hotel Meyerkord, a white building encircled by balconies. Soldier desk-clerks checked them in.

The rooms were regular hotel rooms, with only two sets of double racks to make a military intrusion on the tiled floor. Hanson went into the bathroom and began flushing the toilet repeatedly, chuckling. Oh, man, don't overdo it, Joshua thought. He began stripping off his utilities. "Seconds on the shower," he called, ignoring the pair of fattish sergeants who were sharing the room with them. They looked like twins, he noticed, in spite of their different features.

"Take firsts," Hanson yelled back, "I'm gonna catch a few minutes sleep. Rest up my dingaling 'til I go out and cover it with black syph and glory and shit." Hanson came out and lay down on a bottom rack. A Vietnamese girl came into the room with some linen. Hanson grinned at her obscenely and she turned her face and giggled. "I'm in love," the red-head said, and the girl left, still giggling.

Joshua stood under the tepid shower, feeling the water slide slowly over his shoulders and dribble down his chest and belly. He stretched his muscles under the water; feeling something tight inside him relax under the gentle spray. There was a crack in the green wall and he could see a small spider by it, watching him. He flicked a friendly drop of water at the insect, but it didn't move. He was aware of his genitals, tugging warmly between his legs. Tug away, he thought, and smiled.

He stepped out of the shower. It hadn't been hot enough to steam the mirror and he looked at his face, reflected. Reflecting. R&R, rest and reflection, he thought, pleased with himself. The mirrored face didn't tell him much. Tanned brown, but no real changes. Doesn't show any more than losing my cherry.

Well, he shrugged at the mirror, what'd you expect? Blood?

He dried off and called out to Hanson.

They walked out into the afternoon, a riot of basic colors clubbing at their eyes. Girls in pastel ao-dai dresses bicycled past or clung on the backs of scooters; neater, sweeter maidens. Ten foot tall Asian lovers glared down from movie billboards, watching in silence as Saigon decayed in last bursts of pustular beauty all around them.

As always, Joshua was startled by Vietnam's reality. The sudden translation of a concept to concrete and traffic and air, a personal Vietman now, made of sights and smells particular to himself. It made him uncomfortable.

By night they were on Tudo Street. They entered under the neon of the Hollywood Bar, searching for all hope.

Hey, the girl said, buy me a drink.

Sure. If you talk to me and see my humanity, and love, honor and obey me. That's all. For 200 piasters.

She looked seventeen, her eyes looking into his, large and guileless. He settled down on the stool next to her and bought her some colored water, looking hungrily at her breasts and the crinkle of the tight dress around her crotch. He ordered a bourbon on the rocks. He wished he had a joint. He wondered if she could get him a joint. He wondered if she could get him busted. He drank the bourbon and asked her for another.

She gulped down her glass quickly and tapped it, looking questioningly into his eyes. He nodded and finished the second drink, then bought them both another. "What's your name?" he asked, conversationally.

"Judy," she said, looking at one of her friends. "I see you here before, yes?" She looked at him. "I 'member 'cause you hansom'."

He smiled at her tightly, a frustrated meanness spreading in him from the drinks and from his inability to speak to her in anything but phrases. To think of her in anything but phrases. "You never seen me in your life," he said.

"Not true. You come . . ."

"Bullshit. I come up-country. R&R." By God, he thought, the cunning oriental spy got it out of me. He drank his bourbon and ordered another. I'd better give her some troop movements too. If I know any. He thought suddenly of the poster that used to hang on the wall of the company office, back on Okinawa. A leering VC, half his face in sinister shadow under a cone hat. Know your enemy, the poster said. Glad to know you, enemy. He asked her to go to bed with him.

She looked shocked. "Wassamatta you," she said, "you wait 'till bar closes."

He finished the drink. "Sorry," he said. "I can't afford it. I'd like to drink alone now. So di-di. Scram."

Tears welled up in the girl's eyes. You're kidding, he thought, strangely touched.

He looked over at Hanson. The grunt seemed to have a high regard for his girl's conversational ability. She was drinking up a payday's worth of colored water. There were large track marks on her arms. The bourbon worked on him. Bubbling free clogged viciousness from my guts. Must be sour, curdled sperm, making me mean. In the corner of his eye, he saw his rejected girl talking to a pudgy American wearing grey-rimmed military glasses and a white shirt. The girl was gesturing at Joshua, tears in her eyes, tugging at the boy's shirt sleeves. Probably her regular, Joshua thought. Oh yes, good, keep face with her. Come on, pinkie, keep a little face.

He pictured the boy, pulled by his thoughts, coming up behind his stool. The girl would be in the background, smiling faintly through her tears. He would spin suddenly on the barstool and slam the heel of his hand against the boy's chin. He could imagine the shock and the sudden numbness in his hand and the boy bouncing against the rim of the bar, his mouth red. Oh shit. O shit, he thought. I have got to get out of this. He gripped his glass tightly. His knuckles stood out and he gripped the glass. He looked around the bar. The boy was still talking to the bar-girl, and she was smiling now. The other drinkers and girls seemed frozen in a tableau, their faces and positions grotesque parodies of drinkers and bar-girls. I can't keep this up, he thought. Pretty soon I'll do something out of character and they'll shoot me. He hadn't loosened his grip on the glass. He clung to the glass. Anchor my ass, glass. Don't let me float away. He heard the conversation in the bar drifting around him, holding him in place. He was sweating and he finished the drink. He looked at Hanson. Kindred, he thought. Kin-dred, the society of the dreaded dead. Christ, he thought, they get the ideology and we get the buddy system.

He stood up. "Where you goin', tiger?" Hanson asked.

"Getting a hat."

"You alright tiger?"

"Need some stinkin' air."

"Got all you need here."

"It's not foul enough Hanson. Smells too pretty in here. Bouquets of roses."

"Bouquets of rice."

"Bouquets of crotch-rot, but I need some stink, Hanson."

"Sure, baby. Take it slow."

He was out the door before Hanson and running, giggling in the sudden coolness of the air. He ran full speed into a crowd of people on the sidewalk, laughing at them. Hanson caught up with him and grabbed his shoulder, looking worried. "I can't," Joshua said, "take a long-faced grunt." Hanson looked at Joshua seriously. "Let's get laid, man," he said.

The driver pedaled through alleys of stained white walls and corrugated tin. The partly opened doors in the alleys showed lighted cracks into mysterious Vietnamese lives; people squatting, cooking, nursing babies, ignoring the Americans. The alleys were ragged holes in a soiled, degraded oriental tapestry. The Marines didn't see the degradation. They thought it intrinsic.

The pedicab stopped in front of a house and they got off. They entered a large stone room, empty except for a few rattan chairs and a torn velvet couch. A shirtless middle-aged Vietnamese man was sitting in on one of the chairs, smoking a pungent opium pipe. He looked through them as they entered.

Two girls were draped over the couch. One was nice-looking, in a thin way. Joshua went for her, cutting Hanson out.

"1500 p's, allnight," the opium smoker said, still not looking at them. "Allright," Hanson said, quickly. Joshua nodded, not wanting to argue, wanting only to get up the wooden stairs that hung uncertainly on one side of the room.

Up the stairs there were a couple of beds, stained mattresses on metal legs. One of the beds had a curtain around it. Like a hospital bed, he thought. He followed her behind the curtain. She drew it around them and sat down on the mattress. He smiled at her; suddenly gentle. She smiled back and began undressing. He stripped off his own clothes and stood by the bed, naked and intent. She looked at his flushed lean face and shuddered slightly. She opened her hand, showing the rubber in her palm, then rolled it down on him. He looked at her brown-nippled breasts and shuddering himself, drew up over her. Urgently, he pulled her legs apart and entered her with no further preliminaries. He thrust at her, beyond her, growled deep in his throat. She gasped under the violence of his shaking body and drew her legs up, bringing her feet down on his buttocks. He clung, hung on to her, pumping, nailing himself brutally to life, clung and came, hated it, wanted to keep the quick under him, never stop. He smelled the odor of the two of them and tried to memorize it with his senses; the scent of living never to leave his nostrils.

She felt some of it, the shaking arch of his body bridging to life from death with violent motion. She had trained herself to stand far away from the ridiculous, buttock shaking act of these foreign soldiers, yet the desperation of this man came through to her. She understood it, enough to resent the symbolization of herself. For a moment she thought she would go mad.

He rolled off her and lay on his back. She slipped the rubber off and wiped him. He sighed and looked at her breasts hanging over him, cupped his hands over her ass. He could hear the sound of belly slapping belly through the curtain, and he laughed. What's your name? the girl was asking him. He caressed a breast interestedly. "What?" he asked, not caring what.

"What's your name?" she said, looking at him seriously, intelligently.

He sat up and looked at her. She began drawing together in front of his eyes as he looked, and suddenly he was outraged at the intrusion of her question and her humanity. "What the hell do you want?" he said coldly. "Why don't you leave me alone?" She continued looking at him in silence and he felt like hitting her. Or crying. "Quit messin' around," he said, and she nodded at him, not understanding the words. He got up and got dressed.

On the last night of their R&R they went to one of the enlisted messes to get a stateside meal.

It was a restaurant really, Joshua thought. The American eagle with a hamburger in his mouth squatting over Saigon. Chewing. The bartender told him that it used to be the penthouse of a Colonel who had gone North.

Inside, the mess was an Army dream of a Playboy club; amber lights playing on the polished floor, a discreet brown bar in the corner, and pastel orientals to take orders. The girls there flitted around like gentle reminders of femininity, and smiled, when they were looked at.

Joshua ate steak and fries washed down with bourbon. He ate silently, looking around him at the faces of his contemporaries. Still reflecting. And reflected. Bad habit, he thought. Tends to become a pain in the ass. He ate his steak. Fattened.

Later, feeling full, he walked out on the balcony and looked down at Saigon. Firecrackers were exploding, mocking little echoes of a war somewhere. It was almost Tet. 1967. The year of some animal or another. Year of the steak, maybe. He looked at the sidewalks below. A little girl was standing next to a pile of tin cans and ashy bottles. Her face was smudged, ashy also, and her shirt held together with one button. She looked up at him and waved. He waved once, then turned his back on the city and went in to the sound of murmuring voices and the rock music from the mess' Akai tape set.

Ben

by George Davis

The Blue Sky is almost empty. I walk to the rear and ask Papa-San to fix some fried rice for me. Then I walk over and sit on the concrete floor near the well. The other G.I.'s have gone to the bungalows to sleep with their girls, or back to the air base. I don't want to sleep with anyone. My head hurts from too much scotch.

Papa-san watches me while he cooks, but I don't want to pretend that I am cheerful in order to prevent him from feeling sad that I am alone.

He cooks over a small blazing fire in a pan which he never sets down unless to add more ingredients. The food sizzles, and he lets the smoke come up into his face as the small flames lick up from a bed of rocks and touch the bottom of the pan. He serves the fried rice in a wooden bowl. I pay him a quarter. There are large reddish shrimp in the mixture but I don't feel like eating.

"Lieutenant?" he says, "Lieutenant?"

I smile.

He goes back to the fire, whispers something in the ear of his youngest son and sends the boy off on an errand. I hear the boy running barefoot on the stones outside the rear compound fence. The old man is plump. The faces of his family are lit by the light from the flames. They sit without eating, without talking; they are simply there.

The son returns with a thin, youngish girl. Her clothing is wet in spots, which makes it apparent that she's been working in a bathhouse. Papa-san pushes her toward me, saying, "You sleep with her tonight, Lieutenant."

She takes the last few steps toward me as if she has not lost the momentum from his push. She is a dainty, eighty- or ninety-pound girl with shoulder-length hair and a small mannish shirt covering her pointed teen-age breasts. She tucks her head and blushes. Her shorts are white like the shirt and she has a Scottish-plaid belt holding them up. She would look tinier yet if she didn't have high-heel shoes on over her white bobbysocks. She is amusingly beautiful. Papa-san and his family are happy that I have someone for the night.

"No, Papa-san," I say.

"She no have VD," he says. His voice quickens and rises to assure me. He shows me her card which has a blue circle on it to show that she has passed her last VD inspection. He takes my hand and places it to my ear. I know I am supposed to take wax out of my ear and rub it in her pussy to see if it burns her, but I do not. "I don't want to pom-pom," I say.

The family laughs at the way I say pom-pom. The youngest son urges me by slapping his hands together to make the sound that two bodies make slapping together.

The entire family has turned to look at me—four children, a wife and a mother. I hear a transistor radio playing from one of the bungalows.

The girl is embarrassed. "We walk," I say.

"Chi," she says, and the old toothless woman sitting on the other side of the flames shakes her head Yes.

"Beautiful, poo ying," I say.

We leave along the back path in front of the dark wooden bungalows where several GI's are sitting out with their girls.

The bungalows are in a row like a series of outhouses in back of an old Southern church. A wooden platform runs along in front of them and a naked shiny-skinned GI runs down the platform to where the vat of water is. He squats and washes his privates, then tiptoes back past us into his bungalow.

For a while the narrow path leads into the jungle before it turns toward the main road. The girl and I hold hands as we walk along the ditch that carries waste from the tapioca mill down to the ocean. The girl laughs and holds her nose at the wet-dog odor of the ditch. I laugh.

For a moment I wonder what would happen if I disappeared forever into the human and bamboo jungles of Asia.

We reach the road and walk along the stony shoulder. She takes off her highheels and walks in her socks for a while, then she takes them off, too. In some places the air is chilly, and in others we walk through warm air. Walking through ghosts, we used to call it down South, before Harvard, before everything became literal and scientific, and then became more unreal than it ever was before, leading straight to Vietnam. Before a million explanations came down between me and what I want to feel, and then all the explanations proved to be lies.

As I walk I feel strangely free, and I dread the thought of going back to America. I don't know how I can ever feel right about America again, after what they got weak-assed me to do over here.

I want to go to graduate school, but I know I'll never sit in a class and learn from a white man. And who will I work for, and where will I go.

The road turns out of the trees and runs along the beach. The gulf is empty and the black morning is peppered with stars. The air on the beach is cool. I feel the presence of billions of people around me whose lives are menaced in the same way that mine is. Like the millions of Chinese who were slaves in their own country for centuries.

We walk down toward the water's edge. There is nothing man-made in sight except for a puny wooden dock where the trucks come down to pick up the ammunition and jet fuel from the ships anchored in deep water.

"Pom-pom?" the girl says in a weak voice and sits down and begins to undo her shorts.

"No," I say, and take out my wallet and give her five dollars anyway. Tomorrow I want to bring Damg on this same walk. We could sit on the edge of this continent which has been kept under the foot of white men until finally China had to get an H-bomb and say, "No more." And the people I am fighting, me, in Vietnam had to say, "You can kill me but you can't enslave me any more."

I look out across the water. Bangkok, Rangoon, Kuala Lumpur, Djakarta, Calcutta—dark music—and then across the Indian Ocean to Africa.

Souvenir

by John Tavela

Sergeant First Class Baniff regarded the figure of the woman he loved with dismay. When he had first been smitten, the woman had been as slender as a wand. The men of the company had called her Sticky-san because of her thinness; later a radio sergeant had decreed that her name must be Baby Commie, not because of her political beliefs, which were unknown anyway, but because he had decided she looked in her black pajamas as skinny as a strand of commo wire. That nickname stuck. Everyone, including Baniff, continued to call her Baby Commie even after her shape began to look to Baniff, who was mess sergeant, like a swollen can of spoiled chicken. Secretly, from the first day he had seen her, Baniff thought of her as Reed, as poetic a name as he could imagine. Her real name was Nguyen Thi Song, but no American called her that.

Baniff's melancholy deepened as he watched her eat. She was seated near the serving line, wolfing the remnants of the GIs' noon meal. Her metal tray was hilly with mashed potatoes, ham, biscuits, vegetables, and cheese. She ate margarine plain, mechanically spooning it into her mouth from a fast liquefying mound between heaping forkfuls of the other food. Sergeant Baniff, nervously flicking sweat from the groove above his upper lip, waddled his own well-larded body to her table when he could no longer stand to watch her further bury the figure he loved.

"Eat too much, Baby Commie, too much. Get boocoo fat."

"You fat, GI all fat, me get fat, too."

"But Baby Commie very pretty, uh, you know, boocoo *dep,* before fat."

"Dep no good live. Eat, fat, boocoo okay live."

"Americans like no fat."

"How come Sar Gen Ban vay fat? Me no fat American go home."

"Maybe you no fat you go with Americans."

"Ha, no American take *Viet,* fat, no fat."

"I, maybe, take, you no fat. I like no fat *ba.*"

"Ha, Sar Gen, me no *ba,* me *co. Ba* got man."

"Husband."

"Okay, hus ban."

"No lie, I take. I like."

"Yo me hus ban? In American?"

"Maybe no fat, maybe husband."

"Yo bullshit me. No hus ban me. All a time same-same. GI go, *Viet* stay."

"No bullshit you, Baby Commie. You thin, me . . . me love."

"What mean?"

"Love?"

"No, me know love boom-boom. What 'hin'?"

"Thhh-in. Mean no fat."

"Me hin, yo take me American?"

"Yes, can do."

"Yo fu nee," she laughed and returned to eating, shaking her head.

Sergeant Baniff watched her a while longer, then walked forlornly to the storeroom behind the kitchen. He counted cans for ten minutes, although he didn't keep track of the tally. He left the storeroom and went to his room through the maze of rickety plywood that connected the mess hall with his quarters.

He sat on his bed and put his face in his hands. He often did this, because he was a very sensitive man. Sensitivity was the last thing anyone suspected of him, a heavy, hairy typesetter from New York in his late forties.

He had been snatched from his job, when a President, hoping to give the war a coloring of dignified seriousness, had ordered the call-up of his National Guard unit. He was, however, resigned to call-ups; this was his third war. He had lost his wife in the middle one. When he had returned from Korea, she was no longer at the address where he'd left her. He never found her, and eventually decided that everything had probably worked out for the best.

Reed was nothing like his wife. Reed, Reed, so frail when he had first seen her. His love had been pure, purely for her beauty, her graceful form, her cascade of shimmering black hair. He had not felt the least twinge of lust, though inevitably that came, too. But she was so delicate, so fragile. Even in his fantasies he was afraid of crushing her and so always imagined her on top, gently rocking on the swells of his corpulence. His love was gentle; his love was magnificent. He had written a poem about it:

Reed in the water
    Dips circles in the big wave
        Swimming to my feet.

He had taken a long time to write it, and he knew it was as good as anything he had ever set in type. Better.

He pushed himself up from the bed and tried to push away his depression. He straightened his jacket, put on his baseball cap, and poked a cigar butt between his teeth. He walked to the Orderly Room and arrived sweaty and out of breath.

"That damn package come for me, yet?" he asked the mail clerk, doing his best to growl.

"I don't fly the planes. I just pick up what's at the APO." Baniff had been harassing the clerk for some weeks; his answer had become standard.

"Kee-rist, Useless, I'm gonna stop feedin' ya, if ya don't come up wit' my mail soon," Baniff threatened through his cold cigar. Oddly, the mail clerk admired Baniff for trying so hard to fit the rotten NCO mold; he actually liked the Sergeant for it, but never passed up an opportunity to give any sergeant a bad time out of strong principle.

"In that case, Sarge," he said coyly, "maybe I got it this afternoon."

"Whadya mean maybe' ya got it?"

"Yeah, well, you know, like there wasn't no rain nor hail nor gloom of night, so it was a little hard doin' my job today."

"C'mon, ya got it or not. I got better things ta do."

"Like playin' grabass with the KP's?"

"Wouldn' you like ta know. C'mon, gimme a break, huh?"

"Would it be sort of a heavy package?"

"Yeah."

"Maybe gurgle when you shake it?"

"Yeah."

"TS. I never pick up packages that are heavy and gurgle. Too much work."

"You . . ."

"Tut, Sergeant B., watch what you say to me or I'll tell everybody you got this here case of Metrecal," the clerk said, lifting the ragged package to the counter.

"Hey, you got no right ta open my mail."

"Sarge, it was ripped like this when I got it; you know how they handle this stuff. Tryin' to get rid of your gut, huh?"

"None a your goddamn business."

Baniff lugged the carton to his room and tore off the remaining paper. There were a few cans missing, but not enough to bother him. He lined the cans up on his table and got the English-Vietnamese Dictionary from his foot locker. He spent the next half hour working on his speech, writing it down in the clownish phonetic language the Army printed beside the Vietnamese words.

When he had finished, he went to the kitchen and led Song to his quarters by the hand. The other KP's giggled as they left, and Song hid her mouth behind a hand. He sat her on a chair and delivered his speech, gesturing repeatedly at the cans on the table. He was very earnest, he thought, but Song was convulsed with laughter during much of his oration. Sergeant Baniff flushed when he was done.

Song smiled and clapped her hands. *"Ha si quan Ban noi tieng Viet,"* she said.

"No understand," he said.

"I say Sar Gen Ban speak Vietnamese."

"From book," he said, holding up the dictionary.

"Vietnamese book vay fu nee. Can go? Have boocoo wok."

"Didn't you understand?"

"Shu, okay me go?"

"Don't you have any answers?"

"Okay."

"I say you drink can, no more fat. Then go America with me."

"Wha? Drink can, no more fat. Okay, fo yo drink one."

"No, you no understand. Take many can make no fat."

"Okay, drink many can. Wan me do now?"

"No, no. You drink four cans a day. No eat other food."

"Okay drink fo can, no okay no eat food."

"You eat food no get thin."

"Me no wan hin, me wan food. So good, you no eat food, drink can, get hin, you like."

"Don't you want to go to America with me to live?"

"Okay."

"Really, truly, I swear I'll take you. Please believe me."

"Okay."

"You really believe me?"

"Shu, okay, go American Sar Gen Ban, right. Me go wok now."

"Okay, Baby Commie, you come I give cans every day. I very happy."

"Okay, Baby Commie happy."

For a long time Baniff sat giving loving looks to the Metrecal; there was a goofy smile on his face. Then he realized that Baby Commie had not taken a can for supper. He grabbed one and bounced joyfully through the passage to the mess hall. As he entered the storeroom, he saw two figures lurking behind a row of shelves. One of them was the First Cook. Grinning, the cook came out from behind shelves, furtively trying to button his fly.

"Malloy," Baniff said, "what'd I tell ya about playin' around wit' da KP's on company time?"

"Aw, Sarge, everybody does it. I get off in a couple minutes, anyway."

"No more, understand," he said sternly. Then he added with a wink, "You wanna mess around, go boom-boom your hootch maid."

"There it is," said Malloy, as he went into the kitchen.

"Awright, getcher gaddamn tail out here," Sergeant Baniff yelled to the KP. "You number ten, no more job."

The girl came out. It was Song. Baniff's eyes filled with tears. He felt suddenly weak and put out a hand to steady himself.

"Reed, Reed, Reed," he sobbed.

"Wha Reed?" Song asked.

Baniff didn't answer. He stood silently. His tears made small dark circles on his faded jungle fatigues.

"Why yo cry, Sar Gen Ban? Ma loi say han job go American. Yo say no fat go American. Yo say vay happy. Sar Gen Ban, Ma loi, Song all go American. Okay? Vay fu nee. Song happy. Song vay happy."

Baniff was bewildered. "What song?" he asked suddenly, angrily. "What goddamn happy song?"

"Me Song," she said softly.

"I no understand," he said to the floor.

"Me, too," said Song and went from the storeroom through the kitchen to the dining hall where she wiped the tables.

Warren

by Basil T. Paquet

In the drainage ditch water Warren could see the Chinook's reflection grow larger. It climbed like a spider zooming from the stained puddle toward his eye, or rather it dropped, and as he straddled the ditch to finger a cigarette filter, he glanced up to see the ship block the morning sun as it landed on the hot pad. He had heard the call come in twenty minutes before when returning some litters to the emergency room.

"Queen Tonic . . . Queen Tonic . . . we have 12 litter . . . 2 heads . . . 5 ambulatory."

He turned toward the chopper, dropping his handful of trash in a massive barrage on a pink gauze pad floating soddenly in the ditch.

"Where do you think you're going?" Sergeant Rednick yelled.

Warren half turned, then turned again into the wind of the blades, leaving Rednick to figure out his actions. He joined a group of hunched olive figures moving toward the cargo doors. Soon he was caught in the rhythm of unloading the litters. He felt his tiredness shift for a moment. An energy burned up his body toward his head. His arms and legs jerked in response, but he felt the motion of his procedures more than their purpose. There was a kind of vague excitement as he cut off the clothes of the wounded, slipped the large gauge needles into their arms, pumped blood and dressed wounds.

An hour later he slanted through the door of his hootch. The room was fairly dark. He aimed toward the luminous cross that hung above the new Japanese refrigerator. He felt the handle, pulled, and found one rusty rimmed Pabst already opened. Before he closed the door he saw below the cross a Polaroid shot of a spread-legged, naked Vietnamese girl. Scrawled across the white bottom edge in red felt tip was, "MOTHER MARY Pray For Us." Warren smiled as he ran the edge of the beer can against his fatigue front. "Billy!" he thought. Turning to his left he saw O'Hara's hulking figure in the corner, moving uncomfortably in sleep. He lifted the can to his lips as he walked toward his bunk, smelled stale spit and rust on the rim, unconsciously wiped it against his trousers, then drank. He took another swig and held the perspiring can to his forehead. Billy's silhouette swung through the door. Warren splashed his beer when Billy came close.

"Drank all my fucking beer."

"Shit! Just brought you back twelve cold ones."

A transistor radio, hung from Billy's belt line. A voice cracked through the static, ". . . somethin' off the Tallahatchie Bridge." Billy snapped off the radio.

"That your picture of the Virgin Mary?" asked Warren.

"Fuckin O'Hara will piss green in his pants when he sees that."

Warren dipped beneath the mosquito netting of his bunk, wiped his wet hand across the poncho liner, and checked his watch.

"You missed breakfast," observed Billy.

Warren pulled at his boots.

"You got anything?"

Billy stared toward an open locker.

"A can of Beanie Weenies or some spaghetti?"

"Beanie Weenies."

"How did it go with those guys on the chinook? Rednick was P.O.'d when you took off. Said he was going to report you for skipping detail."

Warren picked at his toes.

"One was DOA and another was expectant. Rednick can suck off. Fucking mentality of a fucking doorknob. Gimme one of these beers."

"Cold mothers! I told him that the Chinook was more important than fuckin police call. Get a smoke?"

Warren reached for his fatigue jacket, felt a lump, and tossed the bundle toward Billy. He grabbed the remaining cans and walked back to the refrigerator.

"Light my Beanie Weenies for me."

The light again revealed the Polaroid snapshot. Warren stared for a moment at the open legs, the leering smile, the invitation of the pose. The picture excited him. Outside, perhaps in the next hootch, he could hear the voices of mamma-sans, rising and falling in whispered, secretive sounds. He bent to put in the beers and saw dried blood on the knee of his pants. He remembered with a kind of anger the young Vietnamese boy who an hour before had reached out deliriously from his litter with a handless arm and struck him. The boy had screamed. The bandaged soggy stump seemed to reproach Warren for getting in its way. He headed back toward the door with his beer, stepped onto the porch, and searched the sky for a noise.

"Billy, you still going into town today?"

"Yea."

"Good."

Warren turned from a line of Huey's snaking westward a mile away back toward the hootch and looked straight up locating the noise he searched for. A C-47 was dumping insecticide straight down on their area. Warren could see the cloud spreading from the tail section catching the sunlight. He felt a kind of depression, a need for rain; savage, beating rain that would stop the red dust from puffing beneath his feet.

"I'm going for a shower." He angled back toward Billy. "Wait for me."

The Lambretta nosed between a stalled deuce and a half and the on-coming traffic. A mile farther on it rolled to a stop itself, still several miles from the center of Bien Hoa. The driver tried unsuccessfully to start the taxi several times. The heat gathered force, its waves obscuring the rational forms of distant buildings. A large jet lifting from the airport seemed to bend in half in its struggle to escape. Stretching over the taxi's railing, Warren could see its tires sinking into the soft pitch. Half a kilometer away were a string of bars and steam baths, their gaudy signs shimmying in the heat. Billy was cursing the driver and a number of men had gathered to offer their advice. Their faces seemed hostile to Warren, as if he and Billy were to blame for the breakdown. He shoved a bill toward the driver and grabbed Billy by the arm.

"Come on, let's keep going."

The men became excited by the size of the overpayment.

"Christ," said Billy. "What you give him so much for?" He turned back immediately to demand change. Warren shouted. The heat robbed the shout of its power but everyone was startled by its suddenness.

Warren and Billy started toward the distant houses. Billy was playing with the holster of a .45 he kept strapped inside his fatigues. His entire shirt was wet and the straps of the shoulder holster shower clearly, bulging the skin, disfiguring his back.

"Trouble with your titties?"

Billy's young plump face grinned back, the sexual allusion pleased him. He opened his shirt front squeezing up his fatty, hairless chest with both hands. The harness obscured the right nipple.

"Suckie suckie, GI?"

"You're fucking obscene."

Behind them the Lambretta coughed to a start. Warren felt the heat with each effort to speak. Words were hard to summon and harder to control in his dry mouth. A movement caught his eye as he worked some spit into the shape of an expletive. A cattle egret landed in the wet field to their right. It strutted through the young rice a few paces from the path that led to a pastel blue house. Through a window Warren could see a shelf of bottles and a bottle-shaped sign. The sound of the taxi faded toward Long Binh. The string of bars seemed too distant.

"Let's try to get some beer in this house. It looks like a private club."

"Nothin' to lose."

The bird flew at their approach, arching sharply over the paddy. Warren lost sight of it as he came within the shadow of the house. The lattices and casements were painted in yellow and red. The bars on the lower windows were a bright pink. They called through the door in unison. An old woman appeared with a shuffle.

"Sah-yent Andy sen you?"

"Yea, yea. Andy sent us. You got anything cold to drink? You got some beer?"

"Sah-yent Andy got everythin' here."

She scuffed toward the liquor shelf. Beneath it was a row of glasses on another shelf. To the right was a large and fairly new refrigerator. Warren could hear movements on the floor above. He motioned Billy toward a table and chairs. The formica top was stained with blurred rings from previous glasses and cans. One of the rings had not yet completely dried. Again a noise sounded upstairs and to the right. The old woman was coming with a couple of cans of Budweiser and the glasses on a tray. Billy set a five hundred piaster bill on the table.

"You pay MPC," the old woman informed. "Sah-yent Andy say GI pay MPC."

Down the hall Warren could hear a faucet being turned on.

"Sure, sure."

Billy placed a military bill on the tray. The old woman returned to the liquor shelf and pressed a button on the wall. A distant bell sounded. Down the hall a toilet flushed and began filling again slowly. This noise was drowned in turn by a transistor that the old woman turned on. Someone was again throwing something off the Tallahatchie bridge. The radio droned on.

"Whoever this fuckin lifer is, he's got quite a racket."

Billy had moved to a near corner and was examining a Japanese stereo set. Warren was about to answer but two Air Force enlisted men came down the stairwell.

"Howdy," said a tall tech sergeant. A pudgy freckled E-4 who followed him was busy tucking in his shirt. He wore stateside fatigues which were stiffly starched. A crusted perspiration line like dried sea foam ran around his pits. He was sweating profusely, the fabric was again dampening. Warren raised his beer toward them. He and Billy both "howdied" back.

"You boys come at the wrong time. Girls gotta come to town now."

"You Andy?" asked Billy.

"Yup."

"Nice set-up. Place's got class." Billy eyed a tape deck.

"Extended three times for this fuckin' place. What unit you boys with?"

With his left hand he had motioned to the old woman who then brought more beer to the table. The tall sergeant swung himself into a chair.

"Sixty-eighth Med," said Billy.

"We were on the way to Bien Hoa but our taxi broke down. I spotted the Ba Moui Ba sign through the window and thought we could get a beer before we headed on. You mind? Is this place strictly private?"

"Shit, boys. Always obliged to welcome a few select clientele. Even a couple of fuckin' Yankees. 'Specially if'n they're medics. You boys get your hands on anything you let me know. Andy's always in the biddin'."

The plumbing again sounded down the hall and footsteps padded across the upstairs level just above their heads. The weedy sergeant checked his watch and shouted upstairs.

"Drag asses, girls!"

The pudgy E-4 ran his restless hands through his hair on his way to the foot of the stairs. He called in a high pitched voice, repeating his superior's command. The sergeant glanced at Warren and Billy with a crooked smirk.

"Boy sounds like a castrated pig."

He winked and his lips curled higher revealing an even row of yellow teeth. Warren felt the closeness of the air more keenly. He raised the beer can to his forehead closing his eyes.

"You don't look too good, boy. Don't look like you could go a good fuck anyhows."

"No sleep," answered Billy for his friend. "But I'm sorely in need of a good lay myself," he grinned.

"One of the girls is staying," said the sergeant, "you make yourself at home for five bills. That's cut rate cuz'n I like you boys, and want you to start off here right." He waved his beer at Warren, "You kin take a steam bath and massage. The old lady'll set things up for you, but I don't think y'all be wantin to pull her pants down," he guffawed.

They all smiled and the E-4 laughed in an exaggerated high pitched giggle. The girls had started to descend the stairs. The sergeant and his protégé moved toward the back door, his entourage had assembled behind in pecking order, he gave Billy his directions, "Third door down on the left. She's a good clean piece."

Warren could hear the sergeant's orders to the old woman muffled through the engine of a three-quarter ton truck. Billy was already on his way up the stairs. Warren could hear the old woman's shuffle again. He measured the steam bath against the ride back to the base and a cold shower. He looked at his watch and thought, "The water tanks will be empty by now!"

"You come mamma-san," the old woman motioned. She busied herself closing the front grate while Warren rose to his feet. She walked back to the refrigerator and took out two beers. Opening both she handed one to Warren and took a gulp of the other herself. Warren followed her through some passages until they came to the back of the house. They entered a large garage-like building which had a row of stalls. Rusted pipes followed down the wall. In a few places remnants of asbestos wrapping hung stiffly down like jack spaniards' nests. A steady dripping at the far end sounded. The air was cooler but the smell was of sweat and dirty linen. The old woman entered one of the cubicles and started turning steam handles. Warren moved toward a window to the left and pushed a wooden shutter open. A large Chinese rooster patrolled the back yard. His tail feathers stirred the red dust in little puffs each time he changed direction. He pecked at the ground in violence. When a young girl carrying a basket of laundry entered the yard the cock moved toward her, following until it became apparent she was not carrying any slops. She moved to a large basin that sat beneath a faucet and began washing. Her motions assumed a rhythm. Her small slim body moved in quick jerks as she pushed down on the cloth she held. Her black silk pants were large and loose, but where the water splashed them they clung to her thin figure. She turned to put aside a piece of wash and Warren could see a small breast outlined through her white tunic. A hand touched his sleeve in a gentle tug.

"You want steam bath massage?"

The crinkled face looked up at him. The suddenness of her approach had caught him off balance. He could feel the embarassment on his cheeks. He had been caught staring at the girl by the old Vietnamese woman and this angered him. He turned toward the sound of the steam, unbuttoning his shirt front as he walked. He faced the wall as he undressed. The old woman made him strangely self-conscious. She was collecting his clothes off the chair where he had placed them and hanging them up on pegs. Her closeness was like a further inspection. He plunged into the steam with his beer still in his hand. The warm mist flattened out against his body. He raised the can and found he had dented it.

A low cot with a mattress covered in plastic was in the center of the enclosure. She placed his wallet in a zip-top plastic bag on a table in the corner. Her thoroughness annoyed him more than his own carelessness. The sweat stood out plainly on her face, already running down the creases as if the perspiration itself had carved the lines over the many years. She took a drink of her beer.

"Too hot for mamma-san," she puffed out. Her grin revealed a mouth of betel stained stubs. "GI like baby-san to give massage?" She motioned back toward the window. The sweat rolled down them both profusely. She spread a sheet over the bed, then stood up straight. Her tunic was thoroughly wet and she plucked at the wet front to fan herself. Her look revealed a sureness. "Baby-san give you suckie-suckie for ten MPC. You no tell Sah-yent Andy!"

Warren could feel the tension of arousal in his genitals. He walked to the table and took the wallet and money from the plastic bag. The old woman had moved up behind him. The odor of her breath and body hung closely through the steam. "You no try fuck baby-san! She commanded, "You be number ten." Warren nodded. Her wrinkles relaxed back into the betel red smile. "You number one GI."

Warren turned the steam valve down slightly and moved on to the mattress. The steady hissing made his own breathing seem irregular. His right hand moved to flick a drop of sweat from his nose. He missed and it rolled down into his moustache. He automatically moved his lower lip and sucked in the saltiness. His raised left hand still held the beer. Even in the dim light he could see the dark stain beneath the fingernails. He shifted the beer and sniffed at the stain. Foul. He ran the nail of his right forefinger beneath the nail of his left. He remembered for the second time that day the young Vietnamese boy with the shattered arm. This time however he remembered carrying the small boy to the morgue. The ward had been busy. O'Hara had helped him carry the litter, but had left him to bag the boy on his own. He remembered with both irritation and a queasiness how as he had reached beneath the body to lift, his left hand had slipped into an exit wound.

A hand on his shoulder startled him. He turned angrily. The girl jumped back, but her face showed no real fear. Warren was embarrassed by his own surprise and foolish reaction. He motioned to her. "Lai-Dai, girl-san." She moved forward. The bottom of her tunic was still soapy.

"Me called Warren. What your name?"

His nakedness bothered him. The girl looked above his body

examining the wall behind him. "Nam," she said. Her voice was soft but not tiny. He moved the towel around himself. "How old you, girl-san?" She paused. The steam was starting to form perspiration on her face. The tunic was sticking to her front. Warren could see the dark of her nipples on the slight swells. She shrugged with a motion that indicated either indifference to the question or that she did not know.

He turned onto his stomach and immediately he could feel her palms settle onto the muscles of his upper back. Her hands felt so much larger and stronger than they had looked. Soon she had set up the rhythm of the massage. The flat of her hands came down in quick pushing jabs. Her palms seemed to contain the whole weight of her body. Her movements controlled Warren's breathing. His breaths came with a sexual cadence and above the rush of steam he could hear her breathing. It too, he told himself, was full of excitement. She worked slowly down his body to his ankles and back up to his behind. When she reached this area he was fully aroused. All his tiredness left him in his excitement, and he eagerly swung his body around. He was breathing heavily. His genitals and his whole pelvis moved in continuation of the motion she had established. He searched her face for some recognition of his excitement. She looked at the wall. He directed her hands to himself, and they responded with a quick rubbing motion. Her top was completely soaked. He realized that she could not have been more than twelve years old and this excited him even more. She knelt on the edge of the bed and her left hand moved toward his chest to steady her position. He took it for a movement of response and pulled her toward him. She resisted, but his movement toppled her onto him. He moved quickly tugging her down into position beside him, his hands roughly working the tunic up her body. His legs held her tightly. Her whole body moved with what to Warren was arousal. She seemed to be stiffening, but he could not see her face until he had jerked her clothing off. The blouse came over her face with a slight rip. Her face was a mixture of terror and anger. She said nothing. Her teeth bit her lower lip fiercely and deep intakes of air flared her small nostrils. Her ribs swelled with each rapid inhale. He loosened his hold. She spat the words at him, "No fuck you." He was humiliated. He lay flat and she resumed her kneeling position on the edge of the bed. Her hands moved back on him picking up the mechanical stroke, but he could feel the tiredness edging up his legs. His penis was becoming flaccid in her hand. He became incensed and spoke through his teeth.

"You suck now. I pay mammasan. You suck."

His right hand came up to her shoulder. She flinched from his grasp and bent lower while she watched him carefully. Her eyes no longer showed no emotion. She took a corner of the sheet and wiped off his penis, using her spit to moisten the head. He was becoming fully hard again, and with the touch of her mouth and her rocking motion he felt himself grow full. He sat up now and spread his legs more. She was forced to move up the bed to accommodate his position. He lay back again but kept his legs spread. From this angle he could watch her motions more easily and they seemed more exciting. He could see his own body pushing into the air and as his excitement mounted he pushed harder. What excited him the most was the knowledge that he would come in her mouth. He could feel the start of the rush, the extra tension. Suddenly she pulled her mouth off and worked his genitals rapidly. He grabbed her roughly between the legs as he came. She cried out, but mananged to jump off before he could get a firm hold of her. He felt the sperm land on his legs. She turned at the door before she left. Her face carried the same indifferent look but her eyes were wet with pain and hatred.

He wiped himself with an end of the sheet. He could feel the humiliation rising. He picked up her tunic and went out to the window. The young girl was washing her hands and rinsing her mouth at the faucet. She turned, her nakedness in the strong sunlight seemed at once natural and a violation. She seemed even younger as she approached without fear. Her lips were swollen from their encounter. She took the blouse as he handed it out to her and slipped into it quickly. Halfway across the yard, the rooster charged out to meet her. She spat in Warren's direction. Small puffs of red dust rose from beneath her retreating feet and the tail of the rooster.

A motion caught Warren's eye. To his right a cattle egret came out of the sun. Landing forty yards away in the rice paddy, it started strutting toward the house through the shallow water and wilting heat. Suddenly it fook to the air again, frightened by the overflight of a cobra gunship. The giant shadow rushed across the paddy and the egret wheeled in flight. Warren watched the bird's retreat. A kind of depression held him, or perhaps it was thirst, he reasoned, following the bird's flight toward a distant tree line.

Warren and Billy could feel the morning sun already heating their backs into a sweat. They stopped at the string of faucets beneath the water tower and washed. The cool water splashed across their faces. They stood to let the coolness run down till it wet the tops of their trousers. Their fatigue fronts were open, their dog tags hanging like amulets.

"Harassment, it's just goddam harassment." Billy took a balled olive handkerchief from his hip and swiped at his freckled nose.

Warren held his hands under the water, scraping the dirt from under his nails. He found a sliver of soap stuck between the pipe and a piling and rubbed till he produced a sweet-smelling lather. "It don't give a shit," he said, raising his nails to his nose and sniffing carefully.

"I can take work!" Billy took the soap chip. "I can work like a mother. But this harassment bullshit, these senseless details! Well, F.T.A." He threw the chip at a lizard crawling up a cross-beam. "Back home I held two jobs, but they was important work. Good pay. I was the best man in the shop. On the way up."

"No hair on your ass, huh?" Warren held an innocent smile up for Billy's inspection. The handful of water caught Billy in the mouth. He sputtered after Warren into the latrine.

"No! No shit Warren. I worked hard, was even planning to get married."

They settled onto the boards, taking berths near the door.

"Who'd marry a piece of shit like you?"

They both wrinkled their noses at the stench. Warren pushed the door open and jammed it with a pencil in the crack.

"Christ, they haven't emptied these things in a week." Warren looked down between his legs through the pear-shaped hole. The sodden mass of waste was nearing the top of the severed oil drum. Flies buzzed around beneath them. "Barrel's full of shit."

They sat staring out of the door toward a high barbed wire fence some fifty meters away. Behind it were a series of low canvas tent tops that puffed in the slight breeze. The sides were rolled like sleeves and they could see the canvas cots, and the few basins and tables allowed to each group of wounded prisoners. A breeze rose almost violently. It pushed the latrine door back on its inner tube hinges. Warren held the pencil in its place. A metal basin blew off one of the tables and rolled to the barbed wire. Voices swept past, carried by the wind.

"Monkey chatter," said Billy. "Same-same monkey!" He pointed, his finger poking from a wad of paper, toward a prisoner amputee who moved in a crouch toward the basin. The wounded man's movements were slow. He placed a single crutch out and hopped unsteadily. The sound of scraping metal lifted into the dry breeze as the pan rolled against the wire. The breeze pushed it still further and the prisoner fell as he tried to reach for the container. His blue hospital pajamas stuck to the wire. "Poor fucker's unbalanced;" said Billy. "They should've blown away his other pin."

Warren laughed out loud. "You're quite the fucking humanitarian, you are. I suppose they'd get bread and water from you?"

"Shit no! Peanuts!" They tittered in unison. In the compound two prisoners under the direction of a corpsman lifted the man off the wire. The group returned slowly to their tent. A small blue tatter fluttered on the wire. Warren narrowed his eyes and stared till the cloth became a bird and the puffed olive turbans, bush.

"Fuck!" Warren muttered, "you know I've been thinking about home. How things are looking back in the world about now. There's woods near my home. In the middle of them is a small meadow. Hasn't been farmed for years. Used to go there hunting rabbits and birds. Even went back there before I came over. Fucked more there than I ever did in bed. I used to keep a pack of rubbers and a bottle cached in the bushes."

"You're a real nature boy you are. I like my ass in bed."

They lit cigarettes as they started to walk toward their hootch. Dry February winds blew small devil dusters across the open quadrangle. The breeze stopped; the sudden heat sagged the canvas, then the tents billowed in an undulating motion that made the camp swell and fall like a monster buried in the land. Heaped with red earth, it struggled to emerge, shaking the dirt from its olive back. Coming from the opposite direction was an old man stooped under the load of a stick hung with wire baskets. Dark brown objects moved in their cages in frenzy.

"How can this guy stand to be near that many rats?"

"Somebody got to catch the fucking rats. Besides, this guy probably sells them to the other gooks for food."

Warren frowned, "Even gooks don't eat rats."

"Man, when's the last time you had garbage detail? These fucking people will eat anything. Didn't you ever smell that shit mammasan eats. I told her she had to eat outside. The stink made me sick." Billy put his hand to his stomach, patting his paunch tenderly. The old man moved to the side to let the soldiers pass. An odor hung heavy as smoke. The rats surged in their cages. Their chatter rose in chorus as a gust swung the load toward Warren and Billy. They stumbled against each other trying to avoid the rats. Billy cursed at the old man who failed to acknowledge the abuse and moved on with a steady swaying motion.

They settled in front of their hootch beneath its overhang. They rubbed cold cans of beer against their faces and chests and drank in long draughts. Billy went in to turn on his tape deck. Warren ran his fingers through his thick black hair and studied his chest and stomach. He was very proud of his large chest and narrow waist. He felt his stomach muscles to see if any fat was developing. Music fell out of the tent like a heavy object, rolling out across the yard. The volume dropped as Billy adjusted his machine. He stepped through the opening.

"Fuck! I wish town was still on limits. I could go for a piece of ass."

Warren chewed on his nails, cleaning each meticulously before he raised it to his mouth. "Me too. I was talking to an MP last night. You know the one guarding the VC with the head wound? He says we're due for some trouble on New Year's."

"New Year's already gone by!"

"No man, the gook New Year."

"Fuck, I hope it don't last too long. I'd like to get into town before my prick atrophies."

"You mean before you yank it off?"

They both laughed loudly at this, feeling a warmth and friendship in the remark. The kind of intimacy and special feeling that you only feel for an Army buddy, thought Warren as he received Billy's playful punch in his shoulder. They settled back against the walls of the hootch, staring vaguely at the horizon where aircraft moved constantly at differing speeds. Before them in the distance lay a major part of the large encampment, its buildings covered with the red dust that brought on their great thirst. Everything took on a sameness at this distance. Like death, thought Warren, and he fought back the image of the young VC he had bagged the night before, his nostrils clogged with blood and this same red dust, his caked protruding teeth thrust out of a mouth that hung open in a snarl. Warren squinted his eyes to make the planes and helicopters become birds.

"Cough . . . again . . . again."

Warren could feel the stickiness on the palms of his hands. Through the abdominal pad he could feel the loose guts forced up with the effort. He shifted his left hand to hold a basin. A fly landed on his right hand and began to feed. When the wounded soldier finished spitting into the basin, it was filled with a swirl of blood and mucus. Warren brushed at the fly which had moved onto the bright pink of the pad. He finished taking the wounded man's vital signs and moved out the back door of the quonset. He leaned heavily on a row of metal containers filled with disinfectant solutions which splashed against the far side. The waves came back with slightly less force and spilled onto the front of his trousers.

A few miles away on the northern perimeter some flares went up, dull competition to an eastern horizon that already displayed a jagged rip of red and yellow. He swished some solution in the basin and dumped the contents in the drainage ditch. He felt around in the bottom of the far right container, fishing up an assortment of medical equipment. He cleaned these methodically while watching the sky. He liked to time this unpleasant duty with the sunrise. The sky was bulging at the crucial point. Warren stalled his return to the ward, searching the bottoms of the containers a last time. His hand caught a small curved object, a tracheotomy tube. He pulled some old adhesive tape from around the neck, slid out the canula, and pumped the metal tubes vigorously beneath the water. At last the sun heaved up out of the dark mountains that edged the coast. Its bright red drained within seconds along the whole length of the sky. It became pale even as it grew to its full circle and soon the red stain had seeped back into the earth. Large grey clouds rushed in quickly and blotted out the last colors, then the sun itself. He eyed the extent of cloud cover, measuring it. Don't get your hopes up, he thought, and turned back into the ward.

Within an hour the sun was baking the laterite into still drier dust, and Warren watched it puff from beneath the boardwalk as he and O'Hara carried a body toward the morgue. He watched O'Hara's heavy back rock with the motion that the litter seemed to set for itself. The dead woman bounced slightly with each step and as she landed a light wave from the pool beneath her body washed toward the front of the litter. Small amounts fell with each jerking step and O'Hara held the litter back away from his fat buttocks to avoid the unpleasant wetness.

"Just kick the door," ordered Warren.

"I can't. There must be another body in front of it."

An SP4 came around the side of the small building. "Hold it boys, I forgot to tag this here DOA."

"You don't have to block the fucking doorway," shouted Warren.

The SP4 slid through the narrow opening. They could hear the litter slide across the floor. The door opened and the young soldier bowed low in awkward humor, swinging his arm before him in an exaggerated sweep. "All yours, gentlemen."

Warren and O'Hara stumbled through the door with their litter. Warren's hand hit the brass catch plate solidly as O'Hara slipped in a wet patch and nearly fell. The body rocked unsteadily. The pool of half-congealed blood slid onto the floor. Warren caught the falling body with his right hand and the litter with his right knee. They lowered together and slid the litter into the center of the floor. Warren closed the door.

"Christ! get the lights," said O'Hara. Warren had stooped to wipe his hand before going for the switch. "Christ, Warren! Get the fucking switch." O'Hara was stumbling in the dark. The litter came with force against Warren's boot and ankle. He reached quickly for the switch. The light caught O'Hara, already near the door, clawing the air. He had forgotten the fat medic's panic of corpses.

"Calm down and help me get this broad stripped."

"I forgot my gloves."

"Look O'Hara, I already worked over, forget your gloves for once and help me bag this gook."

"I don't touch nobody dead without gloves." He moved quickly out the door, his heavy step clattering boards in both directions. Warren moved around the body, pulling off bandages and equipment. He took out his scissors and began cutting off the remaining clothes. The woman had been hit twice. The exit wound in her back had caused the massive bleeding. He examined her stomach. A single small hole was placed neatly between some stretch marks that ran up from her hips. Her face was horribly disfigured with swelling. He reasoned her attack. The first shot through her left side had spun her. The second hit her at about the right mastoid and never came out. Somewhere inside it had churned up what knowledge, what sensibilities, what emotions she felt. What was left was a ripped and dying body that had fought against death for half a day. Warren cut off the blouse. Two loose breasts shifted slightly as the bloodied cloth fell from them, sagged heavily with the weight of death. Pools of blood were already collecting beneath the skin's surface. Her color was pale yellow, but the lividity tinged her with a blue and purplish mottling that made her seem almost white. Warren was moved by this fact. She seemed so young, so light. He moved his hand down to pick a dried blood spot off her right breast.

Then he went to the pile of body bags and selected the cleanest one. He unzipped it and laid it next to the litter. Usually if left to bag a body alone he would merely swing it into the bag half the body at a time. Now he slipped his arms beneath the legs and shoulders, lifting gently, and going to his knees to lower the full corpse into the bag. He pushed the head beneath the upper part of the bag and the feet into the lower. The limbs were already stiffening. He folded the arms across the breast demurely, and stared for a moment at the body. The lack of hair around the groin intrigued him. He knew that Vietnamese women had little hair, but it allowed him to think of her as younger. The right breast sagged from beneath the palm of her left hand. Warren closed the hand around it, and stepped back again. He could hear the boards rattling. He zipped up the bag quickly and waited for O'Hara to come through the door.

"Finished already?"

Warren examined the fresh blood on his hand, trying to determine how much was his own from having struck the door catch. O'Hara adjusted a new pair of rubber surgeon's gloves around his plump hands. "I couldn't find the right size." His hands played with the flaps on his fatigue front.

"Help me put her back on the litter."

Together they lifted the litter into the racks and slid it to the wall with a solid bump. Warren waved his reddened hands toward the pile of clothes and the mass of congealed blood on the floor.

"Clean this shit up. I'm going off now."

Warren walked toward the cluster of hootches that sagged in the intense heat. Beneath the dusted canvas tops were the louvered wall boards and behind them the restless bodies of night crews, bunks, lockers, and short-time calendars. He passed close by a bunker. A strong smell of weed and urine came from inside the piled sand bags. Voices resumed once he was past. He stepped into the low walled urinal that stood fifty meters from his own quarters. The urinal tubes slanted up like mortars from the stained concrete base. He could see in the distance a C-47 circle carelessly, its Vulcan guns churning out long bursts of fire that seemed to almost float down to the earth. He aimed at a half-shredded cigar butt stuck to the tube's screening. Give 'em hell, thought Warren, stepping back quickly to keep the overflowing urine from spilling on his boots. Flies infested the area. They crawled on the screening and tubes, buzzing loudly when disturbed.

He stopped at the beer tent, purchased twelve cans from the girl who worked behind the counter, and ducked out the front flap. No one was nearby. Only at the far end of the quadrangle could he make out the figures of a sandbag detail moving with an exaggerated slowness. He stepped quietly into his tent. He could see nothing for a moment and waited till his eyes could adjust. He did not want to risk stumbling against anything and waking the sleepers. He moved to the refrigerator and placed eleven cans in noiselessly, feeling around the top for the opener. He felt the wooden handle and a piece of paper through which the metal was pushed. He brought it back to the light of the entrance and read.

couldn't wait for you
Smoker got the run to
Saigon. had room for
me and Tony.
Billy

He went back into the semidarkness and sat at the edge of his bunk. He felt betrayed. No one had even thanked him for working over his twelve-hour shift. It had been so long since he had been out of the hospital area. Jesus Christ! He spoke out loud, then searched the squat room to see if there was anyone asleep whom he might disturb. The room was empty. He cursed and pouted over his beer. He thought of his friends riding to Saigon. He pictured them in the bars laughing, drinking, retiring to the rank cubicles where young Vietnamese women waited. He reached into his shirt pocket for a familiar pack of cigarettes and lit one. Warren felt a building frustration. He undressed slowly, pulling off his boots and running the sweaty socks over his swollen feet. He toed his way into his rubber shower clogs. Their worn shape felt cool and familiar. He moved to the corner of the tent and pushed his hand into the dank folds of the canvas. He found the plastic cigarette pack and carried it to the front of the hootch. He looked over the quadrangle and saw the distant sandbag detail. Three kilometers above the eastern perimeter, he could see a flying crane carrying the wreckage of a Huie. It hung beneath the giant mantis shape like a crushed insect. Warren slid a joint out of the pack and lit it with his cigarette. Closing the plastic case, he moved again to the corner, taking deep drags of the joint. He stuffed the pack into the folds. He exhaled when he reached his locker and pulled out his toilet gear. He wrapped a large towel around his waist and positioned himself again at the front entrance. He did not want to risk being caught smoking dope and losing his chance for an R&R. He finished quickly, taking in the smoke in large amounts and holding it only briefly. He took another can of beer from the refrigerator, and headed for the shower room. The temperature was climbing. He could feel the combination of the alcohol and the drug reaching his head and lifting him a little beyond the heat, the sweat that rolled down his body, and the dust that clung to the dampness on his legs and feet. He stepped into the shade of the building and laid his towel and kit on a bench. He stood directly under a nozzle and turned the tap. A trickle of water fell. He moved down the whole row of nozzles turning the taps each time. His hand moved roughly against his chest where a small amount of water had fallen. So many months, he thought, the same routine, the same fucking shit. He rubbed harder, smearing the grime of his hands into the hair of his chest. He felt giddy now and stopped to smell his hands. There was a light odor of marijuana, but the strongest smell was of chemicals. He remembered the dead woman and again in his mind she assumed the look of a young girl. Warren closed his eyes. She took on erotic postures in his mind. He held his left hand to his mouth in a fist and pushed. He felt the wrong images were flashing and a scream was working its way up his throat. The taste of blood washed into his mouth and he dropped his hand quickly and opened his eyes. The cut he had opened at the door of the morgue had started bleeding again. He smeared it against his belly and chest, then down over his genitals. He caught himself in a giggle and quieted it. He wanted a shower badly and wrapped himself up to go and search for water. The drugs had reached their full power and he felt beyond his high a sense of both belligerence and adventure. He headed for the noncommissioned officers' and officers' showers in turn, but found that they too were run dry. He turned back toward his hootch in a rage, feeling the need for another beer. He stopped again at the urinals. The cement felt slippery. Warren searched the sky for activity and stepped back too late. He laughed at his own clumsiness and leaned against the entrance post. The urine felt sticky between his toes. To his right he could see a group of mammasans hanging out wash and he remembered the water tower and outlets at the far end of the quadrangle. He stopped for another beer and headed for the clothes-washing area. The sandbag detail had moved on. He passed their shovels and the pile of sand. The women chatted beneath the lines nearby. He cut between a bunker and a storage building. The area was deserted. He ducked through the low entrance of the washing hut and went to the first faucet. Nothing came. He walked to the far end and found a steel medical supply container filled with clear water. Warren stepped out of his clogs and unhitched his towel. He knelt beside the large container and splashed some water over his face and body. It felt cool to him and he drank a handful. He wet himself thoroughly and stood to soap. The air was close beneath the canvas and he moved to the wall, where a space had been left between the louvered boards and the two-by-fours that held up the low canvas roof.

Outside, several yards away, a woman was washing clothes directly beneath the faucet at the bottom of the tower. She moved each piece that she finished scrubbing to another container, then bent over the first again. She would rub the fabric against itself then plunge it into the soapy water. Her blouse was wet and transparent. She was unaware of Warren's presence and moved freely. Warren became excited. The woman's movements stirred a sharp memory and heightened his appetites. He remembered the girl at the whorehouse, months before the quick upsurge of fighting and the Tet offensive had put the town off limits. He had seen her at this very motion and it had aroused him then too. He started to lather his body and matched his movements with hers. His mind flashed with pictures of the girl over him. He recalled how he had wanted to touch her, to feel her body. He tried to remember the feel of a woman's body. The woman stood and walked closer to the hootch. She was only feet away. She bent to sort a small pile of clothes. Warren could see her body plainly through her blouse. He remembered the woman that morning, how close he had been to her nakedness also, how he had bent over her. The pictures of the women converged and Warren confused them in the figure crouched a few feet away. He was intensely excited, and worked his hands over himself. He came just as she stood and turned back to the containers of clothes. She did not see or hear him and resumed her work. He watched for a few minutes more, then finished washing himself with cool water.

By the time he reached his hootch he was again covered with sweat, but he lay on the silkiness of his poncho liner with little thought of the heat. He drank half of another beer and fell asleep thinking of the girl, promising himself he would make it back to Andy's. He would satisfy himself there if it took a month's pay.

Warren sucked at his beer, while staring down at the scene below. He was waiting for the plump prostitute he had chosen to appear with another cold beer. A warm late afternoon breeze blew against his nakedness carrying a scent of mud, dung, and buffalo off the nearby paddies. He studied his chest, puffing it out and sucking in his belly, watching the sweat roll down through the dark hairs, admiring his own slender waist. He looked out to his left where loud voices lifted from an Army recreational facility and washed over the clump of tin-roofed shacks that surrounded the compound. Soldiers lounged with drinks in their hands near the swimming pool. At the compound's edge he could see a football arch above the fence line and fall. The unseen players shouted game chatter, their voices higher than the market sounds of the people below.

It was Warren's first day off in weeks and his first time away from the hospital and base in months. He had planned it all for so long, and had even passed up an opportunity to go into Saigon that day. For what?, he thought bitterly. He had taken a taxi straight from the gate to Andy's club in Tam Hiep. He had brought enough money to buy the girl outright, and he was disappointed when he found the house half blown away, its pastel walls covered with splattered mud from small craters in the paddy and large-caliber bullet holes. Behind the house he found the steam bath section completely demolished, the twisted pipes jutted in vague directions like snapped stalks of dry weed that had lost the instinct to climb toward light. In the blackened shell of the back building Warren found a shattered washbasin and wondered if the girl had been killed. He felt cheated by this turn of events. A mixture of displeasure and need had directed him first toward the American compound and later to the nearby massage parlor.

He had spent his day sunning himself, drinking, and staring at the bar girl who served drinks at the concession near the edge of the pool. He had watched the shadows of a tamarind stretch its coolness till it completely enveloped him. Through the dense symmetry he could see the few remaining pale yellow flowers that hung from isolated branches. He had passed below the tree on his way out, and pulled down one of the last blossoms. It lay in his large hand, crushed by his effort, the red veins bright against the pale yellow. The dark pods of the tamarind already dominated its feathery leaves.

He had walked to the nearby parlor where he now watched from its windows, finishing his warm beer, idly stroking the hair of his chest. Beyond the compound fence, topped with barbed wire and jagged glass that predated the Americans, were the hovels of a few families who worked within the facility and a string of whorehouses. The hootches ran close beneath the window from which Warren watched, and he could see figures move behind the ragged cloth that hung as a curtain in the window of the nearest hut. Beyond these lean wrecks of tin and scrap wood, the rice paddies ran toward the Dong Nai. In the distance Warren could see the dark mangroves along the river's banks and the sun's late rays urging all the wetness of the surrounding land into a glitter. It dressed the mud-colored water in a refreshing camouflage.

He shifted his attention to the house below. Chickens scratched in the dirt yard. A hand pushed back the rag curtains. A girl threw some water out the window. Warren could see into the house. She paused briefly and stared back up at him. More water splashed out, scattering the chickens, and the rags fell into place.

He heard his whore coming up the stairs, humming a tune and tinkling a glass against a bottle. He returned to the narrow cot and sat on its edge as she entered. She smiled and placed her tray on the small night table. A foil-wrapped condom lay beside the glass on a hand towel. The girl lit a wick lamp and turned it very low.

She pulled Warren onto his stomach and began to rub him down. The alcohol had dulled his senses and desires. He lay wondering why he had come to this place. The girl worked in silence with curt instructions, slapping and cuffing his flesh, working his back into awareness. By the time she turned him over the room had darkened. In the distance they heard an M-16 fire. Both looked to the window when a flare went up. They moved to the casement together, looking across the lighted fields. In the far west only a sliver of light remained. Above, the brilliant phosphorous lamps floated earthward to the rice fields. Warren saw the dark line of mangrove again as the flares fell their last hundred feet.

He turned to the girl and studied her in the phosphorous glow. He put his hand on her breast and felt for the nipple. She muttered and slapped his hand. Light danced on the rag curtains below them. A figure crossed behind the dim veil. Warren thought of the young girl at Andy's. He felt again a sense of having been cheated. A single shot sounded dully from the direction of the river.

The girl led him back to the bed. She played with his genitals and unwrapped the prophylactic. Neither of them spoke. He motioned to her to use her mouth and promised an extra payment. She bent over him as he leaned his back against the wall. Somewhere outside a baby started to cry. Warren could hear voices. They talked in loud whispers. Across the room the wick flickered. A spider lowered itself near the lamp, its shadow grotesque and enormous on the opposite wall. The girl fidgeted with him busily. He felt only a dull throb.

She wiped her mouth on the towel, and drank from his beer. He grabbed the bottle and pushed her away roughly. Voices from the alley, the girls shuffling clogs across the floor, the child's cries— sounds met and disassembled. He understood nothing. The girl left the room, pulling a sheet across the entrance. Warren wiped the bottle across his chest. The crying continued. It was muffled, like an animal at a great distance, its voice rising.

Extract

by Wayne Karlin

A red circle glowing just in front of his consciousness. He fought to hold on to sleep, knowing he would lose. The red circle grew larger and brighter, and he resentfully felt the sleep leave him. He blinked his eyes open and stared into the Duty NCO's flashlight. "Get that thing outta my eyes," he said sharply.

The light lowered slightly. "Come on, Martin. It's time," the Duty was whispering. His voice was low with pre-dawn reverence.

Joshua hunched under the rough green blanket, feeling some sand that had been caught in the sag of his cot grate into his spine. He squinted at the Duty, making him into a dark train locomotive silhouette, his flashlight the menacing headlamp. He saw something white extend from the dark form and he opened his eyes. It was a clipboard. "Initial it, Martin," the Duty said, "I ain't got all morning." Joshua took the offered pencil stub and initialed the pisscall sheet next to his typed name and the time. The Duty, absolved of any more responsibility, nodded at him and left the hootch.

Joshua sat up. He saw Sam standing at the other end of the hootch, his naked black bulk lit in flickering red by a candle. He watched as Sam pulled on a flight suit and took his messgear down from a nail, clanging it, oblivious to the sleeping shapes lumped on their cots. Joshua glanced around at the interior of the hootch. Ten evenly lined cots under bare tin walls. It looked like a skid row transient hotel that had somehow trapped and held on to its guests. A place for old men with spit on their shirts, he thought angrily.

Sam finished dressing and walked over to his cot. "You gonna get some chow?" he asked.

"Naw, don't guess so, Sam. I'll meet you at the flight line."

"Your stomach, man." Sam squinted at him. "You sure you're okay?"

"Yeah. Fine. Just I had some kinda dream and it's still hangin' on me, you know."

"Yeah?" Sam shifted on his feet and his metal cup clanged against the metal tray he was dangling from a piece of hanger wire. "Alright. Catch you later," he said, then hesitated. "Listen, 'tenant DeLeon said to be sure and get .50's for the bird, 'count of we're going North. Don't let the armory stick you with no M-60's."

"Sure thing," Joshua said, and Sam turned and left.

Joshua lit his candle and sat naked on the edge of his cot. He rubbed his face repeatedly and looked around him. After a while he got up and started to get dressed.

The sun had just started to rise from the South China Sea. It barely lit the flight line, just turning the night time black into grey and not yet bothering with colors.

Joshua had finished struggling the heavy .50's into the armatures set behind the open front ports of the sea-knight. He enjoyed the feel of heavy metal slipping well into position, but hated to feel the sweat start and spoil the long cooling of the night.

Now he stood in front of the operations tent, a hot metal cup filled with black coffee stinging the small cuts in his greased hands. He stood and looked out at the helicopter mat. The dawn light made the CH46 helicopters look like a neatly lined platoon of sinister grasshoppers. Ready to jump on command. Wonder if they know who commands. Or care. Joshua sipped at his coffee and let his mind wander with the sun's rise.

He looked at Sam, up on the green back of number seven, peering at the engine. Looking head on at the helicopter, he could see the barrels of both guns sticking out of the side ports, perpendicular to the plane.

The pilots began spilling out of the briefing tent. Joshua gulped down the rest of his coffee and ran out to the helicopter. Sam climbed down and stood beside him, wiping his hands on his hips. They stood together and waited for the officers to come out to the helicopter. Lieutenant DeLeon was walking slightly in front, his flight bag slapping against his legs. The co-pilot, a new second "looey" named Anderson, scurried chubbily to keep up with him.

First Lieutenant DeLeon walked behind his bushy handlebar moustache. He had cultivated it carefully over the last few months, and couldn't help feeling that it completed himself nicely. He was a tall, dark man and his zipped-up flight suit accentuated his leanness. He pictured himself as he walked; a montage of the moustache, the helicopter waiting for him, and the crewmen standing by it.

The officers arrived at the helicopter, and Anderson climbed up to begin the pre-flight. DeLeon briefed Sam and Joshua.

"Sir, you said somethin' 'bout going to the 'Z again? Yesterday." Sam asked.

" 'Fraid so, Corporal Deeson," DeLeon said, smiling. "We have an extract up there. A recon team."

Joshua was staring at the Lieutenant's face. The sickness he had been feeling all morning was bursting in strong bubbles in his stomach. The face seemed to him to be strangely translucent, almost gaseous behind the solid moustache, as if only the anchors of hair were keeping it from being blown away. The lips in the face were moving, rubbery and androidlike, and Joshua watched them in sick fascination, not hearing the words coming out. He was sweating heavily, the sweat spreading unevenly over his skin, like a dirty film of soot. We're dropping some passengers at Phu Bai, then continuing to Dong Ha, DeLeon was saying, his voice distant. They look like nylon, those moustache hairs, Joshua thought, like each nylon hair was glued separately into each gaping little pore above the officer's lip. He could feel the soft weight of the nylon hairs encircling his skin and snaring him, weblike, to the lieutenant. He felt lifeless, a small particle carried helplessly on DeLeon's words. He saw the lips moving and noticed dully the ridge of yellow cottage-cheesish material between the gums and the teeth. More teeth showed suddenly as DeLeon grinned. We'll be passing over some of those fucking villages, he was saying, and if we get any of that fire we've been getting, don't wait for my permission to return it. Do it. Waste them. Don't worry 'bout women and kids. Littledinks growintobig cong. Use those fifties.

Must come with pubic hair, then, this cong.

Joshua watched as DeLeon climbed into the helicopter. He still felt detached from the entire scene, somewhere beneath it. "Josh," Sam said, bringing him back, "still here?"

"Yeah."

"No shit. Let's get some fresh air, man."

The barrel of the machine gun bisected a piece of blue sky and hung threateningly over the landscape. Joshua looked out over it. The country north of Hue had broken out in thousands of Vietnamese grave-mounds. They flew over the stretches of sand and graves, then changed course farther inland, where the country became shining brown mirrors of paddyland. The helicopter's shadow covered then uncovered some cone-hatted farmers. They didn't look up.

A village was coming up, green cauliflower trees and brown huts making an island in the mirror-expanse of the paddies. Joshua leaned forward to get a closer look, as DeLeon brought the helicopter to tree-top level. The maneuver was supposed to confuse oriental snipers, the technological roar of the engine startling them, and the helicopter gone before they could get it together.

The helicopter was moving fast, maybe 100 knots, yet Joshua's gaze fell and wrapped itself in the doorway of one hut. For a suspended moment he could see the doorway as clear and as still as if he were walking up to it on the ground. The brown-yellow thatch of the hut stood out starkly against the green around it, the contrast making it seem more solid and substantial. He felt a sharp twinge of connection with the hut, its solidity filling the hollowness of his sickness. A woman was squatting on her heels in front of the door, absorbed in mixing something in a bowl. Joshua imagined he could see her betel-nut-blackened teeth smiling at the naked child playing next to her in the yellow dirt.

They were passing over the village and the passage tore at him. He felt their transience in that moment. They were just a loud noise and a green flash in the sky, gone too soon to be remarked on. Their loudness was only, after all, a child's cry to be noticed, a child's threat if ignored.

The grasshoppers were scattered all over the ground at Dong Ha. They began circling in, and Joshua opened the breech of the .50 and took the belt out of the gun. He was startled by a sharp blow on the back of his helmet, and turned fast to see Sam glaring at him. The crew-chief swore and threw Joshua's ammunition belt back into position. He nodded at Sam and slammed the breech back down, then cocked the gun, twice. He stayed behind it as they landed. DeLeon's voice was crackling in his ears over the intercom, just hop out and refuel, the crackling said, we're going right out.

They disconnected their gunners' belts and intercom wires, and went out the front hatch. Joshua ran and got the fuel line while Sam opened the tank. He put the hose in the opening and poured gas in. Sam was shaking his head at him. "Sorry I hit you," he yelled over the engine noise. "You should know better than to unload 'fore we touch down here. This ain't Danang."

"Yeah. Sorry, Sam," he said, meaning it, "I don't know where my head's at today." Sam shrugged, then grinned at him. Joshua grinned back, then felt the fuselage of the helicopter jerk up, full, and he stopped the flow of gas. He ran back with the hose, then back to plane, entering and buttoning the hatch up behind him.

Force recon was working squad-size ten-day patrols around the DMZ. It was nerve-wracking, isolated work, and the men were always glad to see the helicopters come for them. They spotted the HU1E gun ship covering the area, first, then heard the slower whop-whop of the sea knight as it came into view. The larger helicopter touched down in the middle of a protective circle of recon-marines, and the circle broke off and began running, orderly, over the downed rear-ramp of the helicopter. The plane took off, fast and without incident.

A sergeant with a five day beard insisted on shaking hands with Joshua and Sam, before settling down on the red-webbing seats. Most of the squad began falling asleep immediately. Joshua glanced at them, then looked back out over his machine gun. He was in time to see a series of quick flashes on the ground.

There was a vibrating bang towards the rear of the helicopter as something hit. The recon men snapped awake, except for the sergeant, who was smiling in his sleep. Joshua felt them staring at him as he swung the gun around and began returning the fire. His tracers curved lazily towards the flashes, bracketing them. He heard Sam open up at a target on his side, and then the ground-fire stopped abruptly. He saw the HU1E diving below them, strafing, then firing a rocket. Right on time, asshole.

Sam motioned to a recon-man to stand by his gun, then ran to the rear. The engine sounded strong and steady. "Nice shooting," said DeLeon's voice in his helmet. "Any damage or casualties back there?"

"Nossir," Sam answered, "Nobody hurt. There's a little hole portside, but nothin' vital I can see. Engine sounds fine." Sam ran easily back to his gun, nodding thanks to the recon-man.

Minutes later, they were at Dong Ha. They dropped off the recon squad and the HU1E, and took off for home. Joshua felt better. His mood had disappeared in the fine feeling of competence from the shooting.

He relaxed, feeling sleepy, methodically, automatically, scanning the country below. He divided the area passing beneath him into segments, then, beginning at the front of the helicopter, would scan each segment in turn. He was almost unaware of what he was doing, the slow lazy routine of watching reducing everything to a comforting technique. The helicopter droned, and he was a lazy, functioning part of the drone.

He shifted his sight to the front of the helicopter, and his complacency left him. Cauliflower trees and a village coming up fast.

He saw it like that: the helicopter suspended in space and the village attached to some moving assembly-line strip of ground that was drawing under the aircraft. For adjustment. It didn't surprise him when he saw a string of tracers flash up from a clump of trees near the village.

"Gunner, didn't you see the fire?" said DeLeon's voice in his helmet. He didn't answer and they were drawing out of range. I'm going around, the voice kept saying, let's take care of those people. He looked at the umbilical cord connecting him to the cockpit. The cord was attaching him heavily to DeLeon, a hair, a thing of flesh making him a functioning part of the pilot. The hollow sick feeling returned and welled in him, spilling from his pores and dirtying him. Martin, the voice in his ears said, you have the first shot. The village drew under the helicopter. There was no firing from below now. Somebody was probably getting hell for opening up on a single helicopter. Getting hell. Getting hell and he was the deliveryman. He pointed the barrel of the machine gun a little below and to the left of the area he wanted to hit. Like training, he thought, dully. There was nobody in front of the doorway now. His fingers touched the butterfly trigger, a butterfly touch. He hesitated. Sam was watching him.

Ben

by George Davis

The street is silent. I feel almost as if I'm floating through the night air with stoppers in my ears. Everything seems far away. I don't want to think about tomorrow.

The African Star sits on the main street, but farther down, in a quieter section behind a small garden. It is owned by three black ex-GI's who got out of the Army and stayed in Bangkok.

The place looks good, better than I thought it would. I go inside. Warm. A lot of laughter comes from upstairs and I can hear a live jazz band playing. I can tell by the sound that they're black. The downstairs room is about half-full. I find a table, sit down, and order a drink. More music and laughter comes from upstairs whenever the door at the top of the stairs is opened. People come in and go straight upstairs. I wish that I was in the mood for a good party. The noise reminds me of the Hollywood Club in Washington, but the downstairs room of the Hollywood is long, while this room is square and darker.

I remember how the guy at the top of the stairs at the Hollywood would take your dollar and stamp your hand so you wouldn't have to pay again no matter how many times you ran in and out. And we used to do a lot of running between there and Chez Maurice next door, and the Bohemian Caverns around the corner on U Street, Ninth and U Street, or Eleventh and U. Damn, I can't remember, and we used to do it almost every Saturday night when I was stationed at Andrews.

A tall bright-skinned black man comes in the African Star with three Thai girls following him. The bartender knows him. They joke. The bartender is a slender Thai man. The three girls perch on three barstools while the two men talk across the bar.

The bartender digs behind the counter and brings up three packs of black market cigarettes. He gives them to the girls and they slip them into their handbags. The girls sit on the stools and talk among themselves while the two men continue talking. Red slacks, blue slacks, mini-skirt with nice little legs spinning and wiggling.

The bar is made of blue mirrors, and there is a long blue mirror along the wall in back of the row of liquor bottles. A blue ball made of octagonal mirrors spins above the bartender's head.

Several GI's sit with their girls eating soul food in the dim room. The door at the top of the stairs opens. Laughter comes down followed by a round, laughing black GI with a cigar in his mouth. "Hey, Nick, my man," he says as his head emerges out of the stairwell.

"Hey, my man," the tall guy says.

"What's happening?" The black man is wearing a silk suit.

"Nothing."

"Nothing? Man, I thought your name was synonymous with what's happening." He slaps the tall guy on the shoulder.

"Shit, not me."

"Three foxes." He looks at the three girls.

"Friends and cousins of friends," the tall guy says.

"Yeah, how about that."

I listen rather mindlessly to their conversation, happy to be hearing familiar tones and familiar rhythms. A young-looking black man sits at the far end of the bar, drinking by himself. He has long well-shaped sideburns. The waitress brings my scotch and water. I give her a dollar, and she gives me change in baht. I watch her small hands counting out the baht on the tabletop.

"Have you heard the band at the Lido?" the tall guy asks. I begin to drink slowly.

"Where're you from, my man?" a voice very close to my ear says.

I look up and see it is the young guy from the far end of the bar. "Washington, D.C." I make a sign for him to sit down.

"Greensboro."

"Close."

"Neighbors. What's happening?"

"Nothing."

"Yeah, I know this shit's a bitch. Army?"

"No, Air Force."

"I'm Army, infantry, Vietnam. What're you, in CD?"

"No, I'm a pilot."

He leans back and takes another look. "Oh, shit, a glory boy. Officer."

I laugh.

"Wilton Smith."

"Ben Williams."

"Yeah, so you an officer?"

"I guess."

We sit and talk for a while. The waitress brings two more drinks. "What do you fly?" he asks after a while, as if he has not let the thought out of his mind.

"F-105's."

"That's nice. Super Thuds," he smiles. He drums his fingers on the table for a moment. "I was going to be an officer, but I had to drop out of college—A & T."

"It's not that much difference."

He laughs. "No, man, there's a world of difference. It's a whole different war down in the mud."

"I'm quitting flying anyway," I say to put myself back on equal footing with him.

"Yeah." He drinks slowly. Then he leans back and drums the table. "I haven't been in combat in twenty-one days," he says, as if to put himself ahead of me again. "I been AWOL twenty-one days. I'm not going back. They don't even know where to find me, and if they wait a few more days, I'll be in Sweden somewhere," he whispers as if he trusts me but does not trust the people who might overhear us. "If you a cop, then you a cop, but I ain't going back. Not alive, I ain't."

"I'm not a cop."

"Well, an officer might be the same thing."

"Shit, man, why would I turn you in?" I say to turn away some of the growing hostility in his manner.

"I don't see why you would go back. They gon' put your ass in jail. The minute you tell them you ain't gon' kill no more of these people they gon' put you in jail."

"I don't feel like running away."

"I want to live, man," there is rage in his voice now. "I want to live. Shit."

"We been running away long enough," I say angrily.

"*You* been running. I ain't been running nowhere. I was born in the shit and I want a chance to live. That's all. I shot a kid, man. I shot a little Vietnamese kid right in the back, man. The night before I left the 'Nam. I was on patrol in a village near Thuc Yen and this little kid came up to me in an alley and asked me did I want a shoeshine. And sometimes they have bombs in those little boxes. So I told him to set his box down and back off, and he turned and ran, and I shot him in the back." His voice cracks and he is silent for a moment. "Then I went up and looked in his little box and do you know what I found?"

"I don't know."

"Shoe polish, man. Not a goddam thing but shoe polish. I went back to base and packed my shit and left. I ain't ever gon' kill no more innocent people, man. And I ain't going to no jail either. I'm still young."

"Okay."

"Not that I'm coming down on you. I thought about the shit too, but if you go to jail, you just as well be dead. Just as well call yourself a dead martyr, and we got enough of them. Don't go to no jail on a bullshit tip, man. I been in jail. You die in jail. There are some Buddhists on Rama One Road near Wat Suthat who can help you get to Japan, and up through Russia to Sweden." He stands up. "I'm going to go back to my hotel," he says. "I didn't mean to come down on you so hard." He laughs. "Ain't your fault that you an officer."

"Good luck," I say as he goes out. I sit down and think about all the black men who have been hitting the road, catching trains. Then I think about all the black men in prisons or on Southern prison farms. I try and weigh one group against another as I pay my check and go out the door.

I go back through the late night streets of Bangkok. I stop at a small all-night coffee shop in the Loom Hotel. I sip the coffee slowly, and think. Then I catch a cab back to our hotel. Damg is asleep when I get there. I turn on the small lamp on the dresser. She is small and beautiful in the dim light. I go into the bathroom and write a note by the small night light above the mirror. Then I pack my things, leave the note and a hundred dollars on the dresser, go out into the hallway and pull the door closed behind me.

The Rabbi

by Barney Currer

Even Sergeant Coates, who had originated the nickname, was not really sure why Lieutenant Rowan was staying in Vietnam. "Must be the money," he would say sometimes. "Goddam Rabbi, I ain't never seen him spend a red cent on anything he didn't have to, and officers make damn good money over here, with no taxes. Probably hates going back to the World and having Uncle Sam dipping into his pockets again." Other times it would be the opposite tack, "That Rabbi's a foxy dude. You watch, though. One of these days we're gonna discover he's been shacked up with the sweetest little slanteye in Saigon, just keeping it quiet. Look, nobody's that straightarrow unless he's got something to hide."

Similar conclusions, evolved on a somewhat more sophisticated level, were what capped the speculations of each of the seven captains who had commanded the Saigon Military Police Detachment (Provisional), and Lieutenant Abe Rowan, over the past twenty-five months. You did not extend your year's tour in Vietnam for no reason; those who did, and the reasons they gave for doing so, followed a predictable pattern. Most would stay over a few months in return for a five-month-early discharge. The rest extended for Combat Zone Pay, or because they were living with Vietnamese women the Army would not let return with them.

Sergeant Coates was your textbook example. He had chosen the Army over jail after a knifing in Louisiana; volunteered for Vietnam after his initial MP training at Fort McClellan; settled himself Downtown with the Saigon Detachment and was now living, supposedly in secret, with a brown-skinned fifteen-year-old who, he claimed, was expecting his first child. He was twenty-two and already head of Rowan's platoon; there was nothing for him at home but a police record.

Well enough, Coates was a man you could figure out. But then that only made Rowan's behavior more perplexing. It was also a bit irritating. There were plenty of opportunities open to you as an MP. Downtown—good reasons for staying on—but Rowan had availed himself of none of them. He did not drink, or buy stereos with his ration card, or work the black market, and while it was true he had saved a great deal of money, his attitude made it obvious that this was a mere by-product, rather than the purpose of his long stay.

Having exhausted all the obvious possibilities, you would turn up his little white card to see if maybe he were Career Material, working under the shadow of his Efficiency Report. Again, no. Your Career Man had his eye on making some rank; Rowan, who could have made captain had he put in a twelve-month extension, seemed content to extend only four months at a time, and remain a first john. There were other things, too. He was scrupulous and patient, but he did not know how to get along with the men. His celibacy, for instance; the men resented it. With his rank and position, he could have his pick of the girls on Tu Do Street; yet Rowan had not been with so much as an occasional girl since his arrival. Sure, an officer had to remain somewhat aloof, but then again, the men didn't go for plaster saints. They liked to have their fun and they liked to think the lieutenant would horse around occasionally, too. That sort of thing meant a lot to them. But Rowan did not seem to realize, and his platoon had taken to calling him "The Rabbi" behind his back.

No, Rowan was not of the Army mold; even his background did not fit. Your Regular Army officer was, typically a no-nonsense, brass tacks sort of fellow. He had taken management or engineering in school or, if he didn't go to college, had married early and had a family to support. Rowan, on the other hand, was a Dartmouth man with an English lit background, no family, and, beyond an extraordinary competence, no apparent interest in the Army. *His* idea of a good time was learning Vietnamese. He seemed a natural college professor—his background, his interest in language, his patience—and you had to wonder what the hell it was that was keeping him here.

Abe Rowan arrived in Vietnam half a month after the 1968

Spring-Summer Offensive, a fledgling officer suddenly ordered overseas after a rash of MP casualties. The lieutenant whom he replaced had been killed in the street fighting in front of the American Embassy. Saigon, then, was an arena of distrust and adrenalin, where a loud backfire was enough to jerk heads a block away with apprehension. He lived in a hotel Downtown and worked in the barricaded MP headquarters by the docks. He memorized the city map, nervously following the daily movement of red trouble-spot pins. He set up patrols and checkpoints religiously, made his rounds in the gunjeep four and five times a day. His first commander lost his foot when his command vehicle was booby-trapped. In the three weeks before the replacement arrived, Abe did not sleep more than two hours at a time. Then, after four months, when hostilities began to wane and curfew receded, he found he had come to know Saigon-Cholon more intimately than he had ever known person, place, or thing in his life.

Suddenly, almost overnight, the tension seemed to fall from the city. Morning intelligence reports ceased to be two-paragraph horror stories; AWOL's and off-limits troops were being spotted in places they would not have dared venture two weeks before. The nightly violence on the blotter report—traffic accidents, stabbings, drunken disorders—seemed, in a strange way, comforting after months of unexplained fires and street bombings.

In accordance with unwritten Army doctrine, the stiff checks and routines set up in crisis were never officially rescinded in periods of calm, but merely allowed to atrophy, through a general laxness, to an acceptable level. The tiresome business of checking credentials of the thousands of Vietnamese who streamed into Saigon daily was left to the local police, and long, involved driving beats were shortcutted to include only those areas in close proximity to the GI bars. New replacements entering the Detachment would learn the shortcuts from their predecessors and abbreviate them still further; the officers, in turn, inspected less, and each successive Detachment commander spent an increasing amount of time on the rooftop lounges of the Rex and Brinks Hotel BOQ's, where he was reasonably available in case of trouble.

Abe Rowan was the sole exception. In October he was making the same elaborate rounds he had drawn up for himself in June, stopping off at checkpoints he was well aware his subordinates were not visiting regularly. Unless he felt a neglected checkpoint was vital to central security he would not send a report down to Coates for action; it was just as well, at most of these places, that the troops did not come around more often than they had to, for few besides Lieutenant Rowan would be tolerated.

Abe had survived Tet and felt, somehow, as though he had inherited the entire city and its secrets. Avenues and buildings he had once past at the risk of his life he could now visit, investigate, with impunity. He knew the face of the city as he did his own; the day was his mirror, time for him to admire the strong features and worry over the blemishes, the slow rectification of which provided him with a sense of time that was lacking in the circular days and the unchanging Asian climate.

Early mornings were most pleasant. He would get up easily at five o'clock and tour the city between six and nine, when the temperate night still crouched in the blue shadows and the thousands of cackling motorbikes had not yet spread their glaze of half-burned gas through the boulevards. He would make the drive out along Duong Cong-Ly between six and seven; earlier than six, darkness masked the buildings, after seven the boulevard sprouted the angriest and most impossible traffic in Saigon, and he would have to battle his driver to keep him from ramrodding the jeep through crowds.

At six, too, Abe could tolerate his driver's daily comment on the state of Duong Cong-Ly and its attendant French buildings: "Sure musta been some place before the gooks got ahold of it." The buildings seemed stoic and white in the mornings, mortified spectators at their own decay. Their lean, flat sides desolved into a patchwork of tin-roofed shops and lean-tos set angular from the buildings to the old, broad sidewalk, leaving only a thin strip of concrete available for pedestrian traffic. Spider-legged Vietnamese men nodded in the seats of their pedicabs, waiting for the crowds to flush with the first heat of day.

Downtown had many faces: the Rex Hotel BOQ with its perimeter of whitewashed cement-filled oildrums and the sullen MP in the concrete kiosk; the Continental Hotel with its open air first floor, a hush of darkness and calm; the grey stone opera house, elaborately carved, empty; the Vietnamese Parliament, scrubbed and white and curved at the entrance like a mosque. In the park square facing the parliament, bordered by tamarind trees strangling in pavement and smoke, a statue of two beaten steel soldiers were charging—apparently—the front door of the parliament. Abe had taken pictures before, but the statue was too large and too distant from the building to convey the irony implicit in their positioning.

Centertown was where Duong Cong-Ly took a jag around the Central Marketplace, a huge circular semi-structure made tentlike with individual additions of plywood stalls and pressed beer-can tin. In the mornings Abe liked to walk through parts of it, before it began to fester with people and the ubiquitous smell of fish and warm urine. The first time he had passed through he had forgotten to remove his pistol. The shopowners, bird-limbed women with dark eyes like laboratory mice, had watched after him with smothered horror. Thinking back on it, he began to understand, and never went armed again, although two of them in particular never forgot, and would bury themselves in their work when he was around.

Uptown was Tan Son Nhut Airbase, a jumble of prefab-and-concrete military structures laced with the dull wood jungle of peasant shacks, all circled, loosely, with barbwire. Tan Son Nhut was not considered an American military establishment and so those who chose to live on the premises could not be excluded. There was a stucco Catholic church and a graveyard, overgrown with weeds and surrounded five times with barbwire, as though to prohibit the escape of a ghostly insurgent. The arena had once been a village, but with the influx of Americans the shacks had come to be inhabited mainly by camp followers and petty capitalists selling trinkets and cheap, handmade jackets. The Vietnamese Air Force Officer's Club, a low, French structure circumscribed by a decaying wall, was where the girls were. Once in ignorance Abe had gone in to inspect. It was dark and close and smelled like cling peaches packed in heavy syrup. A girl with a blanched, designed face like a kabuki mask had literally shoved him into a seat and began to work her fingers into his trousers. When he got up abruptly and strode to the door, she had screamed the most vile obscenities after him, and for the rest of the day he found himself unable to think.

He began to speak a halting Vietnamese. At night he would use his roommate's tape recorder, blushing at the quacking which sounded more like an arrogant parody than an earnest attempt at the language. It was over a month before he would allow himself to say good morning to the mammasan who came in to shine the officers' boots. For all his defective squawking, she understood him, and was so delighted she replied to his good morning three times.

When he had perfected his handful of stock text phrases, he took to the streets; hearing him, they would smile with pleasure, taking pains to reply in short, banal sentences they thought he would understand. Within a second month he had become surprisingly adept at the smallest of small talk: the weather, one's health, inquiries after relatives. He had heard that Vietnamese officers, proud of their English, resented being spoken to in Vietnamese; the rest, however, reacted to his poor phrases so enthusiastically, he began to feel he had never, not until now, really known the Vietnamese. When he had ten months in, he impulsively filed for an extension of four more.

After half a year of relative calm, there was much that was new in the city; Abe began to feel regularly that he was "just now" coming to know Saigon well. He enjoyed the afternoons when the clean, beautiful Catholic children of the officers and government officials were released from their school, flooding the streets at four in their white uniforms. On Sundays the older daughters of the same officials would dress in pastel *ao dais* and stroll in the parks or the zoo, watching abstractly for the scarce young men who were not in uniform and seemed of their class.

Other events happened with military regularity. The first Monday of the month, the armored busses would roll up to the Vietnamese Naval Training Center to drop their complement of new recruits, rural youths, nervous and overdressed in pipestem trousers and Hawaiian print shirts. The next day he would see them lined along the tab of grass by the waterfront, dismally learning saluting and facing movements. He began visiting on these afternoons with Commander Thong, who directed the training and who told him about the new recruits in impeccable, if unidiomatic, English.

"It has been a fortunate occurence for us that this month we have received a great body of our recruits from the Mekong Delta," he said one muggy July afternoon. "You may understand that these men are more knowledgeable in river operations since they have grown up in families who are dependant upon the river for their livings. Did you know that it is not difficult for us"—he indicated himself, a Vietnamese—"to tell from which location our men have been drawn? It is as you Americans can know whether a man is from your north or your south. But understandably you are unable to know the people of the regions in a single year."

In the early days of training, when all the recruits were bunched together on the spit of grass, the two of them would stand at the overlooking window, and Commander Thong would point out differences in size, hair, and features that were obvious even from 100 yards away. When he was sure that Abe was not showing mere indulgent interest, Commander Thong displayed a series of photographs he had taken of men he believed to be typical of the various regions. "It had once been my plan to explain the photographs to my American advisors, but they are busy men and I am not sure they would want to spend time studying photographs. It would probably not help, I have decided; there are many northerners here who are loyal to our government, and my photographs might give the wrong impression."

There were, of course, differences Commander Thong appeared to see which were not apparent to Abe. Generally, northerners were taller, stronger; southerners had wide faces and lips; Delta dwellers had large feet and hands. But distinctions blurred with the mixing of races: Abe could not yet tell a tall southerner with a trace of Cambodian blood from a northerner of pure Vietnamese stock.

By the time his second four-month extension was approved, Abe had come to recognize many of the broad distinctions, could spot them in faces on the streets. Certain strains were so very obvious that it seemed almost unbelievable he had spent over a year in the city and had not recognized them beyond being individual tiles in a brown, anonymous mosaic. Chinese, Cambodians, high country, Delta—faces seemed to leap out at him, the way, as a child, the features of the American Indian had become recognizable after he had gotten to know one.

He brought his new talent, after a delay of months, to the bars he inspected. He visited the bars once a week—Sergeant Coates took care of the other six days—before noon when business was slight, and occasionally on the last three days of the month when there was no business at all. Three strips in town bore the most watching: Tu Do Street, where bar tea cost four and eight hundred piastres a thimbleful and was considered—falsely—to be an officers' hangout; Plantation Road outside of Tan Son Nhut, frequented by airmen and MP's; the string down the block from the Saigon Finance and Disbursing Office, where everybody went after getting back pay. They were all as predictable as barracks, stucco and wrought tin on the outside, plastic and plywood inside, with names like "Playboy Club" and "Sweetheart Bar" and "San Francisco." Before ten the doors would open but no business was expected. Vietnamese children in shorts and porkpie hats worked the floors with their soft straw brooms and the girls would sit together in booths playing fantan and poker, legs drawn up like frogs. He would walk in, look about, leave. On rare occasions he stayed longer. The girls would give him the Regulation Hustle, a concession to the mammasan who ran the place and who invariably looked like Sir John Tenniel's drawings of the Queen of Hearts, but they all knew him and did not try hard. Some of them, he knew, resented him, angry at what they took to be his holier-than-thou attitude. In one of the MP bars on Plantation Road one of them had called him Rabbi, which in Vietnamese came out sounding like "Rav-eye." But they were all hybrids, phony American coeds who talked through their noses, with a traditionally American respect for fast, easy money.

The afternoon before payday, when the Saigon Finance and Disbursal Office was closed, and the girls lolled in front of the bars in a bored display, Abe visited the strip. Many of them called and waved. He waved back, attempted to smile, walking directly to the end of the block, where the first of the bars was.

She had seen him coming and, to her inexperienced eyes it undoubtedly appeared the lieutenant had waved away every other girl on the block. As Abe came up on her, he realized he had never seen her before. Perhaps she was sixteen, a newcomer, apprehensive over the sudden fall-off in business, afraid she would be cut if she did not bring in a couple of drinks. As he approached her, she seemed, almost literally, to swell with pleasure. Her black hair cut and fastidiously set, her eyes made up with whites and glosses, she seemed a little perfumed raccoon. He hesitated, then walked inside. She attempted to lead him; the few girls seated at the naugahyde couch in the corner saw who she had come up with, and smiled.

Pulling his arm gently away from her (he did not like making a big thing of his reluctance with bar girls), he caused her to look up at him. She giggled and urged him, and beneath her eyeshade and lipstick he saw the features of a northern girl. He was so surprised that he sat next to her in the booth, scrutinizing her face. She was as classic as any of Commander Thong's pictures.

"Where you fum, loo-tanan?" She began the series of questions that played from the piano-roll in every Saigon bargirl's tongue.

"Saigon," He said. "I be MP. Where you come from?"

"Ah," she said, coiling her thoughts. She was so new she had not realized the significance of the crossed pistols on his collar; now she was distant and agitated, and switched her feet under the table. "I come—Vung Tau. I have father French, mother she Chinee."

Coates had told him that every girl would have you believe she was either a little French or a little Chinese. This time it was both. He smiled.

"I say you have mother Vietnamese, father Vietnamese. You be born—Hanoi."

The girl's eyes grew round. For a moment she seemed to veer between indignation and amazement. "Ah, nevah happen," she said quickly. "My father be *French*. I no *xau*."

"I believe you do too *xau*," Abe said slowly. "I show: you have north Vietnamese eye, north Vietnamese nose, you be"—he gestured with his palm, indicating tallness—"you be from Hanoi."

She looked at him, clouded with distrust and surprise at his knowledge.

"I know. I can speak Vietnamese if you like," he said in Vietnamese.

She began to jabber fearfully.

"I can speak some Vietnamese only," he said in Vietnamese. "You may speak slowly, please."

"I be good. I no VC. For sure, no VC," she said quietly, earnestly in English.

It was funny, he thought. Here was a girl who would be making her money from being with Americans until the Americans left and the bars closed. But, like the rest, she was comforted by a feeling of her own anonymity, that however Americans would talk or sleep with her, they would never know her mind, her special secrets, and she could keep the lot of them at an exquisite, Asian distance, asking them where they came from and what their names were. Your privacy was remarkably easy to come by.

"I know you no VC" he said, kindly as he could manage. "No sweat. We be friends."

"You have girlfren here Vietnam?" she asked timidly. Back to the classic line, the security of the piano roll.

"Yes," he lied, to cut it off.

"You . . . buy me tea?" she whispered.

"No. I no buy tea," he said and began to get up. Dutifully, she clutched at his arm, gabbling after him. "May your days be pleasant and rewarding," he said in Vietnamese, and left.

Captain Arthur S. Hovey, Abe's seventh, and last, commander, was an overweight, uncomfortable-looking man who had assigned himself the task of Knowing His Lieutenant, and would not be swayed from his chosen course. By now the conflict was being scaled down in earnest and adequate MP replacements, like replacements everywhere, were getting harder to come by. In his first month, acting on a history of blotter reports, Hovey actually did trim back the routing area of the Detachment, reassigning almost half of Abe's old route to the two new platoon leaders, Subbs and McIrwin, and eliminating about a quarter of the remaining area. There was little Abe could do about it; his jeep driver, who had previously spent twice as long on his beat as anyone else in the motor pool, began making thinly veiled threats that if the lieutenant insisted on visiting the parts of his beat which had been eliminated, or redesignated, Captain Hovey would be informed. Captain Hoevy, in turn, had alluded to the fact that if Abe's next request for extension be approved, it was incumbent upon him to carry out the directions of his commander.

The new, abbreviated route was a shortcut to the headquarters paperwork, which seemed to expand neatly to fill out the afternoon. He would sleep in mornings until half-past seven, be on the road at eight and still be back at his desk before noon where an armful of paper was invariably stacked in the center, awaiting action. Hovey would ask him out to lunches and shopping, and for a while his paperwork provided a ready excuse until one day when the sight of dozens of smudged, ill-typed routing forms left him nearly physically ill, and he went Downtown to empty out his mind.

Captain Hovey wanted to buy some of the marginally authentic

Vietnamese prints and paintings that were sold on long boards in the alleys between the bars on Tu Do Street. "You know a lot about art, Abe," he had said. "I want you to help me pick out something Helen would like." When he arrived at the stalls, however, he was attracted to a nude figure with an oriental face and an American body, painted with Day-Glow paint on black felt, and bought it without hesitation.

"I'm sure she'll love it," Abe said wisely.

"Why don't you buy something," Hovey said, gesturing to a row of Day-Glow nudes and tigers. "You're gonna want to have some souvenir of the 'Nam."

"I, ah, don't really see anything that appeals to me," Abe said tentatively. Wrong thing to say.

"I thought you liked the one I got."

"I think your wife will like it, sir. I—I like it, but I don't feel like spending the money."

"Seems like you don't feel like spending your money on much of anything." The grinning, wizened Vietnamese man (Delta region; perhaps a quarter Cambodian) counted change into Hovey's hand and set to sealing the picture in flowered wrapping paper. "You know, Lieutenant Rowan, I've been watching you for some time now." He squinted his eyes, rubbed his chin. Abe could feel him straining at being Psychological. "And there's some things I want to get a few solid answers on."

Abe let out a quiet breath. "Yes, sir?"

"What's . . . what's your *game*?" The captain gave him a piercing look, as though he know himself and was only asking rhetorically.

"My game, sir?"

"Come on, now, Lieutenant. I don't know how your other commanders were, but I don't intend to be coy about this. You've been here *two years* now, and I intend to know why."

"Yes sir," Abe said, and concentrated for a moment. "It's—I guess it's a lot of things, sir."

"Like what?" Abruptly, Hovey changed moods. The change was slightly jarring, like a bad transmission in an old car. "Look. I appreciate your work. The *Army* recognizes the work you've done. What have you gotten, two Army Commendation Medals?"

"Yes, sir. Two."

"That's all fine. Again, not to detract from the Arcom, it's a fine award, but that isn't the reason you're staying here, then, is it?"

"No, sir."

"Then, why?"

"Well, the people."

"*What* people?"

"The Vietnamese people." He had thought of a dozen ways to say it and finally resorted to the lamest-sounding of all: "I like the Vietnamese people."

"Yes?" Captain Hovey expected more.

"And . . . I like Saigon. I enjoy the city."

"For *two years?*"

"Yes, sir," Abe said, his voice warm with anger.

"Well now, that's fine, that's fine, if that's really what it is. Little hard for *me* to believe, of course, but then, I have a wife and children back in the States, which, I'm sure, makes a big difference."

"I'm sure it does," Abe said.

"The reason I ask, though, I think it's fine, your interest in the Vietnamese people, but maybe you're cutting yourself a little short. You could have made captain last year if you'd gone for twelve instead of just four at a time. Now, that's just money out of your pocket."

"I hadn't planned on staying as long as I have. Things just came up and I extended."

"Just the same, you got a little going for you now, and I think you ought to cash in on it. Hear you've taught yourself Vietnamese."

"I know a little."

"Well, why don't you put in a transfer to an Advisory unit. They're crying for Vietnamese-speaking officers. Then you'd really be helping them."

"I don't want to 'help' them, sir."

"But *you just said* . . ."

"I *like* them. I'm *interested* in them. But I don't want to help them in the sense of . . ." his voice trailed off. "It's hard to explain, sir."

"I don't think you really know just what you want, Lieutenant," Hovey said irritably.

It was not a week later that Sergeant Coates' girlfriend was found stabbed to death in her apartment. The second day Coates had missed morning formation they checked for him and found Thanh's mutilated body sprawled over the mattress. No one knew where Coates was. Most likely, he was hiding out in Cholon, among the shanties by the railroad tracks; there was a good possibility that, using the contacts he had made in a year and a half as a Saigon MP he could find friends to get him to Sweden or Canada. What was the touchiest part, however, was that the most rudimentary investigation would reveal that Coates' commanders—Rowan in particular—had full knowledge that the man was living in an unauthorized area, and had never attempted to correct the situation.

"We do have time on our side," Hovey told Abe nervously the morning of the discovery. "It could be four months before this thing gets in full swing. We're checking for relatives and we might luck out and find she had none. Also, since the crime was committed by one of our boys, we can request investigation by a disinterested unit. That'll take time, too. In the meanwhile, we can get you out of here. Sixty days from today you'll be out of the Army."

"You're not going to approve my pending extension?"

Hovey looked at him, amazed. "Lieutenant, do you realize you could be courtmartialed for dereliction of duty? *I* could, too, but I can play dumb. I've only been here two months."

"I'll face up to it."

"No reason to. With you gone I can plead innocent. *I* didn't know you weren't making Bedcheck. With you here the finger's on me."

"I really think I ought to see this through."

"And I don't think you have a hell of a lot of choice, Lieutenant," Hovey said hotly.

Abe's time in Vietnam began to get short, and the Coates case had not gotten out of the paperwork stage. A petition was put up to battalion for a disinterested investigation; was endorsed and forwarded to Group; was referred to Brigade and orders came down appointing the 233rd MP Company (Tan Son Nhut security) to the task. Captain Hovey had immediately written back that the 233rd, due to their proximity to Saigon, was not sufficiently disinterested. The petition had gone from Group to Brigade and seemed now to be lost. No relatives of the girl turned up, and her body was disposed of. Coates was still missing. By the time the Rabbi was finally put on the plane home, most of the Detachment knew that Coates would never be found and the whole situation, in all probability, would never be solved.

Children Sleeping— Bombs Falling

by Quentin Mueller

I remember walking down a street near the riverfront in Danang, Vietnam, and it was in the afternoon and schoolgirls in long sheer white dresses rode by me on bicycles. Old men wearing baggy pants, old women in black silk squatted beside baskets of rice and vegetables they were selling along the walks. The women wore conical hats. They all wore them, even the younger girls. Once, a Vietnamese woman showed me one of the hats. On the inside, a pattern of colors, a design could be seen, painted delicately on bamboo strands. I remember buying one of the hats once. Sent it to my mother.

Walking along, I breathed in the odor of fish and dung that filled the air. The smell of life was everywhere. The Vietnamese had grown accustomed to it. So had I.

I bought a Coke from a peddler and stood watching the fishing boats on the river. A little girl and a boy ran up to me and tugged at my arm.

"Buy ice cream, man?"

Ten-year-olds, I guessed. They carried a dull metal container filled with dry ice and ice cream bars. I gave the girl some coins and she opened the lid of the box. I reached in and pulled out an ice cream bar. The ice cream started to run down my hand. The temperature that day was up over 100. The children laughed as they watched me trying to eat the ice cream before it all melted down my hand.

"You got cigarette?" the boy asked.

"Sure." I gave him three cigarettes and lit one myself.

Walking along with the children at my side. I loved walking with children. We communicated with smiles and gestures.

Walking to the end of a pier, we sat down and the children waved to the old fishermen as the boats passed by. I watched the boy puffing on a cigarette. The girl was wiggling her toes. She put her arm around the boy's neck.

"Brother me." she said.

I took off my boots and wiggled my toes. The girl laughed and it was then that I heard the sound of artillery shells exploding somewhere in the distance. Killing. Killing Vietnamese people. Children burning.

I looked at the boy and girl but they were busy waving at a fisherman. They had become accustomed to the sounds of death. I looked at my boots laying on the warped planks of the pier. My boots were worn out. My fatigues were worn out and torn. My face and hands glistened a dirty bronze. I tried to remember how I used to look before . . . all this. In my mind I had become a permanent fixture in a land slowly being strangled to death.

The girl reached over and wiped some crusted ice cream off my chin. Her hand was dirty, like mine.

More explosions. I watched a supply truck, loaded with munitions, rumble by coughing up clouds of reddish-brown dust into the faces of peasants walking along the road. The peasants carried long poles across their shoulders. Baskets of vegetables were tied on each end of the poles. The truck had a Confederate flag attached to a pole on the front. The flag fluttered in the warm wind. I looked at the little girl. Her long, satin black hair streamed out, caught by the same wind. The boy's hair was the same color but shorter, and cut in bangs over his gentle eyes.

Around us, merchants and fishermen spoke loudly and quickly in a language I never needed to understand. I would smile, or wave.

Sweat ran down my face. My face a dirty river where tears and sweat flowed down into my whiskers.

From a nearby hotel came the sound of music. It sounded like American jazz and laughter. Two officers staggered out of the hotel bar, their brass and boots reflecting sunlight into my eyes.

The boy asked for another cigarette. I gave him a pack of Luckies. Cheap over here. Dime a pack.

"So long, man," he shouted, running off hand in hand with his sister.

I watched the children until they disappeared into the steaming heat of the marketplace. I layed back on the pier and closed my eyes. Tired. So tired.

That night, I waited to board a plane bound for Okinawa. A year had passed. Waiting for my flight. Listening to the laughter of other men, their joking. Cussing. Talk of fine women and lazy days to come. The men were half drunk on warm beer. Wasted. But sometimes the whiskey was good and the marijuana even better. Blot it all out.

I walked off and sat in the chill of darkness on the side of the air field. The night air was thick with the odor of aviation fuel. A phantom jet was taking off, its afterburners spewing hot flames into the black sky. Shaking the ground. Explosions again. Killing.

The pier where I had sat during the afternoon with the children was probably deserted now. River water was splashing up over the planks. A wind had come up suddenly, blowing in off the China Sea. The old fishermen were eating fish and rice with their families. Maybe drinking Thai beer. Smoking.

Children are asleep now. Boys and girls, dreaming of all things nice. Like children all over the world.

And, of course, the nice thing about the story is that now that you have heard it, what happened is part of you, too.

Jim Aitken, Lederer's Legacy

INDEX OF WRITERS

INDEX OF PHOTOGRAPHERS